LAST OF THE
Good Boys

BY JOHN MCPHAUL

DORRANCE
PUBLISHING CO
EST. 1920
PITTSBURGH, PENNSYLVANIA 15238

Dorrance Publishing Co
585 Alpha Drive
Suite 103
Pittsburgh, PA 15238
Visit our website at *www.dorrancebookstore.com*

ISBN: 978-1-6366-1530-1
eISBN: 978-1-6366-1704-6

AUTHOR'S NOTE

This is a fictional narrative woven into the fabric and accounts of true events. With exception to prominent names, personalities and places, assigned characterizations are fictitious and any similarity to anyone dead or alive is unintended and not inferred.

My sincere thanks to all who read and critiqued the manuscript, but I'm truly indebted to the few having sustained interest and opinions that led to the final version. I'll not name names for fear of omissions, but you know who you are.

A special thanks to Dr. Maria Campbell for invaluable advice and editorial direction.

Lastly, I'm grateful to the pilots, the crews and support personnel of the 49th Aviation Company (The Prospectors) in Phan Rang, Vietnam (1966 – '67), for their conversations, stories and photo opportunities. Although many combat assaults and operations herein are historically true and happened as described, for the sake of continuity and the novel form, others are fictional. However, neither are intended to represent an account of any missions flown by the 49th Aviation Company.

The characters of the fictional unit, The 21st Assault Helicopter Company are fictitious as well and not intended to invoke the memory of any person or persons.

For my daughter, Allison,
and to the memory of Jeanette A. Michael,
whose resemblance inspired this story...

Once,
when life was fair
and magic was real,
good boys ruled the world.

GLOSSARY OF ACRONYMS

Aircraft Commander (AC)
Area of Operation (AO)
Army of the Republic of Vietnam (ARVN)
C Rations (C's)
Communications (COM)
Forward Air Control (FAC)
Fucking New GUY (FNG)
Instructor Pilots (IP)
Joint Air Attack Team (JAAT)
Landing Signal Officer (LSO)
Landing Zone (LZ)
Lieutenant (LT)
Light Observation Helicopter (LOACH)
Long Range Reconnaissance Patrol (LRRP)
Military Assistance Command, Vietnam (MAC-V)
North Vietnam Army (NVA)
Officers Candidate School (OCS)
Perforated Steel Planking (PSP)
Rest and Recuperation Leave (R&R)
Southern Christian Leadership Conference (SCLC)
Vietcong (VC)

BOYS OF SUMMER

JUNE 1958

Down in Sandy Bottom, roosters crowed and tree tops stuck-up through a layer of summer fog as morning and light jostled for spaces on the day. Suddenly, a series of raps at the door.

"Who's there?" she asked, while poised for a reply.

"It's me. I came to get Melvin," said the anxious voice of a child. "There's a big accident on the highway—a truckload of eggs turned over," he said in a huff, then continued. "We have to get there before everything's gone."

Quizzical and more composed, she said, "Slow down, young man. What truck and what business is it of yours?"

He managed to catch his breath, and answered, "They're giving it all away before it goes bad. We gotta go and we gotta go now. The other kids are taking the short-cut through the woods!" She is my mother, Claudia, and he is, Tommy, my best friend.

My mom and Tommy stared for a moment into each other's eyes before mom leaned forward and asked, "Tommy Pratt, does your mom understand what you up to?"

"Yes..., ma'am. I asked if I could come get Melvin, and beat the other children there."

I tied my sneakers when Sleep, another friend stuck his head inside the door.

"Hi, Miss Claudia!" said Sleep.

1

Seeing how tuned we were to the incident, mom looked at me, then said, "Melvin, don't y'all get in the way."

Tommy, Sleep, and I weren't first to arrive at the overturned truck. Other friends, Packy, Beenie, and Leo, with his brother Ramey were there, surveyed the carnage. It seems the whole town had picked through the goods, when the seven of us salvaged a wooden crate, culled through small mounds of broken, badly smeared eggs, then retreated to our clubhouse in the woods. In a tiny stream, run-off from the steam boilers at the saw mill, we washed and cleaned them.

Our clubhouse was a shack we built from bark laden boards, scrap from the saw mill just across the railroad track. A narrow, dirt road, bent beneath a canopy of oaks and ended abruptly at an embankment overlooking the railroad and saw mill, formed the eastern border of the woods that sheltered our hide-out. The railroad tracks and saw mill sat to the north. Acres of hardwood and pine trees surrounded the remaining sides—well hidden from the scrutiny of grown-ups or girls.

Leo, at 13, was the oldest among us, his brother Ramey was the youngest at 10. Tommy, Packy, Beenie, Sleep, and I were the pivotal age of 12. Ramey rode the rear of Leo's bicycle, his knees drawn into his chest. When Leo paused, Ramey slid to the ground, then resumed his perched posture. Unable to sit erect, he quickly encircled his knees with his arms. A frail boy, but adroit at maintaining his balance on the rear of the bicycle. Ramey had heart trouble and long outgrew a prognosis of an infant death. However, we cut Ramey no slack for his shortcomings. If we went skinny-dipping, he enviously maintained a lookout for girls or fishermen. When we swiped peaches and plums or sugarcane in the fall, Ramey had his quota, his share of stress and consequences when things didn't go well.

Sprawled as we were in the late morning woods, more bored than tired, we gazed toward the sky at sunshine that filtered through the trees. Essentially, we raced toward manhood having heard from many before us, a need for something pivotal that made life worth living; a yearning, burning need for that something Rain Seed County chose not to provide colored boys. For inspiration, we clung to the certainty of assurances that leaped from the pages of the Bible. In that shaded coolness where summer stood, appeared the mold where such days took shape according to the wiles, wishes and resources at our disposal.

Rain Seed County, Florida, sat far from the powdered beaches of the coasts, but nestled among the rolling, red hills and ancient oaks of Florida's panhandle. A tiny, rural town in a segregated south, an armpit of Dixie and celebrated antebellum values where life too often spoke with an evil choice of words and racist attitudes and practices embraced the law. All manner of things were born and grew well in Rain Seed County, but dreams hatched best in places, far, far away.

My parents, Howard and Claudia Streeter, once harbored dreams, but reality clearly pointed to availability. My mother, a schoolteacher, once dreamed of becoming a dancer, but in her parent's opinion, dancing had no practical benefits for colored girls. My dad, from nearby Creighton County was a welder and worked in a local welding shop. I was the oldest of three children. Ellen, my sister, was eight and Maurice, an infant.

The lumber sawmill and Fuller's Earth Mining courted steady labor year-round, but the bread and butter of Rain Seed County was its truck crops and tobacco. Nonetheless, by any standard, Rain Seed County was a wealthy county, controlled by tobacco barons who owned all essential businesses and had the wherewithal to manipulate a captive force of cheap labor.

Leo and Tommy suggested we go swimming or hunting.

"We can't go swimming. I'll get a killing if my folks find-out," answered Beenie.

"Who's going to tell?" quizzed Leo. Compared to the rest of us, Leo's parents were very liberal minded.

"You know Tommy can't keep a secret," said Beenie.

Sleep sat reclined between Ramey and me and suggested we visit the horse stables nearby and ride horses, but when that didn't excite anyone, we decided we'd go hunting in the deep woods south of town.

We divided the eggs and left to collect our gear, and met later at Mandy's Kitchen, the neighborhood jook, where men in khaki pants played checkers in the shade of trees. We walked past Blanchard's Dry-Goods Store, the tobacco packing-house, toward the outskirts of town. With BB guns, a burlap sack and Sleep's two dogs in tow, we craved the feel of true huntsmen.

Tommy Pratt was our leader. He knew what birds we could eat, how to play a harmonica and when everyone turned and ran, he stayed, explained the broken window. Sleep hunted sportingly with us, but Sleep loved and nurtured all animals. If he couldn't tame, something, he'd let it go. Beenie brought his fishing pole. His folks didn't allow him to kill birds or shoot marbles for keeps. He stumbled slightly, wore his cowboy boots with the pointed toes. Often we wore no shoes in summer.

When Beenie stopped to pick blackberries along a ditch, Packy yelled, "There ain't no fish in that ditch, Beenie, so come on."

"I know that," answered Beenie. "I'm picking blackberries, you knucklehead." Beenie was very muscular for his age. He had a deep baritone voice, was always eating, and quick, to argue, and talked incessantly.

Tommy, Sleep, and me looked for a low place along a fence for Leo to hoist the bicycle across. Beyond the fence, the field sloped gently with wild blueberries and broom sage toward close standing trees with shade at their feet. The smell of pinesap was a constant along with the drift of cinders from tall smoke stacks at the saw mill.

Packy, Beenie, and Leo, with Ramey aboard, headed for the shade, while Tommy, Sleep, and me paused to locate birds nearby. Amid the scream of blue jays, copper-colored BB's rattled in the chambers of our rifles and angst and excitement gripped our faces. Spared were the mourning doves and mockingbirds, and sparrows were often shot and left. Ramey waved us toward the shade, but Tommy, Sleep and I continued toward the thicket accompanied by the pant of dogs breathing. Around noon, we came upon a pear tree that yielded as much green fruit as we wanted, then the pond where Beenie was to fish. We sat at the edge of the pond, ate green pears and watched Beenie drown his bait. Packy was the comedian. His brand of humor poked fun at everything and everyone, a harmless yet negative, probing discourse meant to make fun of your shortcomings. That day, Beenie was Packy's target.

"Beenie, you're wearing out that pole! The fish ain't interested in your bait."

"Ain't nothing biting but mosquitoes." Beenie sighed, then, gave the pole to Ramey.

Packy reminded us Beenie had been kicked out of vacation bible school.

"No…!" answered Beenie.

"You did, you big dummy. Miss Morgan caught you cussing or something."

Beenie protested. "I didn't cuss. She didn't like the way I recited a story from the Bible, that's all."

Shortly past noon, we all crowded in the shade away from the pond, fanned gnats, and had some laughs at Beenie's expense. Ramey labored at the edge of the pond, looked back occasionally, and squinted in the bright sunlight. Soft spoken with sad eyes, Ramey charmed even the staunch old women in church. He looked much younger than his 10 years, yet vulnerable and fragile as soap-bubbles or butterfly wings.

Leo joined the fray. "Beenie, you're not supposed to refer to biblical characters like everyday people. Bible stories don't have 'dudes,' 'babes,' 'jokers' and 'chicks.'"

In his defense, Beenie said, "Miss Morgan told me to go outside and find some manners, that's all."

"You couldn't talk your way out of that one, could you, Beenie?"

"That and Big Maebelle. Now tell us she ain't your girlfriend," Tommy said.

"Y'all know I don't like Big Maebelle!" Beenie moaned.

"She thinks so!" I chimed in. "She's your girl, Beenie. You carried her books from school every day?"

Among very personal secrets was my love for Rachel, Tommy's older cousin. Feelings so improbable, I dared not mention it, ever. For as long as I could remember, mine was a silent, pensive vigil, and utterly private. Rachel lived up north and came to Rain Seed County each summer. She grew up that way. Year after year an older and prettier Rachel arrived. Endowed with years I could never overcome, sentenced me forever to a vacant glance, a polite wave. That Rachel was much older did little to inform me the significance of maturity and intellect. Her summer stays gave her celebrity status as boys her age competed for her attention.

"So what! I carried Maebelle's books," confessed Beenie. "Man, I can handle her," Beenie continued.

"The only time your mouth ain't banging like a bell clapper is when she's around."

They were two of a kind, Beenie and Big Maebelle. To disagree with her, meant you had to fight. With Beenie you suffered through a non-winnable argument.

For years Ellen and I stayed at Beenie's home after school hours. Miss Lula, Beenie's mom, watched our every move via an open window. From that window, she surveyed most of the neighborhood. So, I felt close to Beenie in spite of his cantankerous behavior.

Near 1:00 P.M., everything Beenie and Ramey threw into the pond, the fish went after. Full of excitement, each of us wanted a chance to bait the hook, claim a catch. We left the woods around 3:00 P.M. with cravings of food and water, especially water, as we passed only cornfields and open pastures. We were far beyond the woods when nature began its call. Ramey and Tommy had complained earlier of bellyaches. Now, behind an all-day diet of green pears, feelings of discomfort had each of us in differing stages of the runs.

With the afternoon sun burning at our backs, and pains in our stomachs, we hurried against the need to relieve ourselves and feared a lack of control in preventing it happening voluntarily.

"I don't think I'm going to make it," Tommy whispered.

Leo and Ramey led with the bicycle, Sleep, Packy, and I were next. We saw Leo pull into someone's yard, allowed the bike and Ramey to fall as he scampered to the toilet.

"We all can't get in that one out-house," said Packy.

As Beenie approached us, I asked, "Beenie, what's wrong with you?" I glanced toward his prized cowboy boots. He had a painful look on his face and a walk to match. His arms floated at his sides as if guided by a puppeteer. The grimace on his face said it all, he'd lost the battle to control his bowels, and the flow had settled in his boots.

"Beenie, you smell and you got the farthest to go," Packy ribbed him.

Beenie walked gingerly toward home amongst a swarm of summer gnats.

Sleep's parents, Sim and Emma Gibson, like many, worked in the cyclical shifts of the agricultural seasons. Miss Emma was now a housekeeper for the Atwell family. Some years back, Sim Gibson lost his leg in an accident at the Atwell Sawmill. Severed just below the knee, the stump of his leg rested in the fork of an oak peg-leg he himself carved.

It seems the weeks passed swiftly as the month of June faded into July. The magic that was summer unfolded along with the few remaining days of work in the tobacco fields. Days later, we sat with our ankles buried in cool sand beneath oak trees having long memories. Again, we contemplated the day's activities.

Leo looked over the top of a funny book and said, "We can't go swimming, y'all. Some kid drowned in a pond the other day. We'll all get killings if we go." Swimming at White Mountain, the farthest and most secluded spot was not a good idea either. Weekends, occasionally, families with vehicles or someone with an old school bus, drove a group to the beach at the coast, but that day, we walked to the spring near Sandy Bottom. There a high canopy of oaks draped in Spanish moss, presented a cathedral effect that harbored the coolness of the springs. We sat in the shaded air amid the ripple of crystal water.

"Man, when you gonna grow up and read a real book, get your head out of funny books?" Packy ribbed Leo. Leo had calm, quiet ways. His light skin color, freckles, and stewardship of Ramey, he constantly defended.

Summer had no wish of its own, its smile, its frown, its renewal and fertile gifts, came unquantified, yet complete. For us, summer was the crucible whereby dreams and wishes were fired, hardened into promises, then, pointed the way towards manhood. There beneath the canopy, we gazed among tomorrows for our likeness. With dream-stuffed pockets, we bought into the challenge of education as panacea—that education alone separated us from the adversity of our ancestors. With education, a Christian heart, and the Golden Rule, life's fairness awaited each of us. However, the prospects that equal knowledge and skills translated into equality became a fallacy that died at birth. Against those hot, stubborn days of summer, we looked beyond the high, impregnable walls that surrounded Rain Seed County, and gazed impatiently through the prism of manhood. Our thoughts were, the impositions of manhood were easy and unchallenged, much like a string of summer days and Saturdays that went on forever.

"Did y'all see the Army tanks last night?" asked Packy.

White sections of Rain Seed, sported paved streets, sidewalks and fire hydrants. The courthouse grounds were adorned with statutes that preserved a particular historical pride. The colored neighborhood, its ditches and dirt roads were little more than hiding places for runoff and a litany of debris and sometimes dead animals unable to escape it. But those dirt roads were inviting trails for National Guard Maneuvers and to that date, remained a metaphor for civic neglect.

"That's what I'm going to do if I go to the Army someday, drive tanks. They alright."

Vacant land near our clubhouse became a depository for load upon load of sawdust from the mill, reportedly an effort to control flooding. Many creative projects were born among those piles of fresh sawdust, underground havens, and the likes. The evening in question, the Army reserve exercises included the sawdust mounds and destroyed our underground sanctuary fortified with boards. Neither of us were happy about that.

"I'm going to fly airplanes," I said. "I'll bring my airplane home, give everybody a ride." No one challenged the improbability of my much mentioned boast, nor Packy's. The remarks fell lazily on the stagnant afternoon, when Sleep chimed in,

"I'll have me an animal hospital in a big town, maybe Augusta, or somewhere."

The next day at dusk, we played near Beenie's home. Initially we waited for the cover of darkness in order to hit Miss Louvenia's plum tree. She never ate the plums, no one did. Huge, juicy, yellow plums ripened and fell among the gladiolas and lilies planted below. Any humble attempt that asked to pick them ended with a stern, "No!"

Early the next morning, the unmistaken thud of Mr. Sim Gibson' peg-leg and slight drag of his left brogan, crossed our front porch, followed, by a polite rap at the screened door. Drowsy, but awakened by Mr. Sim's approach, I heard sounds from the kitchen where my mom and dad fed my baby brother. Then the sound of bare feet to answer the door, which was left open during the night to entice a breeze.

"Mable's boy died in his sleep last night," said Mr. Sim.

I heard the remark and asked myself, who was he talking about? Everyone knew Ramey had heart trouble, but Ramey couldn't die. I saw mom latch the screen door, turn, and headed back to the kitchen. I climbed out of bed and followed.

"Ma, is something wrong with Ramey?"

My mom sat, took the infant from my father, and searched for words to console me, somehow explain that my playmate and friend had passed away.

Amid days of mourning, Rachel came to my home. It was shortly before her 18th birthday, although she wasn't much taller than I was. I stood shoeless, shirtless and in short pants, shackled to an appearance as pitiful as Ramey's fate. Rachel and mom sat, planned periphery activities for Ramey's funeral services. Like her high-heeled shoes and nylons, the way her paisley skirt hugged her hips, proclaimed her adulthood, I stood in the tattered remnants of a child. She wore a cotton blouse, sleeveless with oyster-pearl buttons down the back and a wide, Patent leather belt. Her huge, beautiful eyes crowded the spaces on an oval-moon face. When she and my mother finished, Rachel walked through the doorway and onto the porch. I watched as she carefully negotiated the front steps, held onto the porch post until she reached the ground, then crossed the yard. She walked away. Rachel, having reached eighteen meant I'd never see her again. In a deeper place inside me, I knew her leaving Rain Seed County this time, rendered void and colorless my future summers. My love of airplanes and love of Rachel were the constants in life as I imagined it.

That scene as Rachel walked away was the scene I took to the clubhouse immediately after Ramey's funeral. Leo, didn't show up those days before the funeral, but afterwards, he joined us there in the woods at the clubhouse. Still in our Sunday best, we stood, mulled the effects of the services. Beenie was quiet and Packy had nothing humorous to say. As they all clung to scenes of Ramey, I held onto that scene of Rachel, lovely Rachel as she left my home. In an ugly silence that offered no reprieve, but for the scenes of Rachel and Ramey, I thought I'd drown in the hopeless, insignificance of being 12 years old. Tommy broke that silence.

"I didn't look in the casket. I closed my eyes, 'cause I didn't want to dream about it," he said softly.

"I didn't look either," Sleep said, then asked Leo if he looked.

"Sho, I looked! He was my brother! I ain't scared of my own brother!"

We all sat and mulled the same thoughts, the disbelief, the wonder of Ramey committed to death, gone from talking, playing in the sawdust and being called home at dusk. To suppose that Ramey or either of us would some-day die, amounted to awakening some morning to find the world had come to an end. Far away from the burning silence we heard Ellen's voice from the edge of the woods.

"Mamma said y'all come here right now!"

We ignored Ellen's plea for no one moved for an hour or more. Then, we heard footsteps and the swish of branches as someone approached the hideout. Slightly startled, we remembered Ellen's call. We braced ourselves, only to find it was my mom who treaded carefully toward us and not the least bit angry.

"Is everybody okay?" she asked. "Y'all come on up to the house, have something to eat, and get out of those hot clothes."

We each shuffled past her as she embraced us, one by one, then mom gently grasped me by both shoulders, turned me again toward the shanty of a clubhouse and said quietly,

"Melvin, is that my can opener over there? My skillet I been weeks looking for? Would you please take it back to the house?" Although the circumstances softened her remarks, she was not really asking that I return the items so much as happy to learn where they were. For a bunch of 12- and 13-year-olds, Ramey's death offered a new perspective on life. As long as you didn't have

9

heart trouble, polio, or whistled at a white woman, you could live forever. Fresh in the minds of colored boys was the lynching of Emmitt Till.

The song of summer passed like a freight train that wanted to steal away unnoticed—a train that chugged and stopped; slowed by the caution of death that came unannounced in the night, and all the superstitions that surrounded it. Ramey's death taught us a lesson as well. The freedom and challenges of adulthood were non-promises. In all of our becoming, there was a chance we'd never arrive.

At the edge of the fall season, came revival services at church. A collective decision permeated the group as we each joined the mourning bench, a bond far greater than the blood-brother initiations of the clubhouse. A few others and big Maebelle came too. Revival was an intense, concentration of prayers, preaching and worship, aimed at those who sought salvation. The mourning bench was a figurative plateau in life, an anticipated juncture, a crossing where one acknowledged God, Jesus Christ, and the Holy Spirit. There, one accepted Jesus Christ as their savior, and spiritually came of age. On Wednesday, August 4, 1958, we accepted Christ as the head of our lives. Aglow with the spirit and conviction of a new beginning, each of us humbled and visibly moved. A week later, I wore a white cotton robe sewn by my grandmother, was baptized; washed in the blood, and my sins forgiven.

THE NAVY

In September of 1964, I joined the Navy right out of college. I chose the Navy for no other reason than its training cycle was the earliest to begin. With much anticipation, I reported to Aviation Officers Candidate School (AOCS) at Pensacola, Florida. My flight experience upon induction was 56 hours. At the tender age of 19, I barely passed for 15. About that, I could do nothing, but later learned many perceived inabilities about me, quickly defaulted to that vulnerability.

The skies above neighboring cities like Ft. Walton, Panama City and Port St. Joe, offered a scanty familiarity. As flight training proceeded from the propeller driven, North American T-28 trainer to the F-9 Jet trainer, my confidence soared. I was at times, just short of being a hot-shot and openly brash for the training was far from difficult. My flight grade average was consistently in the top five of a class of 32 candidates. Angst was my competitor as each day and every flight pitted an exuberance and its intoxicating rush, all of which said I had finally made it. The blend of dream and reality was volatile, but like catching tadpoles in a paper sack, the bounty was huge, but the choice of vessels spelled disaster.

Beneath an endless sky of puffy, cumulus clouds, an infinite view of the azure blue, Gulf of Mexico swept beneath me. In a squad of F-9 Jet Trainers, I held formation as we circled the training carrier. The first ship in the flight broke formation and headed into a base approach, then final approach, to the carrier deck, the *U.S.S. Lexington.*

"Long Bow, zero-three-two, this is bird's nest. You're on course." As zero-three-two, descended, the remainder of the formation and I, looked on as we continued our orbit of the vessel, then the next ship in order broke formation and followed. "Give it a little power! Hold there!" The voice of the Landing Signal Officer (LSO) aboard the carrier boomed in the headsets. Zero-three-two, touched down briefly and sped across the deck, then climbed back to altitude. In the third position of the flight, I tipped my left wing. "Long Bow one-six-one," the LSO said to me. "You're on course at a quarter mile and looking good. A slight bank and I could see the LSO, the shimmer of heat waves and the tether lines just beyond the fantail of the carrier. "Bring it up," he shouted. "Okay, hold what you got, easy!" As my landing gear stroked the wooden deck, I had but a moment to retract the flaps and power-up to clear the end of the runway

Repetitions of "touch & go," then "carrier landing" exercises, occurred in sets of fives. Flight Training episodes were statistically numbered and logged. In spite of my relative success were personal issues where I ignored military predictability. I avoided boredom, even maximized airtime as I sought to satisfy some individual driven ego. Certainly I was familiar with training ramifications and the importance of consistency, but didn't take into consideration that stats of fives superseded overall achievement and became the determining factor as to who would and would not graduate. I failed to see the big picture. Excited, I lost view of the stringent and often stated lack of patience inherent to the training cycle.

One night I replayed from memory that days exercise and discovered miscues in my carrier landings. On approach, the LSO spoke a dual language, one vocal through the helmet mic and the other signaled by the Fresnel Lens System, a row of colored lights that changed as the airplane entered its prescribed glide path. Approaches at speeds of 80 to 85 knots, the LSO's voice was a second behind the lights. The vector or the colored lights dictated where in the glide path the airplane should be in terms of altitude and distance from touchdown. By the time I coordinated the voice and the lights, another step in the landing sequence should have commenced. Always the LSO was the last word in the landing sequence. His signal and his vantage point on deck committed you to the landing or waved you off.

Henceforth, I concentrated on the Fresnel Lens System and my exercises were consistent in sets of five, including night carrier landings. Still the matter of record was the period in which my repetitions were not in succession. That was the case against me and schedule cuts were due. A simple "wake-up" warning would have saved me, but the war in Vietnam had generated an accelerated course of instructions that called for the best and most alert trainees. The Navy's task was to be swift and impersonal. We were all within one month of graduate training with the much celebrated F-4 Phantom Jet. Following seventeen months of training, I stood petrified among a formation of khaki-clad Ensigns, as each of us hoped, prayed his name wasn't listed.

"Anderson..., Atkins..., Beauchamp..., Simpson...," the duty officer read slowly the names, then my name, they called my name. Later, in a smaller formation, I listened to kind words meant to salvage our pride. Briefly, I stood in the dream that shaped my years of wanting to fly airplanes. I drew inward. Caught with my pants down, figuratively speaking, caught-up in the bountiful success of fellow pilots and me that made it in flight school. Caught as I briefly looked away, unaware of the leak in the sack. In spite of my efforts and my attention to detail, an immaturity shone. Nothing like that would ever happen again. Bitterness boiled inside me, as I hated the system that rejected me and hated myself for having fallen prey to it.

In the aftermath, I drifted aimlessly with no game plan or destination. I slept in bus stations, train stations, and ate from vending machines. I knew I was better than the efforts I'd offered and that alone would be my solace. Like a dingy cast afloat upon an open sea, for days I pondered my fate.

"I'll get it right," I said. "I'll dream the dream again."

TOMMY, THE HARBINGER

JUNE 1966

Home wasn't the sanctuary I anticipated. I went home to cry. I placed my bags in the attic, tried to block-out every trace of that naval experience. Tommy Pratt returned home that week, too. His was not the hope of tomorrow nor that of tattered spirits. Tommy's body came home by rail. News of Tommy's death in Vietnam, hit the small town of Rain Seed County, like a bolt of lightning, a strange bolt of lightning without the threat of rain or roll of thunder.

"Little Tommy Pratt?" someone asked in surprised astonishment. "Why, he was just a boy!" Tommy's death was the talk on everyone's lips. For me, it was a convenient diversion, a tragedy far beyond my own. Under the stare of the summer sun, Rain Seed County resigned itself to the strange death among us. Days later, we braved the heat in Sunday clothing, went to see where the lightning struck, the strange bolt of lightning without the threat of rain or roll of thunder. We gathered to bury Jules' and Beatrice's boy.

My family piled into the old Desoto and drove along the back roads towards the church. Ellen, now 15, and I tarried that morning, in need of flight from the horrors at hand. In an eerie silence, we gazed at the roadside.

"Melvin, where is Vietnam? asked Maurice.

"No place for you to worry about," I answered.

"Then, what is Vietnam?" the child insisted.

"It's a place far, away. A very violent and dangerous place," I answered.

"Howard," mom said, "Make sure Maurice stays inside the church. I don't want him playing around." A waist length garment of white cotton, stiffly starched served as my mom's choir robe.

The old clapboard church, with tall narrow windows brush-painted in pastel colors to simulate stained glass, sat among the trees. The windows were flung open like awnings to vent the heat of summer while mourners stirred the air with handheld paper fans. To the sound of a familiar hymn, we entered the shaded gloom of services. It wasn't until my mother stood to sing the solo she'd rehearsed all week, when my insides shook. That it was Tommy's funeral made the pain all but unbearable. Somehow my mother knew the troubles of sons sent to war. She knew the struggles mothers know. She shared Tommy's loss and that of his parents. I watched as she leaned into the song, closed her eyes, and brought the words to life.

"....Soon-a be done with the troubles of the world,

....troubles of the world...."

However, in the confines of a Negro Spiritual, Negroes didn't just die, they went home. Negroes had a virtual lock on heaven—the ultimate equalizer. Heaven was where a lifetime of wrongs were righted. Having saved-up their glory, they waited now in death to collect.

"....going home to live with God..."

Long before tears welled up in my eyes, or the clinched grip of Ellen's hand on mine, I longed for the funeral to end. My tears were infectious as Ellen, too, cried.

"I'm glad.... you're home," Ellen stammered. Her lips trembled, her voice cracked, betrayed her wish to whisper. Nestled in my presence, Ellen held onto me. I looked at her, wished to lean on the years that each of us had grown and somehow be a buoy at that unfortunate crossing.

We took the brief walk between the churchyard and the adjoining cemetery. Just beyond the shaded reach of graying oaks and nimble dogwoods the bugler played "Taps." Thomas Whitney Pratt, Lance Corporal, U.S. Marine Corps, laid at rest. Shortly, a burden seemed lifted as Ellen tugged at my elbow, slowed my stride.

"I have a surprise for you," she said.

She wiped away the remaining tears from her cheeks and with the softness of that moment and the breath of a rose, she said, "Rachel is here. You remember Rachel, don't you? Rachel Blake, Tommy's cousin from Baltimore?"

"Sure," I answered.

"She's been asking about you ever since she moved to Rain Seed. For real, she's been asking about you, can't wait to see you."

"That's okay, isn't it?" I asked as I detected in Ellen, a measure of disbelief.

Then, something snapped in her eyes and she said, "You ain't nothing special! She's a school teacher, interned this spring." There was a sound of victory in Ellen's voice too. She was tall like me, but until that remark, I thought Ellen had grown beyond our petty rivalries, squabbles, and bickering. As my thoughts turned to Rachel, the mood changed, and Ellen and I approached again the shade of the church.

I listened as Ellen rambled on in her girlish banter. Amid the crowd, friends my age spoke of childhood as if long ago, generations removed.

Like a hum in a song, there came a pall on Rain Seed County, a pall that signaled a great beginning; a drum roll, a harbinger. Tommy was a conscript, his willing attitude typified the romantic lure of war. But like the plume of a dandelion caught in a breeze, or sand castles at evening tide, life appeared to fall apart before our grasp of manhood.

Having filed into the dining hall for repast, I moved about, sampled conversations. Although my flight experiences were victorious in everyone's opinion, monumental and unprecedented in local history, news of my misfortune spread quickly as I floundered in hopeless indecision. My mother watched from a short distance, my weakened attempt at greeting well-wishers, my fabricated smiles, and utter sense of loss. I knew she worried about me, saw as she prepared a plate of food, and brought it to me with motherly advice.

"You'd better have something to eat," she said. "No one is cooking anymore today."

Suddenly, a hand touched my wrist, a soft inquiring hand. I turned and found Ellen, who presented me to Rachel. Often I thought of seeing Rachel again and perhaps, a chance to atone for the silly things said and done while hopelessly in pursuit of her affection.

"Hello, Melvin, and welcome home," Rachel said with big laughing eyes and a look of approval at the sight of me. "Is it the military or have that many years gone by? You're so tall and got shoulders, looking like a man."

"Thanks," I said. "You didn't grow much," I joked.

In the relative quiet of that moment, my pains for Tommy and me subsided. I looked at the moon-faced woman across from me, at the years when I acted as if Rachel was the only girl in the world. Her pert, big brown eyes, brought back years of wanting. Although beautiful best described her, today, the term seemed trite, banal, and overused. In no way did it adequately describe the girl I remembered and worshipped. We talked of old times, tales bogged in summer days when the difference in our age seemed a lifetime. Although still depressed, I basked in those soothing memories.

"You've done well, taken good care of yourself," I said.

A stare of a smile looked my way. Thoughtfully, she said, "Well, thank you."

"You've become quite a woman, Rachel. Then again, I'm not sure if you were ever a child." Her physical appointments long made her popular, but in no way did it define her. I managed to steer the conversation away from me, wondered if she knew how much I still loved her. I saw Rachel look back at me, how she studied my face as she, too, made comparisons between then and now. I looked across the table at the woman who embodied years so powerfully private and precious.

"Mel, how long has it been now? It seems like yesterday, you were a snot-nosed boy that played under the house. Now you fly airplanes. I hear things didn't quite work out. What's next?"

Few were as polite as my family, gave me space, and time to respond. Naval Flight School was the culmination of lifelong ambitions, now I felt as if pinned in the wreckage of my dream, my sorrow morphed into emptiness all full of diffidence.

"I'm still hoping, have a few long shots, but to be honest, I really don't know at the moment."

"I don't understand, Mel, your reluctance to let go. With your experiences, you can do anything."

An hour or more passed as I entertained her questions, but skillfully avoided any real discussion.

"Let's take a ride, if you don't mind."

"I want to go!" Ellen pleaded then hissed when I objected.

I headed back into the church and down the main isle toward the front door where I waited for Rachel. The smell of old wood, the flutter of birds nesting in the loft and sound of the old piano, slightly out of tune, came as subtle memories.

We drove into the countryside towards our old swimming hole at White Mountain. Huge fields of vegetables awaited workers in straw hats and irrigation sprinklers pumped the smell of pond water. White Mountain was a Fuller's Earth Mine with huge trenches dug parallel to one another. Collections of rainwater held by the chalky clay, resulted in a series of clear, blue ponds, each separated by a huge, extended mound of dried, white clay. Rachel drove to the edge of a bluff that overlooked the lakes, and parked.

The place was silent except for the lonely whistle of a Bobwhite bird, the rapid knock of a woodpecker nearby, and the faint smell of magnolia blossoms. One respite from the heat that time of year was afternoon thunderstorms. As if by request, a band of dark clouds appeared, a rush of wind and before long, big drops of rain pelted the car, and the surface of the pond appeared to boil. The rain quickly grew into a downpour, cool, cleansing, and refreshing. Against the rain that fell on the lake, the sound of it pounding the windows and distant roll of thunder, came the smell of Rachel's lavender talc perfume, her sigh, and cunning moves. Her shapely and stunning figure came with great legs, wonderful sculptured calves.

When the conversation again centered on Tommy, Rachel uttered softly, "Tommy…, that's enough about Tommy. We'll all remember Tommy. Tell me about Melvin, what's eating you, and, while you're at it, how in the dickens did you finish college about the time I did? I want to know about your interest in flying, and where did that begin?" The woman in her, the one she'd grown into had spoken, while the girl I remembered came again. Beneath the sound of pounding rain, Rachel paused and summoned my attention.

"You want to hear my life story?" I asked.

"I know your life story," she answered dryly. "But you know…, shortly after I moved here, I stopped by your house… to give my regards…, say hello. I saw all those pictures of you smiling and posing with airplanes. In those pictures, I looked for someone I used to know, instead I found someone else. Since you invited me here, tell me how you got into flying," she asked again with just a wisp of a smile on her lips.

"I'm a better listener," I said, tried to avoid the recollection, wanted instead to remain a mystery. That moment hardly seemed the time to recall any measure of accomplishment. Only the days ahead I hoped, were things I wished to share.

"Talk to me, Melvin Streeter," she insisted. Having said that, she removed her hat, its round brim, half rolled, like the girl on the Buster Brown shoe box. Rachel made herself comfortable, leaned against the door and the seat as if to take a nap. The silky fabric of her dress rose, fell, then flowed over the rounded contours, the shapes of womanhood that never waited for me. The woman in her shouted, churned and billowed like clouds or currents in the surf, unaware, subtle, yet sensuous. Severing my view, I, too, shifted in the seat and focused on her questions. I thought for a moment about the years, the dreams, the good times, and the recent pain of failure. I looked over the years for a starting point.

"I graduated from high school at age 15. Freakish, but I did it. Now it seems I've always been on a quest, rushing towards something. When I entered college I stood six foot or better and was skinny as a rail, when my folks and I took the train upstate where I enrolled in the summer session. My discovery of flight instructions in a newspaper advertisement was earthshattering. It was then I realized my purpose in life, my only dream—to fly—suddenly presented itself. Everything else became secondary. Not once did I imagine that flight instructions were as copious as a classified ad." I hesitated for a moment, surprised at my disclosure, then began again.

"Suddenly, the world seemed too small and the days too short to contain me. Conversations and meetings with flight instructors were surreal, if not awe-inspiring, as I fondled and cuddled my dream. The college challenge became a distraction from my want of flight, but one I had to tolerate. It took all of me to maintain the proper prospective, and some sense of priority. Early signals from home indicated nothing as grand as flying lessons could begin before my second year; and then only if grades remain above par. I, alone, would have to provide the financing. The introductory flight was five dollars."

It didn't come easy, my talk, more like changing bandages as I bared my sensitivities to the world. Even with Rachel, it didn't come easy, but I continued.

"To no one's surprise, I obtained my private pilot's certificate in my second year of college. To the local naval recruiter, I was a novelty, intriguing at first, then the Navy and Air Force encouraged me. I was on top of the world and a little cocky too."

Rachel took it all in, stared into the windshield as the splash of rain faded to a drizzle. Then she gazed intently in my direction, as if she looked inside me, perhaps considered the probability of such change. I, too, watched as she moved, shifted in the seat, admired again the woman she'd become. As I looked on, she smiled at my obvious delight. Once the rain stopped, we walked a short distance over a path of hardened clay to the edge of the lake. Now as an adult, the lake seemed small, demur and lifeless. How insignificant our past, I thought, and how insignificant the relics of that past when a life force so much a part of that past no longer existed. All my thoughts since hearing of Tommy's death culminated there at the lake. I had thoughts of my own death, how real, and how someday I, too, must deal with it. Neither Rachel nor I spoke as we peered at the water for a few minutes, then headed back to the car and the smell of food on the rear seat.

We left White Mountain, the steamy countryside and headed back toward town. Along the way came more stolen glances and a flood of memories and bouts with a savage disparity in our age that precluded anything serious. I was reminded of those early years when we played hide-and-seek at dusk. I remembered my turn to count and seek those that hid and the frustration that developed when I found them but could not beat them running. My memories settled on an evening years ago when I chased Rachel, and in the anguish of failure and the insuperable task of overcoming the attributes of older and stronger limbs, I fell to the ground and cried. I cried because I could not compete romantically with boys her age. I cried because my feelings at that age were strong and real. How cruel the years that separated us and the brevity of her summer stays that would not allow me time to grow up. So driven was I to overcome that disparity that at age ten, I gave away my entire collection of marbles because doing so signified my coming of age. I stood up and moved away from the games and toys of childhood. In that single stroke of benevolence, I tried to cast aside the telltale idiosyncrasies of boyhood and embraced manhood. "Wait for me," the chorus echoed. In addition, ever since grade school, I knew the day would come when I'd confront the subject of my many fantasies. Born from the pains of adversity came a strange maturity. Rachel seemed pleased with her re-acquaintance with a grown-up Melvin, then, she summed up my talk.

"You're an interesting read, but you avoided some things. It's okay, I hope to see more of you this summer."

"I don't want to change directions, Rachel. I'd turn back the clock if I could, take things slower, but I don't want to change careers. I need more time to finish what I've started."

"Mel, that sounds so 'iffy.' I thought you'd stay and settle down," she said, with a hint of disappointment in her voice.

"Do you feel indebted to Rain Seed County?" I asked.

"I like teaching in a small community. I know that I'm making a difference. Am I hiding? Do I have something to fear? I suppose," she said, then, continued.

"I'm glad we had this talk, Melvin. You are quite different, very different. Promise me you'll come by sometime, and talk some more."

Sunshine dissolved the gray skies and the temperature rose again. The wind was gone, and what remained of Saturday staggered toward evening.

Rachel

As the long, hot summer, tighten around me, I waited and wondered how to reassemble my dream. News that Beenie and Leo had received draft notices reminded me of my own vulnerabilities. Lacking anything constructive to do, I simmered; I hid among the places and memories that hatched such dreams. And, there was Rachel. Her presence, stirred into that summer was the salve I needed.

One day a business letter arrived that bore the United States Army's logo. It was the Army Helicopter Flight Program I reluctantly applied for like the Air Force and every other service related program in need of pilots. My secret, I thought, but on that balmy morning amid the drizzle of rain, I watched as my mother moved about the house.

"You received a letter, good news, or bad?" she asked.

"Army," I answered lethargically.

"Is that what you're waiting for?" she asked again.

"Not really." I tried to shrug it off. "The letter is from the Army's helicopter school. Helicopters are a long ways from what I was doing. I'm really waiting for a reply from the Air Force."

My mom looked as if she wanted to cry, but held back her tears, perhaps wondered where had she gone wrong?

"Army, Air Force?" she whispered, raised her arms, and shook her head as to convey her confusion, her disappointment.

23

"Ma, it's a flight program for helicopters, the warrant officer helicopter flight program. Warrant Officers are not commissioned officers. They just fly helicopters."

"I thought you wanted to fly jets! The Navy was where you wanted to be and no place else! That's what you said!"

"I know, momma, but I'm a pilot. Sometimes you don't get what you want."

"Oh! So you understand that, do you?" she asked, then, continued. "Sometimes you don't get what you want, then you move on."

"You're right, ma… I haven't made up my mind yet, but I'm pressed for time. If I turn this down and wait much longer, I could be like Leo and Beanie. As much as I want to wait for the Air Force, I'm scared. I don't care about being an officer. If I have to go, I want to be a pilot. The Army uses fixed-wing aircraft, too. I might get lucky and get into one of those units."

"We'll sit down this evening when your daddy's home. We'll sit down and talk," she said, thoroughly disappointed.

It was suppertime when the family gathered. Evening rode upon winds blown through the screens and an unenthusiastic bark of a hound nearby. The sizzle of battered pork chops on hot grease, billowed from the kitchen. After supper, mom, dad, and I sat and talked in-depth.

"Son, we're worried about the likelihood of you being sent to Vietnam. The Army sends more troops to Vietnam than any service. You've flown a lot of airplanes, you're an engineer for Christ's sake, apply to be an engineer, and avoid that mess in Vietnam. Beulah's boy got his notice today."

"Well, Warrant Officer Pilots don't fight, they don't command anything but the ships they fly. Chances are I'll never see Vietnam."

My parents' minds already poisoned by a reality portrayed each day in the daily newscast, tried again to connect. Momma leaned forward, a needle in one hand and thread in the other, she'd make some meaningless repair in an effort to dilute a painful discussion. She cocked her head, squinted then threaded the needle.

"I remember how excited you were when you first took flying lessons. We all wanted you to be successful and you deserve it. We are proud of you. Things are going to be different this time, I'm sure of that. There's nothing wrong in being ambitious, Melvin, we've taught you that. It's not insensitive your being adamant about what you want, only your timing. Listen to us please and reconsider this."

As if she knew what my choice would be; I think she prepared herself for the worse.

"What happened," she concluded, "to my son, the engineer? Once you had an interest in flying. Now you've become a pilot who's forgotten how to be anything else."

So fixed were the passions of youth that in the tug of ambitions and practicality, the latter had little chance. The call to manhood was silent, a whisper perhaps, but a call nonetheless that demanded attention and presence. For us, the draft came just that way. Individually, it whispered a teasing distraction with disguised evil potential. Collectively it roared like a flood or wild fire as it beguiled and consumed the tender youth unable to avoid its rage. Such was the burden of youth in early summers of our being.

The next day Rachel and I went for a walk as we had on many occasions. Neither of us seemed anxious to admit how gratifying and supportive our rendezvous. Never was there a day when we didn't plan for the next. In each conversation my dreams of Rachel unfolded, wishes long since un-named and undisclosed.

"I still think you'd do better in the private sector," she said. "I can feel you boiling inside, calm only when the subject is flying. The few times I can pull you away, not only am I convinced, but enjoy knowing there's more to you than airplanes. You really going to do it, aren't you?" Rachel asked about my decision, if I would accept the Army's invitation.

"I've got a story, too, Melvin. Like you, it burns. Wasn't sure if I'd ever tell anyone, but lately, hearing you unload, I need to share it with someone— share it with you. I want you to take it with you, pray for me, and forgive me if you can."

"Let's back-up for a moment," I said. "About the Army, only you know I've made that decision. So, what I've said is between the two of us."

I leaned forward for her assurance, when she said, "I knew you were going to take it, Streeter. Your secret's good with me."

"Thanks. Now, why is it you call me Streeter?"

She smiled, raised her brow. "I call you what I want… Streeter. But, if you ever have children, a boy, don't name him Melvin. The name Melvin never grows-up—forever a child." Rachel laughed and staggered away.

"Melvin…, I knew him long ago. The person I met at the funeral is Streeter."

I was not sure how to take her remark. "What is it you want to tell me?" I asked.

We stood now in the driveway beneath a Chinaberry Tree that shaded her porch and import car.

"Go ahead, talk."

"Not now," she said. "I want to take you out to dinner this evening. If my nerves hold-up, I'll say what I can."

I went home, waited as the shadows of evening faded tenderly to night.

I arrived promptly as Rachel and her neighbor talked at the fence that separated their homes. Guided by their voices, I peered into the moonlight that filtered through the Chinaberry Trees silhouetted against a moonlit sky. In the quiet, pleasant evening was a chorus of crickets and frogs as fire-flies or lightening bugs flickered in the night.

"Oh, Melvin, you're here," Rachel said, looking back over her shoulder. "Give me a moment while I get my bag."

Lights flicked on from one room to another, then off in the same manner as she retreated and emerged with her purse. We drove toward Wellington, a town nearby.

"Streeter," Rachel said, "are you going to miss me?"

I wondered how best to answer her question, then she asked again, "Are you going to miss me?"

"I suppose I'll miss everything about Rain Seed County and yes, I'll miss you, Rachel."

She reminded me that February 9th was her birthday, and went to great lengths to ensure I didn't forget it.

We entered the café, a favorite of Rachel's. I studied her face, her huge almond eyes and fragile features; her tiny shoulders, arms, and soft, delicate hands. In a light knitted blouse of green and contrasting skirt, I found her powerfully appealing. Surely, I would come back to this in the future. I would rethink those moments many times, no matter how the evening proceeded.

I had several photos that captured Rachel's many moods. she asked which I would take with me. Again, I did not answer. Rachel reached across the table, tapped my wrist.

"What picture are you going to take with you, Streeter?"

I formed an imaginary camera with my hands and proceeded to make clicking sounds with my mouth.

"That one," I said. "The look I see tonight. That look will always be with me."

It wasn't a lively evening. It was slow and full of questions. Not real questions, but the ones you ask when you hid what you really wanted to say, the kind of questions when a smile was adequate reply, sufficient.

"When you're up there," Rachel pointed to the sky. "It's something special, isn't it? Up there you're unattached. How deep does that run in you? Without roots or conscience, you're like a drifter, one that treasures his lack of stability. What's beyond the immediate goals you've set? How do you know when the goal is achieved, and how do you know when you've had enough? You should hear yourself sometimes as you talk of flying. Not once have you tied it to life as we know it."

In a moment, she caught herself as she realized her ramble, but I was used to it now, her pensive and elongated analysis. I was enchanted by the glow on her face and captivated by wanton memories that over the years grew bigger than life. I was about to answer, but she continued while unconsciously folding and refolded the laminated menu she held. I watched as she fired question after question, saw the sincerity in her eyes, and somehow, knew our link was eternal.

"Why is it I wish you weren't leaving?" she asked.

As she spoke, a profound thought came to me that perhaps summed up Rachel's concerns. Men often hovered above reality, suspended, as they considered what path to take. In that pause, men searched and strained for that all-important dream of their lives. My dream to be an aviator was no different from another who wanted to be an artist or physician, but the fact remained, men were preoccupied, toiled in their suspension. In the meantime, life went on while their personal clocks were yet to begin. It's woman, who stood below, who comprised the sea of reality and it is she who posed the sobering questions that fixes accountability and anchored him in the relevance of the present. Perhaps Rachel was correct to wonder if I understood success or if I knew when to re-evaluate my goal? At what point did the end become the now? How much is enough? Therefore, in the end, it was woman who reached and pulled man to his feet, bathed him in reality and made him be.

The neon light from the restaurant's window flickered like glitter in Rachel's eyes and silence brought realization of the night's impending end.

"If I write you, will you answer my letters, promise? I know I'll miss you, Streeter."

"Sure I'll write. I'm looking forward to seeing what becomes of you."

"I'm not so courageous after all. What I'm about to say, I want you to take it with you. You leaving, takes it away. It means I won't be reminded each time I see you," she said softly.

We left the restaurant, drove back to Rain Seed County. Before Tommy's death and my homecoming, Rachel was content with teaching, worked in the community, and placed anything personal on the back burner. Now her emotions betrayed her and sought my presence, my touch, and what promise I might offer. All summer long, she hid from the memory of passion and its temptations; ignored my desires and that of her own. She forgot words she would no longer say, words reminiscent of things she would no longer do. In spite of having remembered that forbidden passion, she pretended not to.

The night had grown old and quiet except the chorus of insects. When long pauses again invaded our conversation, she knew it was now or never to share her secret. Tears preceded her voice. "I'm not what you think I am, Streeter. I'm a bad person. I gladly take responsibility, my punishment and be reminded my demons are never far away. I'm a bad person, Streeter… I have a child," she cried softly, sobbed. "I … had a child," she struggled, corrected herself. "I…was pregnant once, but it didn't come to term, I had a child…"

She labored in her revelation, so much so, I asked her to stop. Once composed, she continued, but nothing she said changed the way I felt about her. In my opinion, nothing she said made her a bad person. Whatever she was or thought she had become, some spiritual reckoning had occurred. Of that, I reminded her.

"Rachel, your belief in God says you need only ask and it's forgiven," I suggested.

"I wish it were that easy," she replied. "You see, you have a way with me. I listen to you, the way you simplify things, and you let me vent. You always say the right thing. You're the man with all the answers. I'm sure I'll miss that."

I drew her near, kissed her; kissed the many years of wanton, wishful fantasies and she passionately succumbed. She took only what she could repay, said only what I'd remember. For yesterday and tomorrow, carefully I packaged that evening for days ahead. I held her there in the darkness of the car, wished she would hold on; grow beyond the fears of her past. Over my shoulder, applauded the many ghosts of yesterday.

"Rachel, I'm going to a regimented ordeal, full of trying situations. Like the promise you made to God and yourself, I plan nothing less than total subjection.

You know what you want out of life, where you're going, and what it's supposed to look like once you get there. I only know what I want. As for where I'm going, the only control I have is my desire to succeed. I'll simply give it all I've got."

Rachel turned and climbed on the seat; her knees straddled me, then, draped her arms around my shoulders.

"Are you trying to scare me off, Streeter?"

My long legs and knees caught under the dashboard prevented my eluding her grasp. Not that I wanted to, but simply to look her in the eyes and know that she meant every word she spoke.

"You're going to make it this time, Streeter. I'll be praying for you."

Towards 3:00 A.M., having squeezed all I could from yesterday, I walked her into the house. Without any further pretensions or binding promises, I focused on the future where together, time might offer its own solution. How noble, I thought to myself, how noble of me when I reviewed those moments in whatever uncertain times that lie ahead.

SANDRA

Nine weeks of Army Basic Training passed as slow as the growth of ivy. In its pause came letters originally posted to Pensacola Naval Air Station. Letters from Sandra, a girl I dated most in college, caught-up with me. Sandra was a wild-child, whose social consciousness embraced the exploding political ideals of the civil rights movement as well as the counterculture. She now lived in Atlanta, a brief drive from my training site at Fort Gordon, in Augusta, Georgia. The physical proximity inspired mutual wishes to reconnect. With cheerful excitement, we schemed to share a few days and upon conclusion of basic training, she came as promised. We each stared momentarily, remembered, then an enthused embrace.

"Let's go, all this khaki is boring!" shouted Sandra.

In a sun-lit chill of November, I dumped my duffle bag into the rear seat of Sandra's convertible and we sped northwest to Atlanta.

"We have a lot in common, you know," Sandra said. "And I've thought a lot about that."

"You didn't seem to think so in college," I said.

She stared at me for a moment, then pointed her eyes back to the road, before saying, "When you came along, you got into my head, asked a lot of questions. You couldn't understand a person not on speaking terms with their parents. You ignored me, too, Melvin. You always had something going-on, you and your flying. My rebellious but serious nature made a statement, but

31

unlike the other guys, you didn't blow me off when you found you couldn't have your way with me."

"What, then, makes us common?" I asked.

"We're very loyal to our dreams—dedicated, willing to sacrifice the irreplaceable. Those were the times of our lives, college, yet you blew through that experience like it meant nothing."

"And you?" I asked, still uncertain of her point.

"The Civil Rights Movement is at a crossroad, Melvin. Several times, I almost dropped out of college. It's the movement that defines incendiary slogans like 'Black Power.' Someone has to interpret that, some of us have to live among and be part of the grassroots. You, unlike my parents, understood that. A sense of devotion and being stubborn is the sin we share. We refuse to give up. I stand about as much a chance with you now as I did three years ago. Flying airplanes has got you by the throat and you don't know how to let go."

It seemed everyone had my number. Sandra came from a well-to-do family, but more than anything, Sandra was strikingly beautiful. She was a brazen revolutionist, friendly and very popular. Her figure embellished contemporary fashions; mini-skirts, bell-bottom hip-huggers with exposed midsections and bra-less, halter-tops. Her amiable spirit, too often spelled "easy," but to the contrary, her values did not include the promiscuous or thankless indulgencies of that day. Sandra's rebellion was against her middle-class upbringing, materialism, and the West's control and consumption of the world's natural resources.

In contrast, Rachel extended me the lifetime of a boy who saw with the eyes of men—a boy with the heart of a sage, but with the palms of a child, too small to hold such fortunes. Sandra's was four years of warm reciprocated affection, real, yet complex. Since college our contact became infrequent. With her, I spoke my mind. With Rachel, I tightened, guarded my emotions. My love for Rachel had always been opportunistic, though haunting, unrequited and fantasy driven. The scars of wish were deep. With Sandra, life was real time. What I wanted, she only promised. What she wanted I was yet to become.

'What's this thing you have for the military, Mel? The Navy was no good, huh?" Other than the flight school washout, I hadn't shared much with Sandra.

"No good," I replied.

"What does the Army have?" she asked.

"I'm going to fly helicopters!" I fired back.

"Going to fly helicopters, are you?" she said. "People are leaving the country, Mel, trying to avoid the war, and you ask for it."

"Gotta go, Sandra. I gotta get some before it's all over. What brought you to Atlanta?"

"The same as you," she answered. "Vietnam. College enrollment is high, military draft is high and jobs are plentiful. Initially, I came to work with SCLC. In the mean-time, I landed a full-time job and worked my way up to editor in a Publishing House. How long you staying, Mel?"

"I don't know, the weekend, I suppose."

When we arrived at Sandra's apartment, she quickly fixed a meal between jabs, about our days in school. We sat and ate through the same. Her upscale apartment near old downtown looked down on Atlanta, a bevy of efforts to re-make itself, sparkled like some jewel-encrusted labyrinth. I stood at the window and gazed below, and again thought of the two women, Rachel and Sandra. With soft, melodic, jazz in the background, I continued my stare until darkness gave back only the reflections of Sandra and me standing there. The window reflected a look of want and wish, an empty look, long stored amid a dusty be-trayal of achievement. Men who sat alone in bars had that look, as did little boys who stared too long into toy store windows. Sandra's fragrance, filled my senses. I turned, pulled her close and she submitted. Her pointed stare into my eyes conveyed the message that ours was not this time—a message I knew too well. Once I acknowledged that look, all was well. Her look spared an explana-tion—nothing had changed since college. That's who she'd always been for me. So I kissed her and only then she closed her eyes and joined me in a darkness familiar, a darkness that only entertained my wishes, one that finally said I was her captive. Later, she sat between my legs on the couch, her back to my chest, our arms intertwined. Sandra traced the creases in my palm. I think she sensed my disappointment and perhaps a sense of entitlement.

"We've dealt with this before, Mel," she said softly. "Understand that I'm not ready yet, and I want to hear you say that's okay."

"It is okay, Sandra," I said.

"Wait, you said that too fast, Mel…. Don't be upset. I don't want to just have sex with you. I want to win, be what you want, not what you have, and certainly not a …, Popsicle or a slice of gum you shove in your mouth before you climb into one of your cockpits. I'd like to be the moment, not something that enhances it." Her voice dropped apologetically to a harmless purr, then she continued. "I want to be part of you, what you belong to. No man knows me the way you know me. Do you understand what I'm telling you? You've always been someone special, and I was happy being with you. Used to look for you, I drove, I walked, sometimes when I found you, you'd make me wait. I had but a thimble full of patience and entrusted it only to you."

She moaned lightly, chuckled, crossed my arms around her, and continued.

"You've gotten more out of me than any man. I don't want you to be disappointed. I think our time will come. Apparently, there's something out there you want more than you want me."

A bit embarrassed at her candor, surprised at such a personal disclosure, I answered, "I knew your fears of confinement, to be known as someone's girl."

"I bet I asked you out as much as you asked me," she insisted. "I had other dates, but nothing past platonic," she concluded.

"You and I did the big events," I said. "We shared some very special moments, yet it never resembled my idea of a relationship. You and I traveled all over the east coast, from wild parties to various political symposiums."

"I dragged you all over the East Coast!" she bragged, then reminded me how grateful she was for my presence.

That remark brought a playful volley of gentle blows I attempted to parry in a mass of arms, legs, and pillows from the couch. Clasped in a close embrace, we moaned, swore, and rolled in the night.

"What was it you used to call me, Doo-Dah Man?"

"Yes," she answered in fact.

"You never explained what that meant," I reminded her.

"You sure?"

"Yes, I'm sure. Once we talked of love, how you 'loved me, but was not in love with me.'"

"Did I really say that?" she asked in a chuckle.

"Yeah, your exact words," I answered and Sandra's reply was classic.

"Like I said, we have a lot in common; we're two of a kind. Is that what you wanted Mel, a confined relationship? To hear me say, I'm in love with you? Is that it, Mel?"

Dryly and unenthused, I answered, "Let's face it, I was a good stand-in, helped minimize the questions like, to whom did you belong? But you see… I'm a romantic…"

Excited, Sandra punched me playfully, tried grasping my ear, my nose, then a pinch of cheek, something to inflict some minor pain. She needed my attention.

"You should learn to listen with more than you ears!" she said. "Think about that for a moment and all the times me…, Sandra…, chased you. Now, explain my feelings for you. So, you're a romantic?" She continued with a chuckle. "Well…, I think you're a sentimental, self-righteous man in search of romance!"

Laughter billowed in the night as I thought how badly I misunderstood Sandra's sincerity and feelings.

Simply put, I always thought she was out of my league. I never trusted my advances as being effective or her attention as being genuine. In the two years since college, Sandra described our minimal contact as unavoidable and unintentional. She was straightforward and blatant, like the approach of darkness, bold and unavoidable.

In college, fellows who chased and courted Sandra were blinded by their desires or did so with emphasis on social positioning and measuring one's values monetarily. Her looks implied someone used to the extravagant, to lavish living and one who afforded the finer things in life. But those were direct reflections of her middle-class upbringing, the source of her family rift. Sandra bore an acute defiance of such values and presented an earthiness unimpressed with the tapestry and glitz of the world. The likes of her, I had never seen. I saw her first as a hippie, a rich brat, then a serious being, sensitive to the rights and plight of all living things—a beautiful woman illusive and ethereal; just beyond the reach of men and their wishes.

"It seems we're always saying goodbye," she said sadly. "Where're you off to now?"

"Tiger Land," I said. "Fort Polk, Louisiana. Eight weeks of advanced infantry training, then on to helicopter flight school."

"Pilots need infantry training?" she asked.

"No, but if I flunk out of flight school again, infantry is where I'll spend the next four years."

"I'm glad you came, Mel. When will I see you again?"

"Let's stay in touch. Once training is done, flight school that is, we'll get together."

"Leave me behind, Mel, but don't leave me. Don't make me come looking for you either," she concluded. A warm smile lit her eyes, one ready to go solemn any moment.

News from Rain Seed County said all the boys my age had gone to war. The forest was still. No one built tree houses or dugouts in the sawdust. Sleep became an infantry soldier. Packy was in an armored division. Beenie was an infantry radio specialist. Leo became a paratrooper. Among the yellow leaves of hickory, the red and gold of sweetgum trees, our presence seemed long forgotten. The dynamics of manhood, suddenly morphed into that endless string of summer days and Saturdays we long imagined.

RE-DREAMING THE DREAM

The sign arched above the entrance at Fort Wolters, Texas, read, "U.S. Army Primary Helicopter Center." Primary helicopter training, I likened to being a mouse in a snake pit. The Tac Sergeants were pythons who ruled the pit and we, warrant officer candidates, were the mice that lived day to day. Everyone was hounded to the brink of disorientation. A measure of mental stamina and alertness, I found was inherent to any flight training. Only in the classroom setting and only from a few civilian, classroom instructors did anyone receive anything nearing empathy. Jeff Castle, a civilian who taught with excitement and humor, was such an instructor. Castle's voice accompanied me the first time I climbed into the cockpit of a helicopter.

"Flying a helicopter," Castle said, "is a pilot's deliberate control-input while governing the rotation of two sets of rotors, the main rotor system, and the tail rotor system, such that they strike the air at a particular pitch angle to achieve lift and drag."

The first month of ground school was preflight training, the study of weather, the principles of helicopter flight, then primary flight training and flight controls. Gradually, we approached the flight line where everyone tried impressing the IPs (Instructor Pilots) in his initial attempt at the controls. I sought some carry-over, some advantage from prior flight training. Candidates learned to master one control at a time, then takeoffs, landing, hovering, and autorotation, aimed for the magical moment when each

37

would solo. My first turn at the controls in a hover exercise was all but a seasoned pilot.

"The controls we're going to practice are the only controls you need worry about. I'll control everything else. Is that clear?" The voice of the IP was near threatening.

"Yes, Sir," I answered. Controls for flying the helicopter shared the same linkage that gave operation to either pilot. The training model was a Plexiglas, bubble top, craft from the Korean War, the Hiller, H -23. Its mechanical linkage physically attached one component to another to achieve a particular posture of flight. The vibrations were annoying and the delay between input and reaction was slow.

"I'm going to put the helicopter into a hover mode. Using the collective pitch control level, I want you to hold the ship in a hover. You got that? Don't worry about anything but keeping us at a hover, pointing in that direction." The IP pointed to the red markers at the western edge of the training field. His voice boomed in the headsets.

Since the IP had us in hover mode, I concentrated on the anti-torque pedals, left petal, located on the cockpit floor and operated with the pilot's feet. In medium positive pitch, meaning both petals held evenly, I'd retain the desired heading. I thought I need only guard the collective pitch control lever without input.

The helicopter lurched upwards until the IP, yelled, "I got it!" He quickly took control and brought the ship down, just above ground effect and again, said to me, "You got it!"

Emotionally, I was tense, and increased throttle to measure the response of the craft. Nothing happened.

After a moment, the IP said to me, "We are not supposed to be on the ground. That was an excellent landing, but the exercise is to use the collective pitch control in a stable hover. You got that?"

Embarrassed, in my effort, I said, "Yes, Sir!"

"I'll bring the helicopter to a few feet above the ground, you see if you can hold it there," the IP said calmly while I again took the controls.

I avoided over-controlling, tried anticipating the helicopter's movement. Without the emotional tension, I searched for patience and allowed for lag in control-input. Intentionally, I brought the ship up a few feet above the intended hover, twisted in additional throttle and RPM's and the helicopter settled into a hover.

There were casualties in the form of washouts. Any combination of three demerits or notices of pending dismissal, for major screw-ups, and you were history. Such were the elimination tactics of flight school. A predetermined number of pilot positions existed. Not at all unlike the Navy, these were times of war and training offered few mercies. Within the four months that defined primary flight training, each candidate was to solo within 12 to 14 hours of logged time. Those that passed the solo phase earned a bill of confidence and for the first time didn't have to wear their caps backward. As they said, "… having satisfied the basic requirements, we could now play with the Army's toys."

I evaluated my efforts more stringently than the IPs and termed my quest not a relentless, pursuit of perfection, but simply an effort to avoid surprises. I was determined to minimize mistakes, and never again allow anyone to waltz me out the door as a washout. I disliked being predictable, but that was what the Army expected. Later I joined 48 students of an initial class of 120 and went on to the remaining four months of training at Fort Rucker, in Alabama. The training craft at Fort Rucker was a monstrosity that looked like a huge tadpole. It had hydraulic linkage that shortened considerably input to response ratios, but far from the likes of the popular Huey, we all longed to command. Student pilots spent long hours in simulated war games and air assaults as everyone took part in leadership roles, planning assaults, flying lead while simulating real time, troop insertions and extractions, in differing terrain.

There was but one signature laugh in the Army, and that laugh belonged to flight instructor CW4, Jake Habrasham, and without a doubt, the most memorable character in helicopter flight school.

Mr. Habrasham was a solid figure in his early forties. The career warrant officer stood six feet tall and had a thick mane of red hair. Halfway through training at Fort Rucker, I found myself in a familiar yet dubious situation. The training commander, summoned me to a meeting. The sound of drums banged slowly in my head as my nerves tightened. In-route, Mr. Habrasham joined me in a slow trot, no candidate walked in company area. His loose and friendly nature failed to reassure me, for I trusted no one. Near the entrance, rows of stones the size of footballs painted white formed a small perimeter to headquarters. Habrasham paused and slightly tipped his cap, as I entered the building.

"This is no disciplinary procedure, candidate. It's informal, if you will." The gruff, middle-age man in khakis with the bird rank of colonel on his lapel, spoke kindly. A deep sigh and deflating chest spelled my relief.

"Occasionally it is noted when someone with an unusual record is aboard. I'm curious to know why you resigned your naval commission," said the commander.

A bit more relaxed now, I explained my life-long desire to fly. I admitted, too, the resignation was not a smart move, but from the standpoint of a 19-year-old, a naval commission alone resembled failure.

"I came up through the Army Air Corps," the commander began. "Pilots that did not make the grade became bombardiers and remained useful to the program. To fail in one phase of training did not preclude the use of that training in another capacity. We're into something now where we need all the qualified bodies we can get. They spoke highly of you at Fort Wolters and here as well. Answer this for me and you're dismissed. Why didn't you apply for OCS?"

"Sir, I chose the program with the shortest route to the flight line."

Finally, someone cared about the few that fell between the cracks; a spit toward the fire that burned in my guts. No one would ever catch me off guard again—no one. The remaining seven weeks included night flying in simulated assaults that gave each pilot the hours of flying he longed for. As the Hueys came into training use, its difference from the trainers was as vast as a tractor to a sports car. The Bell HU-1 Iroquois "Huey" was the sports car of helicopters. Made of aluminum and magnesium alloy and powered by a turbine jet engine, it would fly at a maximum of 120 knots and carry up to 4,500 lbs. of cargo plus a crew of four.

As spring faded to summer, Rachel spoke tenderly of last summer. Sandra's letters were notes. She kept me abreast of the civil rights movement and the happenings in the streets. Theories abound that the draft became a tool to quell the violent rioting in major cities and the convenience of the Vietnam War created a conduit to support conscription. In late June, under a scorching Alabama sun, the newest class of helicopter pilots received our wings appointed the rank of warrant officer 1. The rank was a license to fly helicopters. I contemplated the changes I underwent throughout those regimented training processes. I lost forever the ability to trust people in general. I lost any sense of humor for fear of appearing immature. Within days, I shipped out to Fort Campbell, Kentucky, home of the 101st Airborne Division Air Mobile. A curious bunch of new and seasoned pilots milled about for the better part of a week, before official language begun to circulate. The 21st Assault Helicopter Company of the Fourth Battalion, 63rd Air Division was mobilizing for Southeast Asia. My burden since I convinced my parents that my chances of serving in the war was slim, suddenly got heavy. Having organized my thoughts, I sought the courage to call home. Beneath lighting from the street corner, I waited my turn at the telephone booth. My carefully planned speech vanished when mom answered the phone. I wished it was dad or better yet, Ellen or Maurice. Small talk eluded me, I stammered.

"Hi, ma, my unit is shipping out, ah in eight weeks."

"Oh?" She acted surprised, as she often did when she knew everything, but made me explain it anyway. I'd rather chew nails than tell my mother I was headed to Vietnam.

"Ah, ah, we're shipping out in eight weeks, ma, we're going to Vietnam."

"You're not going!" she stated and asked all at once. I felt her disappointment in me, her pain and anger. Such news via telephone, what a dastardly thing to do to them.

"I can't help it, ma. I'm part of the unit. Would you tell dad? I have to go. There's a line of people behind me, waiting to make calls."

The pilot next in line, fatigued from standing, knelt, leaned against the phone booth, and looked up from the shadows at me. His piercing stare accompanied my struggle to explain my lack of choice in the matter. His face shared my disappointment and my mother's objections. Perhaps he found words for his defense.

"Now you hold-on...! Just..., hold-on a minute!" Mom shouted.

Then there was silence, more silence as she gathered herself before asking, "Is there someone there I can speak to? ....Howard...!" she yelled, but his reply didn't come soon enough. "Howard....!" she yelled angrily, "....take this phone!"

Dad took the phone and now I had to repeat myself in view of the face behind me. My dad sighed heavily.

"Give us a call when things calm down, when you know more about what's going on," he stalled. Dad felt no better than mom did and knew too well his task was to calm her down. They would talk late into the night, the kind of mumbling in the dark of the house I too often heard.

The 21st Assault Helicopter Company, was flown to California, then bussed onto a troop ship in long, slow moving lines. Once underway, the west coast faded into nothingness and soon we were the only people in the world, upon a ship that sailed into eternity. A few days later, I haphazardly walked into a lounge among men who sat and leaned against the bulkhead, when a voice rang out above the rest.

"This war won't last long! The Navy is here! What cha say, Navy?"

It was the redheaded, chief warrant officer, instructor pilot from Fort Rucker. I shook his extended hand and was happy to see at least someone familiar. Habrasham greeted me like a long lost brother, introduced me and said there were two helicopter companies aboard. With him stood several pilots, recent flight school graduates and impressed with a few "old salts" telling war stories.

I had no reason to suspect Habrasham.

THE ETERNAL SUMMER

SEPTEMBER 1967

Far to the east we went, to an enchanting, beautiful land—just beyond the rim of the world as if to hide the mischief of waging war.

Amid the central plains of South Vietnam, rose the central highland provinces of Ban Me Thuot, Phan Rang, An Khe, Kontum, and Pleiku. None of us understood the historical significance of that region and few were aware our area of operation included such places. Our new home was Camp Holloway, surrounded by elephant grass in the province of Pleiku, four miles from the town of Pleiku. That Camp Holloway recently sustained a mortar attack and was overrun by enemy troops only piqued our interest. Row upon row of tents, or hootches as they were called in Vietnam, each surrounded by three foot sandbag walls, was the sight that greeted us. The first chilling view of Vietnam was the sight of a group of native laborers at work inside the compound.

"Skinny, aren't they?" someone commented as a small group of us stood watching.

"Shit, not inside the compound! How are they able to work inside the compound? They look just like the bad guys to me," another added.

"I don't care what they look like as long as I'm seeing them through the windshield of a helicopter. Keep them the hell away from me," another pilot whined.

Amid days of orientations, safety checkout rides were posted. Standard procedure upon reassignment was a safety check ride to determine one's proficiency in flight maneuvers. At 0:700 I met the unit's flight safety officer, Captain Shields, in the operations tent.

"Ready, Mister Streeter? We're flying guns today, going to shoot up the place a little, give you a feel of the quad machine guns and the Huey 'B,'" Captain Shields informed me.

We knocked the mud off our boots as best we could and climbed into an awaiting Jeep for the ride to the flight line. We rode a tiny trail, marked by water-filled potholes through a field of up-turned tree stumps. At a distance were rows of sandbag revetments or fortified parking spaces for helicopters and level ground where perforated steel planking (PSP) formed the tarmac. I joined the captain in preflight procedures and before long the distinct whine of the turbine engine pierced the morning air as the rotors disappeared into a blur.

The Huey Helicopter had undergone several design changes with newer versions eminent. Its many configurations was evident of an on-going experiment. Our experiences included the Huey 'B,' 'C,' and 'D' models that differed in engine size and rotor span along with slight alterations in the vertical fin among those aspects immediately recognizable. Some gunships or "guns" were the 'B' models outfitted to carry only the pilots, although some heavier armored versions carried the extended crew of door gunners. The troop compartment stood crammed with magazines of ammo that fed machine guns and M-5 grenade launchers. The 'guns' escorted and protected "slicks" or troop-carrying helicopters.

The target area resembled a miniature airport with wide paths etched into the ground. I flew left seat, the copilot's seat in a gunship, the opposite in the 'D' model for troop carrying slicks. Empty ammo boxes like vegetable crates in a garden, marked firing lanes, and intersections. In my delight, excitement and panic fought for attention.

"Okay, line up your sights and we'll make a run. The target is the ground between those markers. This is target practice, not a test. There is no grade. Just get a feel of the weapon systems using live ammo," said Captain Shields.

During preflight, quips about my naval experience baited surreptitious looks as he probed and displayed a thorough knowledge of my personnel jacket and presumed flight capabilities. The quad 30 caliber machine guns, two at each side of the helicopter, employed an aiming device that hung from the ceiling above the copilot's seat. Through its sighting and triggering mechanism in the form of a pistol grip, the co-pilot picked his targets. When not in use, it folded away neatly in the ceiling. The principal duty of the helicopter copilot was to monitor the instrument panel and be ready to assume control at a moment's notice. In the gunship, copilot duties included offensive weapons deployment and in this case included the 40mm grenade launcher. A 7 tube 2.75 inch rocket pod, one at each side of the ship was fired by the aircraft commander.

Captain Shields flew into a huge gully, a dry riverbed having steep meandering clay walls. He proceeded below ground level and flew to the contours of its turns and depths. In an instant, he popped above the ground where the markers suddenly came into view. I squeezed the trigger and the quad machineguns erupted, ripped into the loamy soil. I pushed the pod away to survey the results when the captain said;

"What are you doing? Your next target is coming up!"

A sharp bank to the left and row upon row of markers appeared. Following a thorough set of exercises, the captain climbed away from the field for me to perform a number of flight maneuvers on his command.

"You got it," the captain said, meant for me to take the controls. Later I flew the ravine, also. "Have a go at it. Keep it close to the right side, light on the petals."

I measured my distance from the wall with the leading edge of the main rotor system. The turns came quickly and the weight of the Huey Gunship was apparent and unlike the open deck slicks, but responsive nonetheless. Before long, a satisfied Captain Shields directed me back to base.

"Double 'A,' Mister Streeter, double 'A,'" the captain said. It meant the officer approved my air work.

"Welcome to the Nam," wrote Packy. His letter was first among acquaintances from home.

"Do your best to keep your feet dry and don't take a pass on that daily malaria pill either."

Then, among the letters from my parents was the sad news of his death. Packy, a Marine, died in an explosion near Da Nang. Again, I reached for Packy's letter where among his comedic comments, he still lived and dreamed of life as we imagined it. One moment the warmth of his friendship, a moment later, he no longer existed. Rachel's letter made no mention of Packy, but was full of promises.

"I met with Reverend and Mrs. Lucas to begin talks about, you know what," she wrote.

I walked outside, sat on the sandbag wall and watched the war in the nearby hills, heard the faint sound of a Huey in the night sky and saw beads of red tracers fall into the jungle below. Maybe a crew on base security patrol, I thought. The Huey circled and the night continued to inhale sticks of broken red lines that silently fell to earth. I thought of Packy, the years and summers gone by, and the uncertain role I would play in that war. I watched as yet another Huey joined the night war, as flairs lit up the hillside and more tracers flew in the night. Tracers are bullets that glowed in the dark. Four regular bullets separated each tracer that offered the gunner a point of aim. For Packy, gone were the summers of trial and transition—summers that nurtured little boys and tempered our dreams. Gone now, were summers in time's folly. Tommy, now Packy, essentials removed forever from the cool shade of summer, and days of our youth. Although the war was my opportunity to live my dream, I tried separating the war that killed and maimed from my war of convenience.

The next morning a familiar voice rang out. "What's happening? Navy?" The signature laugh gave him away. It was Jake Habrasham and along with him came my new nickname, "Navy."

His unit disembarked at the ship's first port of call, Vung Tau, and our arrival concluded the tours of those who arrived a year earlier. His transfer precipitated a balance of experienced and inexperienced pilots.

"Mister Habrasham!" I said. "Just what did it take to get you off that beach in Vung Tau? Come to show us how to fight this war?" I mused.

"They told me to pack, didn't say where to—thought you'd have this place whipped into shape by now," the former flight instructor said.

He and several old salts from the troop ship joined the 21 Assault Helicopter Company (21st AHC). The 21st AHC was now a unique four- lift company, with four platoons of troop-carrying slicks (four helicopters per platoon) and one "gun" platoon for escort. The "slicks" had a door gunner at each side of the helicopter, one of which, doubled as Crew Chief, trained to trouble shoot, and make minor repairs. As much as the Aircraft Commander (AC) was in charge, the ship actually belonged to the Crew Chief. His task was to crawl over the ship and log its readiness for the next flight. A ship not airworthy was assigned a red X and noted in the flight log.

Patrick Odine (pronounced Oit-na) was a taut and hardened individual. No one is born that way. For Odine, it took three tours of duty to develop the barbed tongue and assorted prejudices against young, unseasoned, pilots. As the lone colored pilot in the company, somehow, I ended up sharing his ship. There was nothing amiable about Odine, not his narrow, close-set eyes, his dagger and serpent tattoo, nor the curl of smoke from his cigarette. Since it was the platoon leader who made pilot assignments and pilot pairings, there was little Odine could do.

"Gunships are for experienced pilots," Odine said. "No newbie FNG, has the balls or ability for combat flying in a gun ship. That's asking too much. Three fricking tours and I haven't seen it yet. It takes an experienced individual or an extraordinary individual and in my opinion, the latter is in short supply."

I had no interest in Odine's preferences, nor whether I flew 'slicks' or 'guns.' I simply wanted to command my own aircraft as soon as practical. It was late September, the company as a whole had its first mission. The heat and intense sunlight sat poised against the morning's brief coolness. I flew with Odine, the staunch and taciturn Odine. In spite of his personal preferences, Odine, at times masked his feelings well. Never once did I forget whose presence I shared, but once in a while he could be civil.

"Before long, you'll get used to these mornings," Odine said. "They become invisible considering greater thoughts of living and dying and going home again."

I nodded in reply, appreciated the remark.

We pulled on our armored chest protection, called the chicken plate. An enamel coated steel plate curved to fit the torso and hung from the pilot's shoulder.

"For what it's worth, Navy," Odine continued, "I carry standard issue weapons, sidearm, and M-16. That way, in case of a shoot down, we can share ammo. Half the people here have more exotic weapons than a Wild West Show. I don't care what you fancy as a personal weapon, but when you fly with me, carry your .45 automatic, M-16 and plenty of ammo. Got that?"

"Roger that, Mister Odine!" I answered.

Two pilots walked by with low slung gun belts similar to Wyatt Earp, or some cowboy. Another carried a sawed-off shotgun.

"All that is fine as long as you have ammo," Odine said. "But when you're out, what do you do? In a month, you won't see all that. They settle down right quickly."

The wisdom of Odine's years in combat was sharp and clear. He knew that in spite of all its technologically advanced destructibility, the elements and terrain of Vietnam made helicopters highly vulnerable. Helicopters and its crews were prized trophies to the VC.

As the temperature rose, the fuselage made a ticking sound as the metal expanded. With the signal to crank, the helipad came alive with rotors flipping and engines whining. Odine slowly rotated his wrist on the throttle for sufficient RPM's, pulled slightly on the collective pitch control lever and the ship eased off the ground and into the morning air. Odine pointed out the Air Force Base, the twin peaks of "Titty Mountain" and Pleiku, as we continued to climb, then, circled to join the formation of slicks. Our mission was to insert a company of the 4th infantry division into the U-minh Forest, near the Cambodian border, in search of a squad cut off and lost a day earlier. It was not common, but certainly not unheard of for infantry units to get lost in the jungle. Huey slicks, flew into the staging area of the 4th Infantry Division for pickup. The gun platoon, nicknamed "The Vipers," flew at each side of the formation, one above while another flew ahead with a LOACH, Scout in tow to prep the LZ where the troops would be inserted. The formation flew right at 2000 feet, which was effectively out of range of small-arms fire. Odine and I flew at the high position. Above the jungle greens and shaded blues, I held back tides of excitement and the taut pull of panic. The war had arrived as subtle as dawn or dew in the morning. In a flicker of rotors against an endless ripple of valleys came instructions to tighten the formation in order to shorten our exposure during insertion. The four ships of yellow flight led the formation, followed by white flight where Reljac flew co-pilot in the number-two position. Behind them were the four ships of red flight, then Orange, where Belk, the bunk-mate I met on board the troop ship, flew copilot to the flight leader in Orange-one. Through the hail of UHF communications, I followed the transition of events.

"Yellow-one, this is Viper, do you roger marker?"

"Roger, orange marker, Viper 1," lead ship confirmed the marker set by the viper gun ship that flew ahead to prep the L Z.

"That's a Roger, Yellow One." The lead ship was always cautious and aware the Vietcong often used captured radios, monitored radio transmissions and popped smoke grenades to lure ships into an ambush.

The formation settled quickly on the LZ. Each flight, yellow, red, orange, and white, picked their spots and M-60 machine guns from each ship erupted into the tree-line and perimeter of the LZ. The Hueys sat shortly while the troops sprang from the decks.

"Lead out," said yellow flight leader and yellow-two, three, and four roger their readiness and lifted on cue. The other flights followed in concert and in three minutes the insertion was complete. The gun ships, in the daisy maneuver, circled the LZ, ready to suppress any enemy attack. Much like the approach, each flight climbed out low and fast, then flew a short distance to LZ Charley and awaited instructions from the grunt commander, code name 'Strong Man six.' Reljac and Belk walked over to my Huey. Both were my age, but cursed like old salts.

"I'm trying to get the hang of this funny money," said Reljac.

"What a color for money, I mean, Pink! Come on!"

"Check this out," Reljac compared the military script to the Vietnamese currency. "The Vietnamese stuff is weird but it looks more like real money. Hold it up to the sun, got watermarks."

By noon, the only shade in the valley was directly under the helicopters or the ship's cargo deck depending on its orientation to the sun. In a merciless heat, pilots and helicopters sat dormant like huge dragonflies that could spring effortlessly into the air. As a child, I used to clasp a large rubber band over the end of a short stick, stretched it to the other end and secured it in the jaws of an attached clothespin. The clothespin was my trigger. I was ready to hunt dragonflies. Their elongated bodies, its tremble of wings was not so unlike a helicopter.

The next morning, in the dark before dawn, we listened to the mission commander's briefing. Shortly afterwards came orders to crank and we headed for a remote LZ and a rendezvous with 'Strong Man six' and his unit. We flew in the morning's twilight, toward the voice of the scout pilot on the radio as he scoured the jungle in search of 'Strong Man six.' The grunts or infantry soldiers, including the previously lost squad, waited in eight separate groups, along one side of the perimeter and eight more on the opposite side. Each knew what Huey to board, made for a quick extraction.

"Pay close attention, Navy, you'll probably be down there the next time."

Odine motioned toward the slicks settling on the ground. Then the formation reversed its route, and flew back to Holloway. An excited mood permeated the dimly lit officer's club. A fragmented gathering of old salts sat together and the group from Vung Tau sat loosely, but connected by the same conversation. The FNGs recounted their first looks at Vietnam. Frequent deaths of FNGs supported a superstition whereby veteran pilots steered clear of us. The FNG mystique was more than a reason to play clever jokes, it said,

'Hurry, and learn what's going on so no one has to die because of your mistakes.' Names like Milky, Crazy Hoss, Big White, Salty and Deadeye were the results of first impressions, stupid acts, or pranks. FNGs died because they were FNGs. Veteran pilots died because of equipment failure or the enemy was simply better that day. The acronym, FNG, stood for "fucking new guy."

Time seemed bogged in the unchanging elements of a subtropical still life. I had flown with most of the ACs, but lately, more frequently with Bill Wrase. Wrase was sociable, talked a lot during missions. He earned the nickname, "Crazy Hoss."

"Crazy Hoss, huh," I quizzed him. "Where did that come from?"

"My great-grandfather was full-blood Lakota, so they say," he said. "Relatives mention it from time to time. It's the only thing that explains my innate wisdom," he bragged, laughed proudly.

"What's the joke about you and the first arrow shirt?" I asked with a straight face, having heard the joke in partial.

"When I'm razzed, I ask if they know who wore the first, arrow shirt… Custer, General Custer, you get it?" he asked.

I liked Wrase' indifference and his ability to relax. Odine was grim, taunt, and flew in command of his aircraft at all but the most routine instances. Wrase displayed confidence in his co-pilot. Toward evening, after chow, Captain Taylor, a platoon leader, came into the hootch with Wrase trailing.

"Navy, you've got a run to make at first light." It was a milk run or commonly referred to as ash and trash, a one-ship mission to the first Cav division at An Khe and on to the 173rd at Dak To. At first light the following day, Wrase and I tried ignoring a helicopter crash site at the pad the day before. The helicopter and crew limped back to base, but lost all controls near the landing pad. There were no survivors. Already refueled and reloaded with ammo, we went through preflight, then Wrase flipped the breakers, hit the starter button and gave me the thumbs-up sign, meant for me to take the controls.

"You got it! Let's get out of here."

I gently rolled the throttle, brought up the RPMs as the needles in the gauges flipped to safe operating. The throttle worked like that of a motorcycle twist grip. Affixed to the forward end of the Collective Pitch Control Lever that was located at the left of the pilot's seat. A twist of my wrist in one direction increased throttle while the opposite direction reduced throttle. The collective controlled the vertical movement of the helicopter, and resembled a parking brake in a sports car. I pulled up on the collective pitch control lever, which collectively increased power and simultaneously increased the pitch angles and angle of attack in each of the main rotor blades. The Huey eased off the ground into a shallow hover. A slight pull on the cyclic pitch control lever and the Huey crept backwards from the revetment onto the flight line. I caressed the left petal for a petal turn, increased throttle and settled into a hover in ground effect. The gun platoon occupied the rear revetments slightly separate from the rest due to a volatile cocktail that was the ship's fuel, ammo and ordinance crammed aboard. Wrase called departure.

"Holloway Tower, Baker One-four." The company call sign was "Baker."

"Baker One-four, Holloway."

"Roger Holloway, Baker One-four for departure, row-three, LZ English."

"Baker One-four, current altimeter three-zero-zero-two, winds one-eight-zero at zero-seven, cleared for departure, row-three LZ English."

I pulled the collective, nudged the Cyclic forward and the Huey nosed over for a running taxi past the tower and into the sky. The cyclic pitch control lever was for primary directional control, the horizontal movements of the helicopter and stuck up between the pilot's knees. The main rotor system or disk tilted slightly in the direction the cyclic stick was moved, forward, side-to-side or backwards, in the horizontal direction desired.

Over a fog choked jungle, we flew east to An Khe, headquarters for the 1st Cav. Div., then north above the Mang Yang Pass to Dak To. Later that afternoon, Wrase and I flew back to the familiar confines of Camp Holloway. On final approach, all that remained of the copter crash was the stench of burned flesh and a gray and black patch of burned ground.

My mother wrote of dissension among the American public over the validity of the war and, in her opinion, the unfair burden black soldiers bore as well. In her uncertainty, she wondered if some improprieties existed whereby black soldiers served disproportionately in combat units.

"If I had my way, you'd be on your way home or home as you should be," she said.

From my mother's letter, poured the pain and worry they dealt with.

"Ma..., Dad," I wrote in return, "The day to day existence in my unit is far from the dangers conjured by news reports. Our flight safety record is among the best. I fly four, or five hours a day, then I'm back." I fudged the actual time in the air, minimized the danger, played up the comforts of the war zone. "These guys have beer coolers in every hootch, play chess, checkers or card games throughout the night. You see the pictures I sent of children with smiling faces. "

Helms, my hootch mate, had fashioned from crate wood, and stained a marvelous desk and bed-frame. Curious about a bundle left there, I stood, picked up what was an oily rag that concealed a firearm, a .45 automatic. The item was overlooked by those who gathered Helm's personal effects. Helms was copilot in the ill-fated helicopter crash the day before. I dismantled the weapon, cleaned it, and put it away.

THE CONCRETE STRUCTURE

The Eternal Summer had no pause for a Fall Season. Yet, in what would be so, became my season of competency. For my parents, my life and safety was measured daily in the press. A letter from home contained two recent newspaper clippings with photos of downed helicopters. One caption read, 'Shot down in fighting near Pleiku.' Mom allowed the photos to speak for themselves, but asked that I not paint pretty pictures of the war for her benefit.

"Just be careful...pray often," she wrote.

Another letter spoke of injuries Leo sustained. He later died in a hospital in Japan. In the coming days, voices of conscience climbed into my helmet and whispered, "Where's Packy? Where's Tommy? With whom will you share these experiences someday? Beneath what tree will you gather to boast of your much celebrated manhood? Where's Leo?" The voices continued its whisper. Such were the memories of October, the memories of Packy and Leo fixed forever in their youth, never to grow old or be a witness to moments gone.

Rachel's letter shared an idea.

"Dear Streeter,

Much of the news except that of urban riots, centers on Vietnam. You're quite the photographer. I'm sharing with students, the photos that tell the human side of how the Vietnamese live their lives in spite of the war. Keep the photos coming and send some everyday items they use similar to our own.

We'll ask and answer some real questions about Vietnam. Can't say where this is going, but discussions are full of excitement."

A letter from Sandra said, "There are things I haven't the courage to say. It's not that I don't want to share those feelings, I simply thought they could wait..."

Soon, I sank into soothing memories of times gone by, of Rain Seed County, and pretty girls. The fact I grew up in a segregated south meant institutional inequities were commonplace. The military was far and above local politics, but its accountabilities did not prohibit the sneers and polarity that too often existed. I got used to being "out of place." Naval Flight School, for instance.

"Hey, Willie," a cowardly and unseen voice once called out. The name Willie, an epithet, reduced me and all colored men to a caricature. "You really don't believe you can fly an airplane, do you?" Or, "This ain't the hundred yard dash, N———! .... Need brains here!"

My mother's concern grew from a lifetime of improprieties based on race. As early as a year ago, my parents measured my wellbeing for reassurances my priorities were in order. That I could survive was not the question. Their concern was that I not compromise my integrity or home training in exchange for ambitions.

Rumor circulated that another pilot and I would fly courtesy missions for MAC-V. What good things might this assignment deprive me and what undue harm might be in store? A few minutes later, enough of my questions became clear when I learned Habrasham was the pilot to join me. My fondness for him, overcame any head games or questions of race, instead, placed the issues squarely on performance.

"Let's go, Navy," was all the redhead had to say. We flew to the A.R.V.N. (Army of the Republic of Vietnam) camp at Pleiku. That was the first time I met Colonel Stretch, MAC-V commander in II corps. The acronym, MAC-V, stood for, Military Assistance Command, Vietnam.

"There's no schedule or method to what we do. Your patience and skills are tested each flight. You'll miss some meals, and feel cut-off in general. When you fly for me, you're housed at MAC-V. You'll fly unescorted, not knowing when you expect to return. Bring plenty of supplies," he concluded.

We cranked and flew east to the coast. Habrasham was at the controls as the colonel fed him course headings instead of a destination. On board sat a

LAST OF THE GOOD BOYS

haggard American. His beige tropical suit, shirt, open at the collar showed clearly his tan-line. In the spirit of my mother, I tried to understand what I'd gotten into. Once at the coast, we flew south, a mile offshore, past Qui Nhon, Nha Trang, Cam Ranh Bay, before turning west again over the beach and small hamlets. We landed near a picturesque town southeast of Pleiku. "What's going on Habrasham? What's this all about?" Moments later Habrasham killed the engine, waited until the high pitch scream of the avionics shut down, then answered.

"...About... this?" He pointed to the building. "You know as much as I do. But as far as the mission is concerned, it's a piece of cake—a righteous piece of cake, Navy, believe me," he repeated himself.

"You care to say how my name came up for this mission?" I wanted to know. "Who chose me and why?"

Habrasham's face bore a quizzical look as he answered, "I, too, was chosen. Note the route we flew here. Well, we could have flown south, southeast and been here twenty minutes ago. It's a piece of cake, Navy." He pointed to the map at the point of departure and the point of arrival.

"You saying the colonel don't know his way around? That he can't read a map or we took the scenic route to kill some time? What's in there?" I continued to bagger him.

"Whatever it is," he began, "it's real sensitive."

"And how long might this last?" I asked again.

"Not long enough, buddy. Believe me, any one of those guys back at Holloway would curse his grandmother to get this job."

"Sounds like you know something. I'm listening." Habrasham shrugged off the comment, said nothing. I flipped the map onto my knees, traced again the route taken. His finger touched the spot where we likely landed.

"I remember that railroad, but I didn't see any of this," I said, as I pointed to features on the map. Chances are it was the town of Dalat or nearby. If so, he was correct. Our route was far from direct.

The concrete structure was weathered to a dull gray and rose to three levels. The second and third level shrunk respectively in width, each circled with an insulated six and eight-inch conduit. The building had a flat roof, no windows and sat adjacent to a manmade lake. A few hours passed before Colonel Stretch emerged alone from the building. We flew back to Pleiku where the crew had assigned living quarters. For weeks, we flew a bevy of flights to

Dalat and back, each no more exciting than the first. We landed, waited, and flew back. On November 3rd, the Colonel broke his routine and we flew to Tan Son Nhut Air Base just outside Saigon, central headquarters for MAC-V and at that time, known throughout the military as Pentagon East.

At one point the colonel addressed the entire crew, pilots and gunners, then said, "You haven't been told much, mostly nothing at all, but what you've seen and may have heard will not be the subject of idle banter. Do we understand?" We knew nothing and would say nothing about that nothing.

The colonel remained at Tan Son Nhut, ordered us to fly back to Pleiku until further notice. This time we flew north, along the Saigon River, towards route 14 and further north to the southern tip of the valley before I saw familiar landmarks near Ban Me Thout and on toward the beautiful bosom that was the twin peaks of Dragon Mountain. Once at Holloway, our company was in the midst of preparing the largest lift to date. The 21st AHC joined four additional helicopter units that darkened the sky in a massive move of whole battalions of the 4th infantry division and the 173rd airborne, to the hills of Dak To. We landed at a sprawling firebase, unloaded, and repeated our efforts twice more.

The temperature dropped that November evening. Few believed the weather would change so drastically even in the northern parts of South Vietnam. We shivered in the newest of discomforts. A balance of fuel and armaments aboard the gunships became a trade-off relative to the AC. With Wrase, we often flew heavy on ammo and light on fuel. I confirmed the much documented shortcomings of the 'B' model Huey Gunship. Its L-9 engine and shorter rotor span proved harder to hover and strained against the payload of ammo and fuel. The next day, Habrasham and I flew back to Pleiku and the compound at MAC-V. I relaxed, broke open my last can of Vienna sausage. Other favorites from home were Campbell's soup and rat poison.

Rachel's vague list of items for the school project grew in length from one letter to the next. Domestic utensils proved more difficult than imagined to collect.

"I'll go home to Baltimore for Thanksgiving, and I'll continue praying for you," she wrote in immaculate, cursive writing.

Habrasham and I merely flew our missions day and night. Our curiosity waned concerning the faces of strange men and their equipment. The civilians outnumbered the military passengers who, except for the colonel, seemed incidental and out of place. Our hours in the air far exceeded the average hours flown with our unit. I flew at the controls as much as I wished and learned as much as I could from Habrasham. I neared the fabled three-month mark that said, pilots who avoided injury or death during that period had a greater chance of surviving their tour. I had seen death at play, its greed, its smile, and insatiable appetite, yet I bristled with the arrogance of a snake charmer. Among the many bumps along the road of life, few are earth shattering but, occasionally, an incident represented an abrupt departure from the norm. So subtle came one bump that only fate could have summoned.

"...A Look, Looking, and a Look, being Looked At."

On a nameless day in November, Habrasham and I entered the offices at MAC-V. A wood railing maybe 30 inches high separated an open office from the lobby seating. A woman sat at the desk typing. Momentarily, she appeared to acknowledge our presence, but continued her work. Although her look was without expression, a storm suddenly raged inside me. That her skin was as dark as mine did not surprise me, for I regularly saw members of Montagnard Tribes around Pleiku. Her hair was as black as coal and fell about her shoulders and the back of her petite frame. I was visually startled and emotionally confused, as that strange uneasiness continued. My stomach tightened, likened to a fall from a great height in a nightmare. The anxiety escalated to the point I was about to excuse myself for fear I'd faint or become sick, when Habrasham nudged my leg and indicated the colonel invited us to join him for lunch.

The drone of electric fans, footsteps along a wooden sidewalk outside, and the woman's typing were the only sounds I heard. I fought the many assumptions forced into my mind, the mingling of memory, of wishful thinking, and impaired senses made for an irrational state of mind. Her presence flashed a strange bolt of lightning, one without the threat of rain or roll of thunder. In it, I saw a place I'd already been and a feeling of having suffered

59

a great, irretrievable loss. Something said I had crossed a line that separated what was, from what was to be. In the woman's eyes, I saw the threat of tears not yet poured.

Surreptitiously, I swept her presence, then looked away, but like the pull of magnets, my eyes drifted back to her. I felt drawn into a controversy and somehow this woman was party to its resolution. Suddenly, I gazed into her line of vision and she into mine. Our stares were empty, for neither of us seemed present to acknowledge the other. The focus was brief and conscious, but non-connecting. We were entities unreal to one another. A moment later, when I was sure her eyes were upon me, I gave a distinct nod, but there was no reply. Two paths of sight collided and locked onto one another, then torn away. She was real, I knew she was real, yet I struggled to convince myself that she could not be. She looked back with indifference, but nonetheless real.

Unable to escape, I again nodded slightly in her direction, hoped something, someone understood what was happening to me. I couldn't explain such affects, but knowing I needed to, I continued a penetrating stare until she responded with a nod of her own. Finally, an acknowledgement, but in whose assurance of the other? Her huge almond eyes and brown skin as dark as pine cones, looked back at me. The woman looked exactly like Rachel.

I followed Habrasham through an arched doorway, to the smell of food and the tug of anxiety. The dining area had a liberal use of plywood walls, lightly scorched to raise the texture of the grain and a coat of lacquer. A first Lieutenant, perhaps an aide, joined the colonel, Habrasham and myself, at a circular table complete with a white tablecloth.

When the small talk trailed-off, the colonel questioned me on my immediate plans, to which I replied, "Sir…, just a warrant officer pilot that wants to get home and in one piece."

"I can see your rank, Mister Streeter. I'm asking about your future plans?"

"I hadn't given it much thought, Colonel, beyond Vietnam, that is. I haven't had the time to consider the practical side."

"Maybe the Army can provide the practicalities for you," replied the colonel.

Habrasham felt a need to assist his co-pilot and help him understand the meaning of the inquiry. "Streeter here is an old Navy man."

The colonel raised a hand and begged off Habrasham's reply. "Mister Streeter, I am aware of the naval commission you resigned. The Army can and may grant its equivalence. There's a need for good career pilots that want to command."

I sat among two junior officers, yet I became the subject of the meeting. While still ravaged by that strange uneasiness, questions, too, my mother raised, resurfaced.

"I've been in-country for three and a half months with barely 800 hours of flying time. What makes me a hot prospect for command?"

I looked from one half-opened mouth to another, tried softening the remark. Colonel Stretch even smiled faintly before he answered.

"We're always mindful of high caliber men with leadership qualities. To lead is to command. Mister Habrasham knows more about your personal strengths than I. He thinks you're a very good candidate, a good leader. Don't be surprised," he said. "Appreciate when someone at any level is supportive."

The colonel's remark was a reach, an attempt perhaps, to assuage the Navy's decision to reject me. At that moment, his patronization only added to my anxiety. An hour or so passed, and I entered again the open office area, but the woman was not there. I flew at the controls to Saigon that evening, as we soared above the rolling surf with Armed Forces radio tuned in on the headsets.

"What do you know of my strengths, Hab?" I referred to the colonel's remark at lunch.

"Hell, I don't know what I was about to say. You were digging yourself quite a hole there," he answered. "What got into you?"

I did not answer. Surely, the presence of the woman was the reason for my ill feeling.

"Every pilot at Holloway is dedicated to the disciplines of being routine. Like you, they over-came many obstacles to get here, but few have a temperament that starts and ends with piloting. Very few have your impeccable skills. You're the only one screaming to be in charge, the only one I've met whose passion for flying has no rival," he said.

I lived my life without the usual dreams of having fancy things and great sums of money. Suddenly, it saddened me to hear Habrasham say all I ever wanted to do was fly airplanes. How shallow and impersonal I thought. Sandra was correct after all. She and I demanded little, because that was the extent anyone could expect in return.

An evening approach to Saigon resembled any western city as streetlights and electrically equipped homes and businesses lit up the horizon like embers in a fire. After a brief stop, we were airborne again, banked over the northeast corner of the airfield, then climbed east toward the coast and the blackened void that was the South China Sea. When back in Pleiku, we delivered the colonel then flew on to Holloway.

I toiled that night in a sleepless effort. The twilight of day brought some relief, but nothing changed in terms of my memory of that brief encounter. Prior to departing Camp Holloway and rejoin the unit at Dak To, Habrasham and I got word the unit had lost two helicopters. One pilot was dead, while two others sustained wounds that terminated their tours. I lifted into the twilight of receding stars, then ascended to 4000 feet and flew north in a brisk November coolness.

The landscape around Dak To had festered to engulf hilltops and valleys. Bombing and napalm drops churned up the red dirt and defoliated the jungle's trees. Left were broken, dying stumps like so many match sticks stuck in the soil. Fellow pilots sipped coffee and looked through tired enlarged eyes hidden behind dark circles. The hours and stress of combat flying showed on their faces, their walk, and speech, as they said little, instead used gestures of the head and hands. Habrasham and I had flown almost 80 hours in the past week, and only my youth and craze for flying kept me excited. MAC-V liaison officers and advisors generally worked exclusively with ARVN troops. Most pilots, to a man, disliked flying in ARVN operations. Bad stories circulated concerning their behavior under fire, with exception to the most elite units. Few if any pilots in the 21st relished flying for M.A.C-V.

I found a can of baked beans in a box of 'C' rations; a smaller can contained a biscuit, a can of fruit cocktail, and a pouch of cocoa mix. The cocoa is what I was after. In the chilly air, I tore open the pouch, poured it into a cup of hot water. The vipers had lost a gunship, but the pilots escaped injury, and the helicopter recovered.

Hills 823 and 1338 were the subject of briefing that morning with inclement weather conditions expected by early afternoon. I flew with Odine, teamed with a LOACH scout headed for hill 823. Odine and I flew against the mountains that morning, against the mountains and against the clouds, each a more formidable foe. We flew in support of Charley Company, 503rd infantry, as they ascended the 800-foot peak. We flew linked by radio to the weary voice of Grunt-six, the commander, unable to advance his unit pinned in the elements for two nights and a day. The grunt commander spoke haltingly of their predicament. The smell of their dead succumbed to the merciless heat of day, and the wounded, half-alive, drifted in and out of consciousness. Odine and I flew into the teeth of well entrenched, well supplied N.V.A. regulars and let fly an ungodly amount of ordinance that spared the troops on the ground a change in posture, but little else. Then the clouds moved in just below the rim of the mountains and sealed off the valley. In such a low ceiling, only the air strikes continued.

The larger of the LZs could accommodate one helicopter at a time. Chainsaws and explosives flown in to clear and enlarge the LZ's met sniper fire so intense the evacuation and re-supply slowly stopped. Soon, the days became a taxing mixture of landing and cranking, refueling and re-arming, banking and jerking in a frenzy that blurred the senses to a numbing monotony.

In a lull between shifts, I laid half-sleep. The VC walked mortars nearby in search of us. Each explosion came closer in rapid succession, like giant footsteps. Paralyzed with fatigue and choked with fear, I fell sleep, saw bodies that tumbled, and came apart, withered and exploded from the impact of gun ship, machine guns, and rocket fire.

Reljac strolled over to my hootch. Today was his 21st birthday.

"Y'all brought smoke on Charlie today," he said. The gun platoon had beat back every effort made by the NVA units.

"One-eight is broke," he continued. "They won't have that Huey flying for a while."

Reljac and I talked in snatches, watched at a distance a brief service for the dead.

"You flying again with Odine, tomorrow?" Reljac asked me. "Word has it y'all on recon near the border. I'm flying with Big White, trying to extract the last of the wounded from hill 875. That hill is hot, man."

Reljac never mentioned his birthday. He talked softly, exhaled cigarette smoke, looked over his shoulder as two Hueys cranked and flew the remains to Qui Nhon.

As Reljac had surmised, the next briefing had Odine and I teamed again with Frost in his LOACH or OH-6A, Light Observation Helicopter. The scout two-seater with Plexiglas Bubble cockpit and single gunner was the most fearful of flying. Rarely a week passed when a LOACH crew was not downed. We re-coned several miles to the northwest of operations, between Dak To and the Laosian Border. Near the border, we descended and the nimble LOACH buzzed the tree tops like a Hummingbird, looked for trails and enemy stashes. Crabbing sideways, we shadowed the LOACH, settled into a low orbit, ready to crush any response. This practice of 'hunter/ killer teams' was common. The VC transported supplies quite openly across the border from Laos. In a hover mode, Frost encountered enemy fire.

"Get out of there!" Odine shouted into the headset to Frost.

Odine and I pummeled the area as everything withered in a hail of rocket, gunfire and grenades, as Frost and his LOACH spiraled towards the ground. On impact, the gunner staggered from the wreckage, wounded and dragged one arm. I saw no sign of Frost as Odine called in "dust-off," a call sign for a medical evacuation helicopter. In my opinion, Odine flew a shallow approach that provided minimal exposure of the target area. Odine kept the sun at our back, but I was livid, having to watch.

"Why did you pull-up!" I said, then pointed through the windshield, Odine's left, at a stand of trees and logs, for him to fire it up with rockets. Odine again banked against the eastern sky and set up his approach. A trail of sparks and vapor marked the path of the rockets. In a lower approach, I had maximum exposure and adjusted the quads to fire at its most rapid rate, and stitched wide paths among the scrambling VC. Brush and weeds on the ground flailed in the steady stream of fire as large swatches of jungle suddenly became splintered. An evil growl, each burst of gunship fire sounded like that of a monster that puked death and mayhem. I still found targets in the turns when I spotted what looked like rocket fire from the ground.

"Rocket fire, your 4-0-clock!" I yelled.

Odine bottomed the pitch and moved the cyclic to the left, hit the petals and rolled a high, insane bank towards the ground. Four slicks and another gun ship came on station as did two Air Force Sky Raiders, propeller driven fighters that laid down a screen of napalm, then reversed their course and laid a smoke screen. That was adequate cover as slicks inserted their troops within 50 yards of Frost's ship. We remained on station until another Huey with a tether line arrived, sling-loaded Frost' scout and we escorted it back to the firebase at Dak To. I sat pensively, rationalized the good and evil of the day's action. Frost and his gunner were dead. The concepts of reason, will, and rationale, lost their meaning. That day I became an animal and reacted. I was part of a machine out of control, switched on to destruct mode and left on. Our day was done and everyone had gone to chow or prepared to do so when

Odine returned to the flight line and slouched on a spot of ground next to me. He didn't say anything right away, just shared the air.

I'm told, the crew chief had informed Odine that I was still strapped into the seat harness since shutdown. In the crew chief's opinion, someone should check on me. By the time Odine arrived, I had found a spot under the nose of the Huey. I sat in the rapidly cooling air as a ghostly fog settled along the ground. Odine's reputation was one of impatience with a temper to match. He was a self-appointed consummate gunship pilot. When he talked, he demanded your attention. If you screwed up, he chewed you out, then, reminded you that no FNG belonged in guns. Operations would replace Frost and his gunner. The dead among the VC unit would reappear as fresh bodies ready to die again. Nothing had changed.

"Get it off your chest, Odine. Where did I screw up?" I asked, and anticipated some vile comment. I sat beneath the chin bubble with one arm over the front edge of the left skid, poised for the usual assault on my youth and inexperience.

Odine exhaled cigarette smoke from his lungs then field-stripped the butt.

"You did well, Navy—real well," he began. "A cold-hearted killer and that's what it takes to fly guns."

Odine spoke calmly, short of the mean squint in his eyes or the raspy disdain in his voice. "Remember, guns is more than finding targets. You have to minimize your exposure, offer a smaller target, and remember your turns, avoid banking into enemy fire. You're sharp. Out there, I had my targets along with that rocket launcher. Today you showed the mentality necessary for guns. You made a good call, my orbit was high. Good call."

I couldn't believe my ears, nor was I assured the conversation would end so calmly.

Hardened and disappointed, I all but ignored his comment.

"That wasn't mentality on display out there," I said. "More like vengeful aggression."

"That's what guns are, angry aggression," said Odine. "I know that you can fly the ship. The mix of offensive and defensive flying, communications, and accurate deployment of arms are all reflexes. Sometimes thinking takes too long. Its action and reaction that's critical. In my opinion, you're an exception. The navy taught you well, gave-up a good man. I think you're ready for right seat. Come on, let's get something to eat," he concluded.

65

Odine sighed heavily and bounced to his feet. He didn't talk down to me that day, and didn't brush me off with his icy silence. I, too, stood, turned toward the rumble in the hills, toward the days that held me there, and wondered where, might it all end.

In a heap of mountains stood a garden of green, unable to avoid the pummel of bombs and cries of pain. A heap of mornings had no names, mornings barely distinguishable from yesterday or tomorrow, sought some relevance. A heap of empty boots lined in ceremony represented what used to be. A heap of laughs lest the sorrow sat in. A heap of evil in a clash of dreams gone awry, and, a heap of times now, I regretted my lure from childhood, having craved the fortunes of manhood and its perceived freedoms and independence. Now, I wanted to go back, be a child again, to linger once more in its innocent ignorance, go back and make those days last forever.

Crews on night shift dropped flairs that aided troops pinned on the slopes and prevented VC encroachment. Enemy 50 caliber tracers reached into the blackened sky in search of a Huey. The night became a boiling, black soup as vertical beads of bright orange bubbles, arched in a starless sky. On a late November Sunday, rain and dark clouds hung over the valley. A trio of small monkeys, brave or lost, flirted about the camp as I watched through eyes about to close, then, I fell asleep.

On Thanksgiving Day, A FAC (Forward Air Command) pilot, in a single engine Piper Cub, vectored Odine and me to a downed Huey. The crashed helicopter rested in the vines and limbs of the tree canopy. Odine accounted for the crew, then fired a series of rockets. With the nose of the gunship pinned to the target, he reversed his orbit, crabbed flawlessly then, in a fast, low approach, surprised a crowd of enemy troops that ran into our gunsights. I let roar the quads, as rounds pelted the ground and foliage like a hard rain on a dirt road. Nothing the size of a human escaped being torn apart, and driven into the ground. Med Evac confirmed no one survived the crashed copter. When we heard the grunts had secured the last hill, I swaggered about the Huey, examined the new hits. Then, among grenade canisters and feed chutes on deck of the Huey, I sat sadly in a sense of retrospect. I saw scenes of my childhood alongside those of bodies stacked, bodies ripped apart and tumbling in the dirt. I wondered at what cost might I someday flip the switch and regain that innocence.

I needed to look away, to flee the horror camped upon the days, and I found refuge in memories of summers I knew best. Once, as children, my sister and I sat perched upon the steps of grandma's porch, our eyes focused on the dark, drawn to images conjured by Grandma's preaching. There where evening stood, beneath a moon of falling leaves, grandma preached hell, damnation and the wrath of the Lord, talked of fire and brimstone, how God destroyed the world with water, but it would be fire the next time.

Ellen was five, I was nine, as we sat frightened, doomed as we were, to the fire next time.

"I want you to be a good boy and a good girl and God will bless you. Mind your elders and study your books," she demanded.

My evil deeds amounted to having swiped sugarcane from Mr. Phillips garden, killed birds with my BB gun, or caught chewing gum in Sunday school—so in need of repentance to avoid the fires of hell, I cried. I prayed for the saving of my soul. Soon grandma's rocker, her nocturnal rhyme, capitulated to a song of praise.

"…, Guide me O'thou great Je-hova…"

The sound of her voice drifted beyond the porch, to the ears of a passer byer, unseen in the cloak of darkness.

"Alright, Nan!" said an unknown voice.

"….bread of heaven, bread of heaven…,"

Thoughts of Sandra and Rachel refreshed me. Then in the blink of an eye, I stood once again at the visceral edges of reality. What now, of my soul and evil deeds, might I salvage?

XUAN

"Get your gear," Major Campbell, the executive officer or XO said to me. "Find Habrasham, you're due back in Pleiku before dark."

Helicopter units again ferried men and materiel back to base camps. For all the misery Dak To produced, the lives and efforts to take hills 823, 875, and 1338, we gave it all back to the VC.

Upon landing at Camp Holloway, Juan Guerrero, maintenance officer, waved us over and presented Colonel Stretch's personal vehicle, a brand-spanking new Huey Helicopter. Like a Jeep or the tablecloth on the colonel's dining table, he now had his own helicopter for his nocturnal, anytime, one-ship missions.

"You two, are moving up in the world," said Guerrero. "No one else is allowed to touch it. Once we stencil on the numbers and insignia, you can have it."

I opened the door and leaned into the smell of new paint, taut, clean seat harnesses, and a gleaming instrument panel. Habrasham wasn't impressed.

I thumbed a ride through the town of Pleiku where daytime traffic and the presence of military vehicles were common, but the VC owned it at night. In search of mail, I continued eastward to the ARVN Compound and the office of MAC-V. The shaded office of Colonel Stretch was especially nice, its ample screening and use of electric fans, made it quite comfortable. The Montagnard woman sat at her desk flanked by huge sectional maps of Vietnam.

"Excuse me, is the colonel in?" I inquired, not certain if she spoke English. Late sun poured through the screens amid the smell of lacquered walls. The woman looked up as I leaned slightly over the railing.

"The colonel is meeting now," she said in a business tone, yet avoided eye contact. Her voice was slow and articulate but heavily coated in accent. I stole glances as the reason for my visit fell dimly in her presence.

"Is there mail for Streeter or Habrasham?"

Before I could introduce myself, she raised her chin, pointed her face towards me, and said, "Mister Streeter, and Mister Habrasham." She spoke as if familiar with the names. "Yes, there is mail. The colonel has it." Having stammered terribly over the names, she offered no apology as the "S" sound was foreign to her dialect.

In wait, I lingered outside in the evening shade. Minutes later, she appeared at the door. She wore the traditional Ao Dia Dress and conical straw hat as she moved along the wooden sidewalk. In an absence of emotion and without pause, she said, "The colonel is meeting. You come back tomorrow."

The woman in Rachel's body continued past me and away from the complex. I sat until sundown, till the sun rested in the bosom of the Hodrung Mountain, before I gave up, then thumbed another ride, toward the town of Pleiku and Camp Holloway.

Within minutes my ride approached the gates of the ARVN Compound, a checkpoint for civilians. I watched as the Montagnard Woman went through the line and out the other side. The checkpoint had no walls, just a tin roof and a series of stalls that resembled a starting gate for racehorses.

At dawn the following morning, Habrasham and I lifted in the colonel's new Huey and flew to MAC-V. Only the helicopter was new. In the month of December, we flew the same routes to the same locations in the same non-stop marathon. On the 21st of December, I commandeered a package intended for MAC-V and Colonel Stretch. I bribed an enlisted man with access to a vehicle. Beyond the helipad and the MAC-V office stood a row of singlewide mobile homes. They were senior officers' quarters, complete with air conditioning and flush toilets. Vehicles parked at the colonel's home meant he was not alone. I approached the door and gave a quiet knock. With no reply, I poked my head inside to find a New Year's Eve party in progress. It wasn't common knowledge, but I was aware the colonel would be stateside for Christmas and the traditional New Year. The guest included local officials of the Vietnamese Military, politicians, U.S. Base Commands, both Army and Air Force.

My entrance went unnoticed until I located the colonel, who immediately opened the package. With great anticipation and to his surprise, displayed a richly finished glossy, wood, box that contained a large, crystal decanter of brandy. Pleased, the colonel feigned exhaustion and pointed toward a few letters clasped with a rubber band. The brandy was impressive and brought a lot of attention. Moments later, above the drone of several conversations, I heard a female voice pronounce my name.

"Mister Streeter is a friend of the colonel," the voice said.

I turned and saw the Montagnard woman who smiled this time, curious and inviting.

"Good...special...liquor...you give," a Vietnamese officer stammered in English, and raised his glass.

"I hope he likes it," I replied. Suddenly given credit for the brandy.

I faced the Montagnard woman as that flash of a fatal fall, again filled my guts.

"And how are you this evening?" I asked the woman that looked like Rachel.

"I am well, thank you," she answered in an animated voice.

"Would you like some champagne?" I offered, as if I, too, were a guest and free to issue favors.

"No," she answered, but retained her smile.

"Your work with MAC-V, do you like it?" I continued, treaded gingerly. Anxiety became curiosity, then a need to know who and what was she?

"Yes, I like my work here," she answered, then stroked her hair and it fell again down her back.

A few moments passed as I searched for the velvet hook, something with which to grasp truly, her attention.

"I like my work," she repeated herself, repeated her smile and her face trained on mine. She had a soft, slow voice, with words evenly spaced. Her huge, sensuous eyes accentuated her speech as if the words alone had no meaning.

"Your English is excellent," I said. "You can't imagine how wonderful it is to hear a female voice speaking English." A minute observation, but true. Her voice was a small reminder how familiar images are trampled in war. "MAC-V is on top of everything that happens in this war. I'm sure you're well informed."

"The little I know would hurt or help no one," she said. "Maybe it not so good to know everything," she completed her remark.

"You're probably correct, but personally, I'd like to know." With such angst, I held onto her, her moon face and brown skin.

"What do I know?" she asked, again brought a smile to her cheeks and eyes.

The Vietnamese guest, predominately Catholics as evident of their consumption, were a minority in Vietnam, among a native population that subscribed primarily to the Buddhist faith.

Deep within, a struggle ensued as I compared her to Rachel. Again, I was entangled in senses gone wild. Her round face and almond eyes were unlike the distinct slant of the native Vietnamese. She was the same height and complexion as Rachel and apparently the same age, having the same narrow shoulders and delicate hands.

"My name is Streeter, Mel Streeter, and occasionally I am the colonel's pilot."

"Yes, I know you are Mister Streeter. I told you the colonel had your mail. You remember?"

"So it was," I answered, as if I could have forgotten.

"My name is Xûan," she said, pronounced it to sound like the "Sung" Dynasty in ancient Chinese History. One hand held the other in front of her dress and her eyes again were trained on me.

"Well, Xûan, are you civilian or military?"

The hum of the crowd faded beneath the roar of butterflies in my stomach as my nervous feeling persisted.

"I work for the government. I am civilian. And really, you know as much as I," she pleaded.

"I'll not pump you for secrets, but we all know, MAC-V calls the shots around here."

"My knowledge would help no one. I am only staff support," she revealed. "But your job must be exciting," she suggested.

"Well, it helps if you have a heart of stone or no heart at all. It might help to be a little crazy, too, and look to the future with disinterest," I half joked, then continued my baffled look concerning Xûan's astonishing, twin-like resemblance to Rachel.

Xûan focused, then answered, "Your job is unique, one due to your special skills. Many people have no choice in the duties they perform. You work at a task of your choosing."

Her 'S' words weren't succinct, but nonetheless conveyed, nor did I realize she listened so well as to reply in depth and in earnest.

"You're correct again. I'm doing what I always wanted to do, and it helps if you like living on the edge. Just what do you do for MAC-V, since you like your work so much?"

"I translate documents and orders into Vietnamese or from Vietnamese to English, to ensure uniform interpretation."

"Now that sounds like someone who knows what's going on. It's been a pleasure to meet you, Xûan, I enjoyed our talk."

I wished her a happy New Year and likewise to others as I made my way toward the door. I nodded to the colonel who raised his glass in reply.

I left on my own terms, and hoped I planted in Xuan, a hunger, something unfinished, unsaid. Having dealt with the origin of my haunting, its untold reasons and affects remained a source of mystery.

At dawn the following morning, Habrasham and I cruised at 4000 feet south toward Saigon and Tan Son Nhut Air Base. The colonel made no mention of the night before, nor did he seem affected by his consumption. He sat between several pieces of luggage and in a brown paper wrapper tied with a string, was a Montagnard crossbow. A brief visit with his family filled the stare in his eyes. Below, the waters were placid and flat, and in the splendor of dawn, the sun rose, dripping from the South China Sea.

I never learned to drive an automobile. Now, as time permitted, I practiced with a Jeep around the motor pool. Unlike the family Desoto, Army vehicles and their standard transmissions became an annoying distraction for a novice. In a grind of gears and a cloud of dust, the Jeep lurched and stalled in what became a comical struggle under my own tutelage. When the holidays and New Year's passed, Habrasham and I flew again to Saigon to pick up the colonel. Hardly a pleasure trip, we tirelessly monitored each arriving flight and flew out the moment he arrived. We flew directly to Dalat, left the colonel, and then returned to MAC-V. There, the gunners left for their mail and personals but the air turned white in a tremendous downpour and forced them to return.

"Take a Jeep, the colonel ain't here," I suggested.

The gunner then replied, "They'll have my ass for that. If one of you suddenly had a need, nothing would be said."

"Not so!" Habrasham answered in a shout. "This is important and you know I've been fretting about it for three days now."

In a huff, Habrasham rolled off the bunk and reached for his trousers, but still dressed, I relished the challenge of driving in traffic. Rain, washed-out roads and poor visibility, made for an uneventful trip. Once returned, I approached the MAC-V Office and attempted to park the colonel's Jeep unnoticed. I stepped from the vehicle onto the wooden sidewalk and saw Xûan in the doorway.

"Hi, you're not going out in that, are you?" I pointed ceremoniously to the torrents of rain.

Though resigned to the fate of getting drenched, she hoped for a slack in the rain, then answered, "I have to get home, Mister Streeter."

The intensity of rain and heavy cloud coverage created a premature darkness. She had no other choice, for the checkpoint was about a quarter mile away. I wondered if I should take the Jeep again.

"Would you like for me to drive you home?"

In an appreciative smile, she answered, "That is a favor I could not ask."

Both of us caught in a probing stare, one that said any objection she raised would produce another offer.

"I asked you," I said.

There in the shadows of the doorway and roar of the Monsoon, in a presence so familiar, hid the haunting likeness of Rachel. She studied my face as if her answer would appear, she considered my proposal.

"Okay, yes," she uttered.

She adjusted the wrap that covered her arms and shoulder, and climbed into the Jeep. Xûan spoke English well, but used no contractions. Perhaps it was the way she was taught or her lack of practice made her speech animated. The Jeep had no doors or sides. The erected windshield supported the canvas top and did little more than shorten our exposure.

"Did you go away with the colonel?" she asked.

In her mind, my association with the colonel exceeded our routine assignments and bordered on friendship, but in all essence, I was no more than a taxi driver.

"No, I was here," I said, and reached to adjust her cover in the crosswind.

Her huge, dark eyes searched my face. The checkpoint teamed with workers who sought to avoid the soaking rain. As Xûan stepped into the downpour, I drove through the gate and waited on the other side.

She didn't expect I would take her beyond the checkpoint. Unaware of my need for her presence, she spoke sincerely.

"I did not mean for you—give so much of your time."

"I offered a ride. I'll take you wherever you want to go." I slowed the Jeep, indicated I would go back to the checkpoint and the Vietnamese Jitneys if she desired.

"Thank you, Mister Streeter. I tell you where to go."

I drove into Pleiku, turned north of the main street onto small roads then ox trails, before I came to a faded pink house of stone.

"Thank you, Mister Streeter. I will see you later."

She grasped her belongings, stepped from the vehicle, her body bent as if to avoid the downpour. I watched as she passed through the gate and melted into the shadows that surrounded the front door. I sped away beneath a sheltered, blackened sky. In all the excitement, went my promise to return with a bucket of ice for Habrasham. Of that, he reminded me.

"Tell me you got lost or you got laid. I see you didn't get the ice!"

Soaked to the skin, I removed my clothing under his taunting but friendly assault.

"What happened? I thought you went after ice, you jive-time farmer."

"You know, Hab," occasionally, I had a habit of shortening his name, "once you'd go out of your way to be polite, and—"

He cut me short, "You used to make promises and kept them. Now you don't bother to come back—no sweat!"

The two of us growled in friendly swears the rest of the evening.

The following day, I hooked a series of rides to the 4th Infantry Division. Westward, through the town of Pleiku, where the road bent to the south past shanties made of flattened beer cans. Along the slopes sat a seedy group of bars, barbershops and massage parlors with names like "Ooh la-la Bar," "My Bar," and "The Green Door," that catered to GIs. An identical checkpoint fronted the entrance to the Air Base and Camp Holloway, guarded by Air Force Military Police. Beyond the gate, the road forked south to the air base and Dragon Mountain or west to Camp Holloway.

Nestled on the slopes of Dragon Mountain was home to the 4th Infantry Division. I recently learned that my childhood friend, "Sleep," was in the 4th Infantry. The twin peaks of the Hodrung Mountain, "Dragon Mountain," or "Titty Mountain," to American troops, formed a sensual silhouette against the horizon. However, the Hodrung Mountain was much more than a base camp for infantry soldiers or a visual reference point for pilots. For Montagnards, particularly the clans of the Jari tribe, the Hodrung was sacred ground. They long contended, its desecration by the military was simply a slap in the face by another super power with big promises. This mass expansion in Pleiku debased and grossly interrupted the lives of local indigenous tribes, who for the most part intentionally ignored its presence.

By evening, I located Sleep's unit. In a dwelling, similar to my own, Sleep laid prone on a field cart, topped with a thin mattress that drooped over the edges like a muffin. A mosquito net hung crudely above the cart. I moved quietly to Sleep's side and spoke as if it was routine.

"I hear you're the bad dude from Rain Seed County," I said.

Uninspired, Sleep did not move, but answered dryly, "I can hold my own. What do you know about Rain Seed County?"

"I spent a little time there myself," I replied, matched Sleep's mood.

Sleep raised up on his elbows, parted the mosquito net with his left hand, and produced a flame from his Zippo lighter and right hand.

"Melvin! Melvin Streeter! Hey, man! It is Melvin! What's happening, home-boy! Wow, man! What are you doing here? I mean, how did you find me?"

"I'm with the 21st Assault," I said, a bit more composed than Sleep. "We've been flying y'all all over the place for the past three months."

"Wow, Mel. This ain't real! I mean, we're a long ways from home, home-boy and a pilot, too! Every time I got on a helicopter, I looked for you. You got my letters?"

"Sure did," I answered.

Sleep unconsciously nursed his feet when I noticed the blackened effects soldiers got from constant exposure to water. Too often, it morphed into a foot disease called jungle rot.

When he realized I noticed, he said, "They're (his feet) beginning to clear up, no worse than ground-itch," he referred to a foot fungus we often got as children from prolonged wading in stagnant water.

"This is not quite what we envisioned, is it, Sleep? All those years we dreamed of being grown, being an adult, being a man. So much to deal with, we got a lot to shake-off, before we can start again."

Neither of us mentioned the deaths of Tommy, Leo, or Packy, and little could be said that didn't reference their passing. Silently, we made judgements about what each had grown into relative to childhood.

"Nothing's fair in this world, bro," Sleep muttered.

"What are you saying?" I asked.

"You, me and Beenie, if we make it, have another war to fight once we get home. They told us to educate ourselves and life would be different," Sleep concluded. He was sad as result of his understanding of life and wondered where and if he could fit.

"Are you saying the old folks were wrong?" I asked.

"You're a college boy, the rest of us hired on at the mill after high school and learned some valuable lessons. Tell me this, do you think the rungs on that ladder to success will be the same for you as the guy next to you? Not saying the old ones were wrong. We can be humble but never naive. We're no different, times have changed, but we'll be in the same fight. You and I are a dying breed if we go back with the same tactics we learned as children."

Sleep tackled the real questions about life and once again, I saw the ignorance I'd accumulated, how tunnel-vision concerning flying airplanes had masked many attempts to critically view the world around me.

"Sooo…, what's it like flying above it all …? You take care, the VC love taking down helicopters."

"Same old grind," I answered, "I'll be glad when we all get back home. Good thing we came in about the same time. We'll be back on track before you know it." I added.

"It cost to be a man," said Sleep. "This is all part of the package, I suppose, and I can't wait to get home—short-timer! 120 days to go, Brutha! I'll tell everybody I saw you," Sleep laughed.

Sleep and I talked late into the night. A night full of yesterdays, as if we could or wanted to go back and again bury our ankles in cool shaded sand or the feel of warm mud as it oozed between our toes while catching tadpoles. Sleep's keen interest in animals, landed him in the K-9 Patrol as dog handler, an irritating detail for most, but not for Sleep.

WHICH WAY, YESTERDAY?

Sleep and I talked for hours, when suddenly a commotion in the hootch next door became too much to ignore. It never got late at base camp, just dark. As if he stepped from the pages of a fashion magazine, a brother fresh from R&R and the custom tailors of Hong Kong, created a mixture of laughter and astonishment. He wore a navy blue pinstripe suit, powder blue, long-sleeved, dress shirt with a burgundy tie. He also wore alligator shoes and about his shoulder was a charcoal gray, cashmere overcoat. He flipped his Zippo lighter, lit a cigarette, and made a series of turns, modeled his wares. Some grunts from neighboring hootches overheard the commotion and joined us.

"You'd be up the creek if Charlie lobbed some mortars in on us, wouldn't you?"

"Yeah, but I'd be clean!" he crooned, not swayed for an instant. It was a sobering sight. In a momentary stillness, no one found it so strange how he was dressed, only how far removed we were from yesterday and tomorrow. Some guts it took to don such a get-up in the middle of the boonies at night.

"Just in case," he said. "Just in case I don't make it, y'all see the new me!" In contrast of home, any home, the war presented a dichotomy in which everyone lived in constant denial and forced to exist in two worlds, an inescapable present and, the other cast in memory. "The world back home," alone embodied reality. Home encompassed everything good, lasting, and complete. All else amounted to an inferior facsimile especially the present.

Chambers, another member of Sleep's unit, had been in country about as long as Sleep. Chambers kept his watch set on Eastern Daylight Time. Being on the other side of the globe was no reason to disconnect from real time in the world. Frequently fellow GIs hailed him and asked, "Chambers, what time is it back in the world?"

"7:40, last night," he snapped.

"Man, back in the world, people are getting ready to party."

Around noon the following day, the colonel called from Dalat. Instructions included our transport of aluminum tubes that housed blueprints, schematic drawings, or something similar and brought along to Dalat. Habrasham proceeded to the helipad and began preflight, I headed across the wooden sidewalk toward the office. Xuan sat at her desk in the shaded breeze of electric fans.

"Hello, Xûan!" I said.

"And how are you today, Mister Streeter?"

"…Very well, and you," I answered.

Her smile was her reply. Xûan fumbled with the slender aluminum tubes.

"Would you remind the colonel there is an event at the air base tonight. His presence is requested. You, too, will go, yes?"

"Hardly," I answered. "I don't rank, and that's far from the company I keep. Actually, I'd like to drive you home, talk to you for a while."

"Why would you do that, drive me home?"

"I don't know, but I'm bound to learn something." The tug inside me neared panic as it insisted I not give up.

"But why would you suggest such a favor, Mister Streeter? I will manage if it does not pour rain." Seriously, she contested my offer. The aluminum tubes would not be still, they rang softly in her attempt to level them in her arms.

"Then I will pray for rain, lots of rain," I said, desperately tried to inject some humor.

"What will you gain by driving me home?" she asked but did not smile.

Annoyed by the banging tubes, I reached and took them one by one into my arms and said, "I know your name and what you do, but… who are you, and why … are you?"

We exchanged looks as she now reached, as had I and leveled the four-foot aluminum tubes in my arms. I smiled, made harmless my plea, and softened my approach—left an opening lest I loose, the battle.

"With the colonel at that gathering tonight, I could drive you home and we could talk."

Until now, she gave no reason, but didn't back down—offered no smile as to weaken her resolve. Again, her eyes searched my eyes before she bowed her head.

"That is impossible, Mister Streeter. I am sorry. You were kind to help me yesterday. I thank you, but I cannot invite you to my home."

Again, we looked at one another. A piercing unconscious sorrow flooded both our faces.

How silly of me, I thought, to assume that I could simply suggest an invitation and in the same breath it be granted. Now, driven by a particular fear, not one of harm, but a fear ever apprised to the enigma her presence presented. Not once had I considered that she was married, engaged or a woman with children. Since that fear superseded any ideas I could conjure, I would appeal to sincere persuasions, since my perceived charms had no effect. Somehow, I assumed that since she looked like Rachel, she must at least be like Rachel, amiable and available. I dropped my eyes and said,

"I could say thanks for your kindness, Xûan, and be satisfied with speaking to you from time to time. My gain is learning yours and my relationship to this war and why am I here? Convince me our meeting was coincidental and relevant only to that moment back in November. Your presence alone is full of questions." My fears now included a loss of the good will established at the New Year's party. "I don't suppose you understand anything I'm saying, but I'd like to see you, get to know you—know where you're from, and what might that look like."

"You want to hear the voice of a woman speaking English," she said. She remembered my comment made at the New Year's party. If only she knew the reason, the force and dynamic of her presence—so breathless, numb and arresting. A slight change in her body language, the slink of her shoulder indicated a change of heart.

"If I never saw you again, I know I've missed something important, something special," I continued. "So, why don't I drive you home about..., 5:30?" I quickly estimated the flying time to and from Dalat, provided the colonel did not detain us.

In her pause, one full of soft looks, looks of comfort or familiarity without the need of further questions—one full of promise and perhaps her own wishes, she said, "Okay, yes."

I was down the sidewalk and halfway to the Huey when Xûan emerged from the office. I tied-down the tubes, climbed into the seat harness and buckled in.

"You ready?" Habrasham asked.

"Ready, Sir," I answered sarcastically.

Habrasham flew south, down the valley as the jungle in several shades of green, and clustered rooftops, here and there slid beneath us. Recent rains filled bomb craters that looked like broken mirrors scattered over the countryside. I flew at the controls on the return flight, flew the colonel's route, to the coast, then north along the South China Sea. The colonel pulled on the auxiliary headset and I clicked his microphone.

"Colonel, I'm to remind you there's an affair at the air base tonight and a great deal of interest that you be present."

The colonel mulled the point for a moment then said, "A lot of politics, a lot of Press, I suppose. Comments on the Vietnamization Policy, eventually turning the war over to the Vietnamese."

Shortly before 5:30 P.M., I pulled into the MAC-V complex where Xûan waited. The encounter was like a weekend date. My eyes followed her into the Jeep. There were questions I didn't know how to ask.

"Shall we go?" I said.

"Okay, yes." A half-smile looked back at me.

"How are you, Xûan?"

"I am fine," she offered, followed by a broad smile as if it concealed something.

"What is it?" I asked.

"Nothing is wrong. I think you are so very young," she said. Xûan didn't know, but with the Navy as example, my confidence would never again be undermined by perceptions of my age.

"Yes," she continued, "you are so very young to be a pilot."

"How so young am I?" I wanted to know. Curiosity still ruled. Xûan had no agenda and formed no opinion, but my youthful looks were an old problem, an easy target.

"Maybe sixteen or seventeen," Xûan laughed. In spite of her suspicions, without it, my boyish looks took a beating.

"I'm as old as you are, maybe older," I lied, but thought to myself, someone or something opened that door, and nothing, certainly not my age would deny me again.

"How long you been in Vietnam?" she asked, surprised and impressed at my sense of direction and how I remembered the route to her home.

"Four long, slow months I'm afraid." The road vanished into a narrow, uneven trail bordered by wood fences.

"In eight months you go home. You have a wife?" The Jeep hit a pothole and the fishnet bag with lunch pans nearly bounced from her lap.

"No, I have no wife," I chuckled. "Don't you think I'm so very young to have a wife?" I asked, in her choice of words.

"Yes, maybe you too young to have a wife."

"Have you always lived in Pleiku?" I asked.

"No, I was born in a very small village north of Pleiku," she pointed as if it was just beyond the fence. "Where do you live, Mister Streeter?"

"Mel or Melvin, please. Not Mister, okay? And I'm from a small town called Rain Seed County. Like your village, it's very small."

"Your mother, your father, still live there?" she asked about my family.

"Yes, there's a brother and sister too. Is your family here, Xûan?"

"My brother, my mother," she said.

"No husband, you have no husband, boyfriend?"

"No husband and no boyfriend. My mother, my brother," she said over a light chuckle.

I slowed the jeep as the road narrowed from recent rains. Before long, I was at the faded pink house. A low fence bordered the yard. A stone walkway led between a tiny garden of painted stone and rock, to a small concrete deck, even with the ground. Wide bowls made of straw and filled with grain, dried in the open air. An excited child, a boy, stood in the doorway, about the age of two years, clothed only in a tiny shirt.

"Come, Mister Streeter," Xûan invited as we approached her doorway.

Xûan picked-up the child, his eyes pinned to my presence, while an elderly woman peered back from inside. When the woman stood, her silhouette was framed by an open window. Beyond the window was a panoramic view of a rice paddy that loomed for hundreds of yards, sectioned by earthen dikes constructed at right angles. One dike pointed to the kitchen window and ran westward into the rice paddy, to a large stand of banana trees, maybe 500 yards from the rear of the house. The elderly woman had looks of a bygone beauty. She wore a billowing white blouse over black pajama like pants, was the same height and complexion as Xûan and chewed a dark, reddish substance that coated her teeth and gums, called betel nut. I assumed she was Xûan's mother as she paused, studied my presence as if I were a homeless pet found along the roadside, and out of fascination or pity, Xûan brought me home. Although assured I posed no threat, her curiosity was apparent.

"What do I say?" I asked Xûan.

"You say hello," Xûan answered.

With that I nodded, but before I could speak, the mother said, "Hi… you…?"

I smiled, a bit surprised.

"Ceux qui sont noirs," the elderly woman continued softly, rhetorically, to no one in particular. The phrase was spoken out of context, seemingly without meaning, except it did have a meaning. It meant, "The black ones." Without explaining exactly what was black, I was sure she referenced me as a black man. She had spoken in French, and again, I was pleasantly surprised. I searched for the appropriate phrases to transcend the cultural gulf that separated us. I found it difficult not to stare at Xûan, and having noticed she was aware of my gaze, I finally looked away.

"Something wrong, Mister Streeter?"

"Nothing's wrong."

Our eyes crossed paths again, then she pulled the child into her lap and dressed him with short pants.

Caught up in the crossings of Xûan and Rachel, I was unable to separate the two. And again, in a grip of anxiety, I began to second-guess myself.

"A moment ago, I wasn't sure if your mother spoke English and I didn't think it was proper to shake her hand. I feared offending the both of you." I lied concerning my reason for pause, but my reply was adequate considering our understanding of each other.

Xûan produced a long thought-filled smile, spoke to her mother in their Montagnard tongue. The mother answered and to that, Xûan offered yet another reply, which left me curious about their exchange.

"Tell your mother thanks. Tell her I said thanks for a kind greeting and pardon my ignorance."

As the mother wandered into an adjoining room, Xûan said to me, "My mother said you are a handsome boy and maybe too young to be a soldier."

Before I could defend myself, Xûan and her mother again were in dialogue.

"I told my mother, I said the same to you, that you were too young to be a pilot. My mother says you will always be young."

"Your mother is a wise woman, but what does she mean by that?"

"You will always look young, that is what she meant. I think you are a nice man and you should be very happy."

"Why is that?" I quickly added.

"Why? Because you are big and strong. Because you have a mother and a father, sister and brother and very soon you will go home." Her words were soft and compassionate.

A small portrait rested on a table beneath a window. She noticed the photo caught my attention, and said, "That is my brother, another brother and me at Dalat. My brother is dead, Mel. He was a rice merchant."

"I'm sorry. Did he live in Dalat?" I asked.

"No, I attended the University at Dalat. I will show you." She left the room for a moment and returned with a photo album.

"So, Dalat and the University is the source of such good English. Now I understand," I said.

"My English is not good. I do not speak often in English. I forget." She seemed sincere.

"I speak so little English at work. Same words, same documents repeatedly. I forgot so much English."

"We can fix that. You and I will talk, alright?"

"Okay, yes," she seemed satisfied with my proposal.

I browsed the photos of a younger Xûan.

"May I have one?" I asked, anxious for some proof I had not gone crazy.

"You want a picture of me? Why? Oh, no, these pictures are not good," she almost apologized.

The Ao Dai, a traditional Vietnamese style dress, had a banded collar and close fitted top.

The bottom was essentially a pair of pants, but rendered almost invisible by a skirt-like piece that hung from the waist to the feet, front and rear, while split at both sides. Virtually a matching flap of fabric attached at the waist. The entire garment was made of a rayon or silk fabric. White top and skirt, with black pants was a common combination and appropriate business attire. White top, skirt and white pants was semi-formal. Xûan wore white with black pants underneath. I could not overlook how appealing she was, her figure, the outline of her legs and tiny waistline. She was unaware of the strangeness I'd found that was her surrogacy of Rachel.

Cloaked in the coming darkness of Pleiku were many dangers, particularly since I was alone, so I soon said goodbye to the mother as Xûan followed me to the door.

"Goodbye, Mel, I will see you later, okay?"

I picked my way through the shadows and narrow drives to the main-street, then sped east, back to MAC-V.

A POURING OF TEARS

The next morning, having anticipated a late departure, Habrasham dressed and drove to Holloway for our mail. Upon his return, he approached my bunk.

"What are you going to do, sleep your life away?" he asked, then handed me a package wrapped in brown paper and bound with a string. There were letters, also.

"And you look like hell! You look as bad as you looked last night!" Habrasham continued to scold me, while I yawned in the morning air, stretched my limbs, and threw a few lethargic punches at an imaginary, foe.

"Another night's sleep, like that and I'm ready. What's for chow?" I asked.

"Chow my ass. It's near 7:30!" he shouted gleefully and again shoved the box toward me.

"And what does the colonel have in store for us today?" I asked, still yawning, still prone on my bunk.

He looked at his watch before saying, "He's plotted a course to a little place called Yulin, deep into China."

I raised my head slightly off the makeshift pillow and asked in all earnestness, "China... really!"

"Hell no, you Jive-time farmer! We gotta be ready to fly in thirty," he meant thirty minutes. Few things frightened me about flying missions with Habasham, but often my naivety showed.

87

"Well. Why didn't you say so?" I bounced to my feet, got cleaned-up and dressed. We grabbed our gear, the letters and package, then headed for the helipad and preflight inspections.

The package contained homemade cookies filled with walnuts.

"Now this is what I miss," Habrasham muttered the words over a mouthful of cookies. He cleared his throat and said, "You've got a good, close family. That means a lot." He held a cookie between his lips then buckled into the seat harness.

Our instructions that day did not include the presence of the colonel. With the gunners in place, we lifted and flew north, to Da Nang, in search of some industrial instruments lost in shipment. We landed at a tiny LZ at the edge of a sprawling supply depot and searched through binders of shipping manifests. The subject of our quest belonged to the concrete building at Dalat. We moved to another then a third depot before we found it, two narrow, wooden, 6-ft. crates. It was dusk dark when we returned to Pleiku and the MAC-V compound. Anxious, I retired to the billet and the rest of my mail. One letter with the logo of the local high school in Rain Seed County, caught my attention.

"Dear Sir,

Richardson High School and the Richardson High School Sophomore Class extend our warmest gratitude for your help in making the sophomore class' theme and presentation, 'Vietnam, Its People, Its Culture,' week, a great success. The items and photos helped generate hours of meaningful discussion on the Vietnam War and the lives of its people. We sincerely regret the sudden death of its originator and committee chairperson, Rachel Blake, who passed away before the program's conclusion. We thank you for your support of this program."

I slid off the bunk and walked outside, perhaps the information was mistaken. Today was Friday, January 12, and according to the letter, Rachel died weeks earlier. I thought of her troubled past and how close she came to salvaging her life. I walked aimlessly in the dark, unable to cry or grasp the meaning of something so final. As if drunken, I talked aloud to myself, then I cried for Rachel, for death's blind selection. I cried for the dreams she courageously constructed, for Rachel's lack of time to unfold and taste life. Then I cried for me, for my loss. My fantasies of Rachel over the years held more satisfying moments than the few times with her. Until recently, Rachel chose to bottle her life rather than live it. She took the careful route with few chances of failure. A stagnant life began the end of life. A flowing river lived in its continuance. Once dammed-up, it ceased to be a river, and it's dead. Once again, sorrow had come. I leaned against a sandbag bunker and mourned.

"Those old bunkers are full of scorpions. Careful how you lay around them." Habrasham' voice reached me before I could see him. "I couldn't find you. I was about to help myself to another batch of cookies when I saw the letter. I apologize for reading it, but seeing that it was typed …well…, when it's typed it's either trash not worth opening or bad news; it's official," his voice trailed off. "She the school teacher you talked about, sent those boxes to?"

"….Yeah!" was all I could say, then asked him, "Who's monitoring the radio? I'll go and do it." I tried to change the subject as we approached the wooden sidewalk, walked past the colonel's mobile home, the MAC-V office and on toward our billet.

"Were you going to marry this lady?"

"I don't know, I don't know a thing. It seems only death is alive."

Habrasham searched for some words of comfort. "I've heard you talk to the men. I know you understand life's a day to day engagement—nothing's promised. I'm sorry about Rachel. …I'll understand if you want to be alone… but I have a jeep, let's drive over to Holloway, take a shower, have a beer, you'll feel better."

We drove to Holloway, walked toward the hootches, swatted insects, and tried to avoid mud holes in the dark.

"You asked why I chose you as co-pilot on this mission. Why is that important?" Habrasham asked.

"What's more important are the questions I don't ask, such as how are you connected to all of this, Hab? You've got more pull with the brass than any pilot in the company, regular line officers or warrants. Just tell me this, where do you fit in?"

The term "Gooks" was an epithet directed towards enemy troops, ARVN soldiers and Vietnamese in general. About my question and comment, Habersham erupted with his patented loud laugh as the silhouettes of four men came into view ahead of us. The silhouettes recognized the laugh.

"Damn Habrasham and Navy; still flying gooks, are you?" The silhouettes were on their way to the showers. We ignored the remark as Hab considered my question.

"I'm strictly warrant, no more or no less, nothing clandestine—just a job. However, your abilities do a lot for you. That dictates who does what for whom. It's time you take credit for your work. I call it as I see it, Navy. As a pilot, you've got excellent air work. On a combat assault, you're quick and decisive, calm and confident. That's the kind of pilot everyone wants to fly with. You know the stories of pilots going to pieces, scared to death while doing their best to keep the helicopter in the air and dreading the next mission."

"I'm scared all the time, Hab."

"Yes, but it doesn't affect your ability or judgment."

"I don't know, Hab. I've been less than ideal in most cases, and I'm afraid the killing has gotten to me."

"What I said remains. You're a hell of a pilot and I'd rather fly with you than any pilot in the company. You come close to what I was like at your age. My old man used to talk of seeing fires in my eyes. I've seen that fire in your eyes. You're a pilot forever, it won't stop at helicopters. You'll go far—still wet behind the ears, but you'll go far. Let's get cleaned up, stop by the club, and have a drink."

"I'll do just that," I answered.

We parted for our respective hootches.

I didn't make it to the officer's club, didn't help tend the rumor mill nor celebrate the small victories of my fellow pilots. Before I fell asleep, I again thought of Rachel. Later, Habrasham aroused me from a deep sleep and we drove back to MAC-V.

The following day, I received the letter no one wanted to write, the news of Rachel's death. Rachel died from complications sustained in an auto accident. Beenie, too, was dead. He died in a place called Kha Sahn. The war and news of war and children dying created a sense of paranoia in neighborhoods back home. To illustrate the fear and feelings back home, my mother related an incident that ripped apart the community and probably repeated itself many times from one end of the country to the other. Beenie's mother watched the neighborhood through one window, the same window through which she saw Ellie, me, and Beenie grow-up. The approach of the olive-drab sedans were grim teachers. The same teacher that taught willows to weep, the graceful bow of sunflower blossoms, the weighted sag of a ripened fig; their eyes held low like pallbearers. She brandished an apron for Beenie's sedan, with eyes full of tears, attempted to chase it away. Wish, again was reborn. Her wish to hear old words if not from his mouth, once more to scold him for some mischief, but left to acknowledge his death in some hell-hole she couldn't pronounce.

"We're dying from this war in more ways than one," my mother wrote.

The buzz in the officer's club centered on the news of my dead fiancée. A few tables away sat Odine. He and I made eye contact and he raised his beer, presented a nod of sympathy. Amid many expressions of the same, I grabbed a couple of soft drinks and sat with Reljac and Belk until the late hours, then turned in. The next morning I reported to the XO, Major Campbell.

"Major Campbell?"

"Yeah, Navy, how're you doing?"

"Just fine," I answered, unaware my reason for having to report.

The major pushed away from his desk and with his fingers interlocked, cradled the back of his head with both hands. "I'm sorry to hear about your fiancée. I was wondering if you've given any thought to taking a leave."

"No, Major, that's not the case."

"You sure about that Navy?"

"I am sure and I won't be expected for the funeral."

Major Campbell signed a document and handed it to me.

"Go to the activity board and choose an R&R location to commence in three days."

"Major, I appreciate the kindness."

"Kindness, Navy, is not the issue."

The major stood, handed me a copy of the statistics from the previous month's mission reports.

"You and Habrasham have logged eighty percent more hours than anyone in the company. Some of those pilots have already been on R & R. Dak To, took the starch out of all of us. You've had your share of situations, not to mention the current one. It's your choice—I can ground you, or you can take your R & R."

Taipei, Japan, Bangkok or Hong Kong; Australia, Hawaii, and Singapore, among others, listed places eager to host pent-up, saved-up GIs in need of an escape. Perhaps the timing was correct and I would benefit from a change in perspective, if only briefly. I chose Hong Kong, where I'd breathe deeply the air and relax on untroubled ground. I'd hide among the canyons of concrete buildings and neon lights—hide from the memories of Rachel, who grasped for life, for the promise of life that whispered, "Nothing's promised." I'd hide from the steamy dampness, the blinding brilliance of the tropics, and the horrors of war. So cruel was that respite, a teased folly; such strong reminders of a reality I once knew. Caught between the memory of that life and the desolation of war, I'd indulge in the facsimile offered. I'd find a painted face, one whose smile I'd own 'til morning. I'd cherish her laughter, her devotion, question her kindness while reminded, it's almost like living.

XÛAN'S WISH

Dying ain't so bad, I thought, and I thought a lot about dying as we re-entered the tense air space of South Vietnam and Pleiku. Tragedy had many names and as many faces, fates worse than death were prominent. Again, in the eternal summer, having returned from my R & R in Hong Kong, my senses forced me to compare the two worlds, that of Hong Kong and South Vietnam, a contrast most disturbing. Dying ain't so bad, I thought. The idea of being alone, alone in the effects of one's injuries was unacceptable.

Habrasham was not a patient man and the colonel's erratic, if not secretive schedule often frustrated him. When I stepped off the C130 cargo plane at Pleiku Air Base, it was Habrasham who waited there.

"Well...?" He stood with his arms outstretched, and his mouth open.

I simply said what I thought he wanted to hear. "It was really great. How are things going around here?"

"Nothing new," he said, and handed me some mail. "You got a little time, but we can expect that call before long."

We drove around the perimeter of the Air Base to Camp Holloway where I pound the dust and rat turds from my bunk and searched for anything that may have slithered inside.

A letter from Sandra focused on the cause of black folk. She stood in the heightened intensity of the movement and its rhetoric. Once, as students, I accompanied Sandra to Atlanta for a series of meetings for SCLC (Southern

93

Christian Leadership Conference). In one gathering, a debate of careers caught the attention of Dr. Martin Luther King Jr. It became a heated discussion, such that Dr. King intervened having understood our inclinations were to choose "safe" careers rather than one that complimented abilities and ambitions. In an unusual pledge, we numbered about a dozen, Dr. King challenged us to pursue the career of our choice. Upon graduation, those having no success in securing employment in a chosen field, he asked, "…write me here at the center." In a gesture of sincerity, he clutched a list of our names in his departure.

Dr. King was Sandra's hero. His tactics for social change didn't satisfy me. A growing number of activist also had dwindling patience. Even Sandra was torn between the philosophy of her hero and the impatience of the streets. However, Sandra recognized an emerging militancy in Dr. King and tried to convert me to a King supporter.

"Too many of our brave brothers are being absorbed by this war. We need you home, Mel. This is not a fair assessment, but we're fighting a war here as well," she wrote.

The call from MAC-V came in the afternoon and Habrasham and I flew the colonel to Kontum, a short flight, and waited as officers attended awards ceremonies for ARVN troops. In the boredom of waiting, he and I mused about the delights of women. He had no love interest back home. His was Army issue, wherever stationed. He then mentioned the convenience of the fuel bladders and its proximity to his woman's house in Pleiku.

"What is it…a minute, or two from refuel to that back row of houses?"

"Probably," I answered lethargically, as I strained for some comfort in the seat harness.

"Another minute or two and I'm in her hootch," he said.

"House, Hab. We have hootches, they have houses. What you're thinking can get me court-martialed and thrown into the brig. Taking a Jeep, we've gotten away with, but parking the colonel's new Huey in the middle of a rice paddy, an unauthorized flight—man, you got a pair, but like I said, you're connected."

Suddenly Habrasham sat upright and snapped his finger, "That's it…Navy. I hadn't thought of using the colonel's Huey, but that's the best choice. We don't go through operations, and you're apt to see MAC-V vehicles anywhere."

Unenthused about such a flight and concerned about his safety, I asked, "What happens to me, Hab if you don't come back from one of those visits?"

"It's a risk," he said, "but think of what must have happened to me."

Still lethargic, I answered, "I think it's a crazy idea coming from a lifer, but since it's your idea, I'll go along."

When the attraction between Xûan and I became obvious, he remained coy. He and I never spoke of that relationship, only the planning of our rendezvous.

That evening, shortly after we returned to Pleiku and MAC-V, the colonel and gunners departed, then a determined Habrasham pulled up to a low hover and cruised toward the fuel bladders, a series of huge, 16'X30' rubber containers that resembled a giant pillow. Once refueled, he skimmed the expanse of the rice paddy toward the rear edge of Pleiku and circled the cluster of banana trees where the dike pointed to Xûan's backyard, some 500 yards away.

"For visits, we can do this," he said as if to convince himself. "No sweat, we can do this."

We flew back to MAC-V, landed and took the colonel's Jeep back into Pleiku and Xûan's house.

Xûan and I peered through her kitchen window, across the rice paddy toward the banana trees.

"You wouldn't have a pair of binoculars, would you?" I asked.

"No," she answered.

"Can you get a pair?"

She thought for a moment, wondered for what reason, but didn't really care. "Okay, yes," she replied.

"Good"…then I explained Habrasham's plan. "For short stays…if I may?" I added.

Xûan and I devised a scheme, a marker that forewarned the state of security in the hamlet. Then we sat as she guided my head into her lap. Her home was excellent for unwinding, truly an escape from the drudgery and sameness of war. Now that my present had arrived in the form of war, I was relegated to thoughts of the past and simpler times. That more than half my tour remained, meant the odds for survival were not kind. Yet, in a pilot's way of thinking, death was no surprise, only premature.

I rationalized the presence of Xûan, and concluded that it was encouragement to live in the moment because as Habrasham said, "Nothing's promised." My preoccupation with the enigma of Xuan and Rachel was one that burned and pressed, a proposition I alone had to resolve. I now had to accept Xuan for what she was and finally place Rachel in the past. Nearly a dozen times the past two weeks, I drove Xûan into Pleiku and her home. I needed an answer for the fires that raged within me. When we looked at one another, it was like looking into a mirror as we saw ourselves reflected, measured, and presented. The fact we were from worlds apart gave meaning to a curious kinship. In unspoken exchanges, our cultural differences seemed ill prepared to deny a bond destined to grow. What evolved she would not contest and I was yet to understand. Today I deepened the conversation, sharpened my remarks while in need of real answers.

"What am I to you, Xûan?" I sought to measure my presence, my significance and what if at all was fair to Xûan.

She understood my question, now she searched her heart for the courage to be true, then searched her vocabulary for the words that best described her feelings.

"I am practicing my English. When you talk like this, I need words I seldom use. You make me need words I do not remember and some I do not know. I will answer your question."

She left the room briefly and returned with a cloth and a tiny bottle of a clear liquid. Xûan sat and pulled again my head into her lap. She spoke softly, before she squeezed pimples on my face and cleaned them with the ointment. She messaged my face, methodically applied the ointment with the skill of a therapist and the care of a lover. English was not an easy language and an adequate translation for many life situations might not exist.

"You are my friend," she began. "I invited you to my home. I care about you and already, I say I am glad we met. I will be in love and I will be glad it is you."

As if from an assembly line, the words came carefully spaced and stamped onto her gentle voice. The smell of the ointment mingled with the floral musk of her favorite fragrance, was flattering yet austere.

"You mean you won't be disappointed you allowed yourself to get involved?" I asked, then searched her face with a probing stare.

She continued in that calm confession. "What is happening to me has nothing to do with time. I have decided that I want to be with you."

Words I longed to hear came from the heart, and I wondered what I could give back. "Was there someone special in your life, Xûan? Ever been in love?"

"Yes…," she said, "once, that was a long time and we were happy."

"Do I remind you of him?" I asked in sorrow for I presupposed her person was Montagnard, perhaps with minimal features similar to my own.

96

Pensively she answered, "You are not like him. Pham Van was Vietnamese and you are American. You cannot act like Vietnamese. You are not the same."

"Pham Van, was that his name?" consciously I probed, waded deeper into her past. "Think you'll ever get married?" I asked.

"I could marry to a Montagnard. I could marry to you." A smile and brief chuckle followed her statement.

"Would you marry me?" Short of a proposal, I asked if she'd consider such.

"Maybe I would marry to you," she said, again with the smile and the chuckle. "It would be an American marriage, yes?" Then, seriously, she said to me, "Mel, in seven months, you will leave. I will feel bad, but I will be glad that I met you."

"What makes you think you'll be in love?" I continued my quiz.

"I do not make it come. I cannot stop it. I know it will come. If I asked you to go away, it will not stop what is happening to me, so, I want to be with you."

It sounded so simple, her small voice with centuries of discipline bred into it. Her simplistic approach to life demanded no reciprocation. Xûan's efforts and energy focused on her people in an effort to preserve and elevate a lifestyle. The war and its dominance until now, prohibited her return to her village, but in her heart, the inconvenience was temporary and before long, war or no war, she pledged to attend her dream, return and establish a school.

"Are you in love with an American girl, Mel?"

I rolled my head in her lap, looked her in the eyes then looked away. "I don't know," I whispered.

Xûan didn't believe me, so she continued. "Tell me about her, Mel. Tell me…, what is she like? Is she still in love with you?"

For the sake of conversation, I referred to Sandra as I spoke.

"We don't speak of love, but like you, she is very beautiful," I said. "For years she's been like some magnificent animal that roamed freely. The times I shared with her I thought were platonic in general. Recently, she made me understand how special we were. Now she speaks of love and the wish to belong. Like you, she will spend her life in the preverbal villages and towns, fighting for the cause."

"Do you think you will marry her?"

I smiled at Xuan's directness, remembered how I must have sounded minutes earlier. "Once her mind is made up, she won't be single for long."

"How do you mean, platonic…, your time with her?" Xûan asked.

"It was never meant to be serious, only friendly. It took such courage to believe that what little I had going for me would impress her."

"So…, you and her are not in love, Mel?"

"No, we're not in love," I answered.

Life had dealt Xûan a difficult hand. She deserved better. Perhaps for the first time, I wished my accountabilities did not extend beyond that moment, that somehow Xûan and I could transcend the boundaries of war, toward a sense of permanence. Since reality offered no such assurances, I remained in awe of her beauty and the aura of her fragrance.

That evening I had intense thoughts of Sandra, and her efforts to convince me of subtle changes, in Dr. King's philosophy, one that supported her contention he indeed was a militant man for those militant times. In Sandra's opinion, Dr. King realized the times for reform had all but passed and the word "revolution" would best fit the needs of a restructured American wealth, its economics, and political power. My thoughts were, if her hero flirted with militancy, he flirted, too, with suicide and great disappointment if he thought America would someday wake up and redistribute its wealth. To do so, to think so, was beyond radical. In my opinion, Dr. King's non-violent doctrines depended upon docile persuasive appeals for concessions. To facilitate some measurable changes in the near future, a more radical appeal was necessary.

Days, perhaps a week later, Habrasham and I refueled and flew near the stand of banana trees and landed. I wondered about Xuan's village of birth, the one she talked so much about and felt indebted to return after the war. She belonged to a clan of the Jarai tribe, one of many tribes and interethnic groups that I and American Troops lumped into a single category of Montagnards. In general, they occupied the central highland provinces from Ban Me Tho to Phan Rang and Kontum. Together, the tribes numbered around 900,000.

Xûan watched our approach through the binoculars, then skipped along the dike towards the Huey and climbed aboard. I joined her on the deck of the cargo bay, leaned my head into her lap while she stroked my boyish, hairless face.

"Someday I'd like to visit your village?" Xûan seemed puzzled by my request.

"My village is very remote, Mel." Once she explained the difficulty in getting there, she seemed rather enthused about the idea.

"Would that cause problems, my going there?"

"No, but it would take all day to go—and another to return. What will you do there, Mel? Why do you want to go?" she asked.

"I want to see the things I like about you, learn what you were like before, and what you might become."

"Maybe yes, maybe no; my village is not the same as Pleiku, Mel. It is a very small place, simple people who farm and raise animals. There are no roads, no automatic water, houses like my house, or places to buy food." She almost apologized for the rural isolation and near primitive way of life.

"That sounds like my neighborhood," I said.

"Oh…, no, your neighborhood is very different, Mel! You live in America."

So misinformed, I thought. Perhaps some glossy page from a magazine of chrome and glass formed her impressions of Noble America, its perceived notions of justice and equality.

"Not so different," I said. "Much of my neighborhood is footpaths and dirt roads. The people are warm with simple lifestyles, too, and many of their homes do not compare to yours. Like your people, they, too, rise in early morning, wear straw hats, and work tediously in some form of farming. Not so different." It was not easy to accept my comparison, but she believed me.

"Your work, Mel, will it be in your neighborhood, your town?"

"I don't think so. Flying is all I've ever done, and the only thing I know how to do. Will you write to me?" I asked.

"Okay, yes!" she answered gleefully, then pulled back her hair, fashioned it into an attractive bun at the back of her head. "When will you come again, not fly like today?"

"I don't know. It could be tomorrow," I hoped.

When Habrasham arrived, I helped Xûan from the deck of the helicopter and watched as she walked along the dike beneath a darkened sky as her figure faded smaller into the shadows at dusk. Once strapped into the seat harness, I flipped the breaker switches, squeezed the start button on the collective pitch control lever as the groan of igniters gave way to the scream of the turbine. As the RPMs came up, I evened the petals while Xûan slipped into her back door. I skimmed across the rice paddy, banked against the row of houses and climbed out of range of the refueling area.

THE TET OFFENSIVE

JANUARY 1968

The month of January ended the annual tour of duty for a third of the company's pilots. Odine, with whom I had flown a great deal as co-pilot, was among them. After a staggering four tours of duty, he called it quits.

"I want the first assignment that gives me the AC status," I said to Habrasham.

"Don't get your hopes up too high, among the new guys will be plenty with comparable hours, but you know our AO and that's key," he confirmed. "You're not letting Odine's opinion about young pilots chase you out of the gun platoon, are you?"

"No way," I answered. "There are two more rotations in our tour. I'll have my choice."

Habrasham left to join a poker game and I headed for the Officer's Club in search of Reljac or Belk.

Neither was in the officer's club, so I sat and clutched a soft drink when one of the newly arrived officers, a colored, 1st lieutenant strolled in. He looked around as if he wanted to buy the place, gave a chuckle and walked over to me.

"You're the one they call Navy? I'm Steve Thompson," he said and extended his hand. "Everyone asked if I met you. I should have known why."

We shook hands.

"My pleasure, have a seat, LT," I said.

The lieutenant appeared to be in his mid to late twenties, a muscular build and just under six feet tall.

"We roughing it now," he said, smiled and continued to case the joint. "I hope it gets better than this." He glanced down at my nametag and asked, "Where you from…Streeter? What kind of drink can I get around here?" He meant alcohol.

"Beer, sodas, or whatever you bring," I answered. "I'm from Florida, five months in-country."

"I'm from Cleveland initially," LT. Thompson added. "But my dad was a career man. Name an Army Post, chances are I've been there… ever been to Cleveland?"

"Never have," I said. "You with the group from Korea or Germany?" I asked, having heard there was a mixture.

"Germany, been in-country for four days. Thought I had a shot at the 1st Cav … Been stuck in Cam Ranh Bay, and an ear full of that Tet New Year warning. Four days waiting for a flight and here's an air base with all kinds of aircraft." Thompson then looked me in the eye and smiled. "I've seen the new duty roster," he said. "You're now second platoon, AC."

"Ah…, thanks for the news," I said in a broad smile. "And where did they assign you?"

"First platoon, as of this morning."

"Everyone's keyed-up about the Tet New Year. If I didn't know better, I'd think it was just another detail," I said. The Tet New Year marked the Vietnamese Lunar New Year. It's like our New Year, but commenced the last of January.

"Heard a lot of good things about you, Navy," Thompson smiled broadly. "What's that you're drinking, a grape soda?" he asked, unable to see beyond my grip on the can. "Care for another one?" Thompson stood and approached the bar, bought a Schlitz and another grape soda for me.

Thompson had a host of specialized certifications; airborne jump school, jungle survival school for pilots, and a black belt in martial arts. A first lieutenant in a captain's slot as platoon leader meant a promotion was forthcoming. He'd command a platoon of four helicopters and crews. That he was a brother was supportive—some place to go when there was no place, someone to talk to when there was nothing to say. The truth of the matter was, all the new pilots were FNGs and they, too, had to appease the Gods of life and death as had the veterans.

Later that morning, Habrasham and I went over to MAC-V. Flight plans included Kontum again. Colonel Stretch and a bevy of ARVN Officers prepared inspection tours of ARVN outposts.

"Dammed if I'm looking forward to this," Habrasham whined as we crawled over the Huey in preflight.

I stood atop the Huey with a view of the wooden sidewalk that extended from the mobile homes to the helipad. The sidewalk was meticulously built amid a series of trees and in a downpour, it saved the trudge through eight inches of mud.

"I see the chief and gunner, coming," I uttered. "You think we'll be back before dark?" My mind was on Xûan and like Habrasham, I wasn't excited about today's jaunt.

"You know things can get wacky with the ARVN Units," he answered. "This prep for the Tet Offensive, who knows what time we'll be back?"

ARVN Commanders seldom got proper credit for their triumphs, and many of them sported huge egos and an arrogance that claimed the war was theirs to manage.

The crew chief and gunner arrived and locked down their M-60 machine guns and each, a string of frag and smoke grenades. The colonel, with three ARVN Officers climbed aboard as we cranked and flew north, to Kontum, and an ARVN Outpost. About four platoons of ARVN Soldiers stood in formation. As I sat up my approach for a grassy patch to minimize the effects of rotor wash, one of the ARVN Officers went ballistic. In the best English he could muster, he directed me to land squarely in front of the formation. Amid a torrent of sand and debris, the formation inhaled the swirl as the ground commander presented a salute until Colonel Stretch and guest approached. Just out of reach of the rotor wash, the sand, and dust, the officers spoke for a few moments while the formation weathered the elements. Then the officers including the ground commander boarded the Huey and I flew along the perimeter of the compound as instructed, permitted their inspection as the ground commander explained the gun emplacements, enemy obstacles, and claymore mine defenses to his superiors. The inspection lasted all of thirty minutes when I again approached the formation and the ground commander returned to his men. We flew in and out of several outposts that day, none more considerate than the first.

I passed through the MAC-V office that evening like a pupil with a classroom crush on his teacher. Unable to get Xûan's attention, I gave up to finish my flight log entries, only to look up moments later as she stood before me, tempestuous and disarming.

"How long have you been here?" she asked me, having circled the wooden railing.

"A few minutes, no more," I answered in a stare.

"Did you say hello? I did not see you," she continued.

"Yes," I lied. "Have you thought of me lately?" I asked her.

"Yes, I think I made a big mistake. I invited you to my home," she teased.

"Do I get to drive you home today?"

"Maybe," she continued her tease.

"Xûan, sometimes it's difficult to understand how all of this…, you and the war, that is, is really happening. Real life, is fleeting, but when you're around, I'm certain that life as I once knew it is still possible."

She looked as if she understood my distress, considered what the war must be like for me, then answered, "Thank you, Mel. I already explained my feelings and why. Yes, you may drive me home. I will wait here for you."

Later, I feigned an emergency and took a Jeep from the motor pool. I picked up Xûan at MAC-V, but when we approached the familiar checkpoint, the ARVN MP didn't wave me through as usual, instead, stepped to the Jeep and said, "9 P.M. curfew—stay alert."

Xûan climbed in and I sped away, wrapped in her presence and the visual accent of Rachel. At Xûan's home, I looked past the house to the backyard where a water buffalo grazed. Xûan's infant brother toyed with the beast and the beast obeyed. In a steady breeze, the banana trees waved at a distance.

"What do you see?" Xûan's voice came from behind.

"Just admiring the view."

She stood next to me as the wind toyed with the flaps on her dress, before she touched my elbow and invited me inside where I shared photos of my family.

"Why do you look at me that way?" Xûan asked.

"Someday, I'll answer that for you."

"Your sister is beautiful and looks like your mother," Xûan added. "Will she be tall like you?"

'Tall, but not quite as tall," I answered.

"No photos of your girlfriend?" she asked.

"Maybe the next time I'll bring those photos."

"You, lie," Xûan said, looked again at the photos. Someday I would bring Rachel's picture and watch her reaction, but not now.

"I told you my girl is probably seeing someone else. She is very pretty, but Beau Coup butterfly." That was a French/English term, slang, meaning literally one who invites many men, having no particular loyalty.

"Beau Coup butterfly, ha! You go see bar girls, Mel?" she asked rhetorically. Xûan recognized the lingo used by GIs and bar girls. "You have a girlfriend in Pleiku, Mel?"

"You said I was too young to be a pilot, too young to be a soldier, too young to be married, so, I must be too young to visit bar girls."

"Bar girls do not care how old you are," she concluded.

"Is there one you recommend for me?" I asked.

"I do not!" she exclaimed.

"Then I'll stay away, and as your mother said, I'll always look young; frustrated as hell, but young."

Softly, as if it really didn't matter and as if she really didn't believe me, she said, "You, lie."

I looked at the Jeep parked at the roadside as two Vietnamese Men walked past. The grunts often shared a common enemy practice whereby the VC removed the pins on hand-grenades and strapped a rubber band around the lever, then dropped the grenade into the gas tanks of military vehicles to explode at some undetermined time.

"Are you okay, Mel?"

"No," I answered, then corrected myself. "…Yes…I'm okay. The Jeep…, I really don't have permission to have it."

"Come," she said, "…sit. The Jeep is okay."

Xûan sat, placed my head in her lap, and spoke as she again squeezed pimples on my face.

"Not so many, Mel."

"What is that you're using?" I asked.

"Medicine, now be quiet or get some in your mouth. You have very nice teeth, Mel."

With small hands she painstakingly nursed my acne and made innocent comments. She filled the palm of her hand with ointment, rubbed both palms together, then gently massaged my face, or did she caress her own needs?

Her hands addressed my need of repair while her eyes sought a place for me. The woman whose attention once eluded me and later brought pain and anxiety, now held me and spoke to my needs, my wants and my fondest fantasy.

Quietly, I laid as thoughts and ideas wandered through me. I wondered what effect this situation would have on our lives as she nursed the last vestiges of my adolescence. When her huge eyes caught my stare, she sat back, temporarily engulfed in a smile that bared an awful shyness.

"When will you come again to see me?"

"I don't know, but unless I'm flying, working for the colonel is b-o-r-i-n-g."

"Were it not for the colonel, we would not have met, Mel."

Serious now and so unlike me, I said, "I'm not so sure about that. I think it's for you I came. This is something that began long ago. I'm sure you don't understand that, but as I said in the beginning, we both came to Pleiku. Anyway, is that beginning to mean anything to you?"

Xûan stared at a point in space and said, "Other than the sound of a female speaking English or an escape from the war, what does it mean to you?"

Once again, that inner voice spoke for me. I could not imagine having said such.

"I've always been interested in you, since we were children." The words referenced mine and Rachel's childhood. "I'm the one that loved you, remember? Old enough to want, wish and remember, but not old enough for you to care." I played with her in that one-sided tease she would never understand. "You once told me a joke with a curse word in it. Do you remember? You made me swear and cross my heart, never to tell a sole."

"I think the medicine is making you sleepy," Xûan answered. "Maybe you are a little crazy, too. Yes, I think you are too young to fly so much. When you are not flying, Mel, will the colonel give you time off?"

"I get a day off, now and then, sometimes," I said.

"What do you do, Mel, on your days off?"

"I'm learning a little about photography, bought a new camera, and I sleep a lot. I don't get much sleep otherwise. My next day off, I'll spend with you."

"But Mel, I work, how would you spend your time there?"

"We'll get away. I can fix it, I know people with connections."

She was puzzled and I lied, but the point was to know the extent of her desire, given limited activities and no place to go. I was grateful for her concern, her sensitive show of feelings, and her calm, quiet demeanor.

Soon I had to leave, so I stood, felt her hand on my back as if guided toward the open deck with no porch.

"When is your next day off?" I asked.

"In two days. Will you come then?" she wanted to know.

"If I can," I answered, but knew I would slay a dragon if need be.

The next day I hooked a ride over to the 4th Infantry Division. A deserted compound greeted me, a few rear service personnel and grunts convalescing.

"I'm looking for Gibson. Is he around?" I inquired.

"Oh…, I remember, you're Gibson's friend. I guess you haven't heard…. Gibson missed the pick-up on a sweep two days ago. They went back for him, but couldn't find him."

"Naw…, I'm talking about Gibson…, Carl Gibson… short dude…," I explained, not convinced the grunt meant my friend.

"Yeah, I know," the grunt said.

"That's his bunk over there," I agreed, it was Sleep's bunk. "What's going on, and when did this happen?" I asked.

"During an extraction at LZ Baldi, Gibson had the dogs as usual, and one of the door gunners waved him off because the Huey was full. Actually, the first chopper had been hit and couldn't get off the ground. That caused some confusion in the other assignments and guys scrambled. Charlie hit us with small arms fire from all over the place. Next I saw, Gibson headed for the bush. That was two days ago, around 1600 hours."

It was unreal, the thoughts I had to consider. I stood, reshaped my cap, and thought the worst. It was a platoon of my unit, the 21st, that made the extraction. I heard talk of the enemy encounter and firefight. Once back at Camp Holloway, I approached the XO. "Major Campbell," I said. "I understand an infantry soldier from the 4th failed to board one of the choppers during an extraction a couple days ago? Did we send anyone back?"

"The gunships stayed on station as long as it took to salvage that broke Huey. They looked for him, but failed to locate him," Major Campbell replied.

"Major," I began, "this happens to be a home town buddy of mine. It was our extraction, is there something we can do?"

"I heard it was a dog handler. That's your guy?" the major asked.

"Yes, Sir, the best," I replied, but there was no need to embellish Sleep's qualifications, nor his long personal relationship to me.

In a small show of sympathy Major Campbell walked over to the operations map, our area of operation.

"We don't initiate missions, Navy. We fly in support of infantry. Okay, right now there're eyes and ears in that area, a LRRP patrol. These guys are good. They've seen him once and can probably put a finger on him. They may already have him, but he is not their mission."

None of the talk made sense if the answer was still no. As a child, Sleep was fearless. He always had something wiggling in his pockets, a snake, a frog, or a baby rabbit he'd chased down. My parents questioned him thoroughly, then allowed entry in our house. All he wanted to be was a veterinarian. As dog handler, I felt the odds were in his favor.

Shortly after 4:00 A.M. on January 30, the town of Pleiku, the Air Base, and various military installations erupted in explosions. Traditionally, the Vietnamese Lunar New Year celebrations combined the significance of Christmas and New Year's Day. In January of each year, a week was set aside for festivities, family reunions, and the honoring of ancestors. That last week in January, 1968, communist troops, under a self-imposed cease-fire, suspended the war. In a sinister move, among thousands who traveled, came well-laid plans and minions to execute the Tet Offensive.

Trucks headed for the flight line, moved down the isle of hootches as pilots quickly climbed aboard and headed to their respective stations. Habrasham and I lifted for MAC-V. In the dark of morning, we flew without marker lights, saw at a distance a dull glow against the night sky that was the town of Pleiku, ablaze. The colonel, in full battle gear and an armload of materials, stood at the helipad. He climbed aboard and Habrasham flew immediately to Dalat. The long suspected Tet Offensive had begun and by daybreak, more than a dozen cities in South Vietnam had been attacked. For four days, coordinated skirmishes continued until the communist forces were either dead or simply dispersed into the population. Another four days passed before the colonel was prepared to return to Pleiku. We lifted off into the night sky, again less the marker lights until out of range of ground fire.

"Monitor any radio transmissions," the colonel ordered. "I'm afraid this is not the end of it."

Habrasham waited until the colonel was out of sight before he muttered exhaustedly, "Who's going to hear the damn radio?"

I, too, felt the weight of fatigue from long hours, in the air.

By morning, it was eleven days since Sleep disappeared, and nine days since I last saw Xûan. I wondered how each fared in the attacks. MAC-V, in a flurry of activity, braced itself for additional attacks.

"You are not sleeping much, are you?" Xûan asked. She noticed the strain on my face.

"Not much. How are you? Is everything alright?"

"Will I see you later?" she asked in a hurried whisper, not able to talk.

"I'm not sure. Would you tell the colonel Habrasham and I are here?"

The colonel appeared distraught as well.

"Mister Streeter, how soon can we be airborne?"

"Right away..., if that's what you want, Sir."

"I'm heading that way ...Let's go!" the colonel said and stomped through the doorway.

"Yes, Sir!" I snapped and left the office.

We flew the colonel to II Corps Headquarters and waited most of the morning, then flew back to Pleiku and MAC-V. From the air, Pleiku was a mess, as jagged walls and roofless structures stuck up from foundations burned black, while natives picked through the rubble. The colonel retired to his trailer and I entered the office in search of Xûan. She approached me, elated at my presence and held my arm tightly.

"My mother and brother left town, Mel and I stayed here at MAC-V all week. I slept in your bed, among your things," she concluded.

"And how did you know it was my bunk?" I asked, amused by her choice.

"I know your things," she said, confidently. "I have not been home. People are missing..., Gone. No one can sleep," she said.

The morning brief unveiled a multi-staged combat assault at LZ Charlie, northwest of the town of Ban Me Thout. My first combat assault as aircraft commander was filled with distractions and the plight of my friend, Sleep. I dared not write home and mention what I knew. As co-pilot in the gun platoon, I seldom got close to the grunts. Now I saw their faces, the faces of brothers, the black soldiers, many who populated the grunt units. During the second insertion, again I flew in Yellow Flight, the number four position, as we flared for touchdown. Within three feet of the ground, the grunts were off and ran for the perimeter. As the lead ship signaled to lift, a volley of enemy gunfire erupted near the LZ. Solinger, flight leader in Yellow-one, nosed-over as Yellow-two and Yellow-three reported hits. Then I reported hits, as rounds lashed the Plexiglas windscreen as if someone slapped it with an oak switch. Other rounds ricocheted or spun their way through the fuselage. As my platoon climbed back to altitude, I made a hard bank behind Yellow-Three and awaited the gunner's status of hits on the ship.

"Anybody hit?" I clicked the mics.

With an "all clear," and no structural damage via the gauges, I climbed to the rear right of Yellow-three as the platoon now flew in the opposite direction of incoming flights, parallel to the LZ, that stair-stepped to the ground below. I looked to my right, across the cockpit and down into the LZ, at the three o'clock position and saw a ship in white flight as it exploded against the ground. I quickly turned my head, as not to see, but in the darkness of my clinched eyes, I saw it anyway. Jamison, my copilot, gazed into the LZ.

"White-Three is down," was all he said.

In a heightened sense of chaos, the gun platoon flitted like a swarm of wasps when an enemy 50 caliber machine gun erupted, captured everyone's attention on the ground.

"I want that 50! I want that 50 out of commission! Have you located it?"

"Viper-one to Six," I heard Wrase on FM, trying to raise Grunt-six, the ground commander. "That 50 is on your east flank in a pile of logs, but he's more interested in us right now."

Wrase banked, rolled his gunship, and Sanderson rolled in from the opposite direction and lit-up the position. The 50 caliber went silent. We flew to a marginalized LZ and landed, waited should the need for a quick extraction arose. When the gunships approached, I knew at last, we owned the LZ. Habrasham came over, wiped his forehead with a dingy handkerchief and leaned against the deck with a long look on his face.

"What does the newest AC think of flying slicks?" he asked.

"Formation flying. Finding my spot and holding it," I said. "Inside turns, outside turns, trying to keep-up... good work-out! Generally we flew but two formations, the string formation or stagger-left formation. Stagger turns required precise positioning in the formation while giving the ship to your rear and easy target to maintain his position."

In a few minutes came names and faces of White Three, names we'd already forgotten along with photos they may have shared, wishful plans, relatives or children.

Once back at Holloway, I walked into the operations tent.

"Major, anything on that grunt MIA? Are there plans for a search...? Does anyone care?"

"What do you want, Navy..., a platoon at your disposal?"

"No, I need your Jeep. I have to see the colonel at MAC-V."

The Major was relieved, and gladly gave up his Jeep. It wasn't the colonel but Xûan I longed to see.

Fellow pilots in my former hootch in the gun platoon celebrated the arrival of Sanderson's belated birthday cake and insisted I stopped in. I joined the small ruckus amid the smell of cigarette smoke, stale beer, and a group of guys I missed being around.

"Navy, you're holding up the cake cutting. Let me show you something," Sanderson yelled. It was a large rectangular cake, and by some miracle survived shipment with a few cracks, broken in places but hadn't crumbled.

"You guys are all over my birthday cake!"

On the top of the cake were caricatures of helicopters and the pilots that shared the Hootch. I saw my likeness prominently represented in chocolate, with the name "Navy." Sanderson's mom had a message for everyone in the hootch each time she wrote. We were all her boys, and she insisted we each came home safely.

THE MONTAGNARDS

I left with my personalized hunk of Sanderson's birthday, sheet-cake and drove through Pleiku, toward MAC-V. Just beyond the ARVN compound, I saw Xuan as she approached the checkpoint. Her conical hat hid her eyes, shaded her face from the afternoon sun. As I slowed the vehicle and paused before her, she looked up, pleasantly surprised, then climbed into the Jeep.

"You been away, Mel?" She spoke in her slow, careful voice, so full of pause and patience, like the yawn of morning unfolding.

"How have you been?"

"I am fine. Thank you for coming for me."

I drove around bad places in the road and headed up the small trail, saw that she stared, and I wondered about her thoughts.

"Everyone is afraid," she confessed concerning the Tet Offensive and attacks on Pleiku.

We arrived at her house, found it deserted but undamaged. She opened first the shutters, then the rear door, as light chased away the shadows and fresh air mingled with the smell of charcoal.

"My mother and brother are not back," she said, then with one hand, she lifted her hair as the breeze caressed the back of her neck. She then sat, looked at my face, at a few small pimples.

"Are you tired, Mel, are you sleepy?"

I did not answer her questions, and said little since we arrived. I was tired. I was tired of the war, of the routines with no hope of change. I was tired of doing anything but flying.

I pulled Xûan's face to mine and kissed her lips. I kissed her repeatedly until she framed my face with her soft, brown, hands and kissed me back, then she whispered, "How long can you stay, Mel?"

"I don't know, for as long as you like," I answered the look in her eyes, her sigh, and then kissed her again.

"You stay here, Mel. Stay with me…, okay…, yes?"

With rapid breaths, she caressed my head. We laid entangled in the strands of her hair, entangled in the fates of time and circumstance when someone outside sought my attention, sounded the horn on the Jeep. Xûan stood and went to the window, turned and told me it was my friend Habrasham. I walked outside as he leaned on the hood of the Jeep.

"We better talk, Navy. Like flying, when you hang out like this…, best you have some kind of cover, someone should know. I thought we had that." He was disappointed, but his concern went deeper. This, his second tour of duty taught him the dangers of hanging out in marginal secure provinces.

"Her folks panicked and left town for a while and she's scared," I said.

"She's scared! We're all scared! There's a war going on and whatever she's afraid of, you better be afraid of too. You can bet they know more than we do."

"Okay…," I mulled over the points he made, and leaned against the hood of the Jeep. "Take the Jeep back for me. I'll stay the night."

Habrasham gave me a hard look, an "I don't believe you" look.

"I'll be alright," I assured him.

"You son-of-a gun," he laughed. "Get in and I'll bring you right back."

I looked back at the house, as Xûan stood in the doorway and wanted to explain.

"Come on, get in. You'll be back before she knows it," he growled.

"Where are we going?" I asked.

He turned onto an adjoining road and came to a house within a stone's throw of Xûan's house. He jumped out and went inside, then returned with his sidearm, and web. He tossed the gun into my lap, climbed in again and switched on the engine.

"It's not much, but you can make some noise if you have to," Habrasham said.

114

When I returned, Xûan had closed the shutters and the doors. She stood with glassy eyes as I closed the door behind me. In my grasp, I held her as firm as the stare the first time I saw her. The wet of her tears on my cheek, the wet of her mouth upon mine, the long trembling sighs she blew past my ear. From the thump of her heart came the dance of desire and the need to belong. I searched her garment, confused by its strange construction, for I found no buttons or zipper that lead to the body underneath. Completely baffled, I discovered her smile gazed up at me.

"Montagnard women remove their own clothes," Xûan said.

"And, I have seen simpler puzzles," I answered.

She went into a room, changed into a gown of cotton and reappeared in a doorway that had no door, only a curtain that she parted with her hand. That she said nothing, was everything that invited me in.

I followed the crumbs of femininity as if there existed no roots to my want and wish. There, I was summoned warmly by sensuous shades of black, brown, tan and bronze. In the haste of passion, I pulled from her the gown that entangled us and saw her as I imagined she'd be. Amid scenes in her Montagnard dialect she retreated to places familiar, places sovereign, safe and secret. In a gentle grasp, she guided me to her hidden places, welcomed cravings of my own and shares of waxing. Xuan peeled away all hanker painted on the days as we each plunged toward the soft, moist depths of surrender.

How strange yet familiar my arrival, the way a river plotted its course, the way light or darkness filled spaces, I'd found my way. In the gentle grasp of the river, its ebb and flow; I waded towards a distant and beautiful shore, a river full of rivers bent, fell and moaned beneath me. I reached for the curving shoreline, joined its rhythms, its buoyancy while avoiding other faces in the river. And before long, like a helium-filled balloon, once restrained with a string, it surged and tugged, took but a sigh to free its grasp, then soared unbound and loose. A joy she'd known before, she now revisited. In a pleased yet exhausted tone, the woman within made incoherent sounds of rapture.

Quiet and content, Xûan leaned into my body, avoided my eyes yet searched my heart for approval, for requite and certainty as to her indulgence. She dragged her hands over me, slowly, the way blind hands read braille. In the dark of the room, she did not fret my gaze. I caressed her many shades of consent, kissed the brown of her, the black of her, her tan and bronze. Barely above a whisper, Xûan talked to me in that soft, slow-paced manner of hers.

"Mel, I have a confession. I did not tell the truth about my life. I will tell you now. Okay, yes?"

Surprisingly, her voice trembled in an effort to maintain a growing confidence.

"I am sorry, Mel. I lied to you. I did not know how to say, 'yes' to you and 'no,' to me and it still be true. I did not imagine it would come to this. Tram, my brother, is not my brother. Tram is my son. Pham Van, the man I stood with in the photo made in Dalat, was not my brother. Pham Van was my husband, Tram's father. He is dead."

She spoke slowly, still at a whisper.

"Please, forgive me, Mel. My husband was a rice merchant and would not support the VC, so they destroyed his business. Later, he still would not store food for the VC, so they killed him and Pham's father. His mother later died, too."

Xûan's husband died before their son, Tram was born. Since she, too, feared reprisals, she, her mother, and Tram, moved to Pleiku. Vietnamese women were expected to marry only once in life. They became part of the husband's family and subject to him. Since her arrival in Pleiku, Xuan avoided relationships. Her education was a remnant of a program under the French occupation of Vietnam that provided teachers and schools for Montagnard settlements. Many, Vietnamese trained abroad, in France, but the social fabric of Montagnard life was a close-knit affair where few chose to live so far from the family group. Although Xûan chose the University at Dalat, the distance remained great.

"Mel?" she whispered.

"Yes?" I answered.

"I am sorry, I..."

"No, Xûan, there's no reason for you to apologize, least of all to me. You've given up a great deal, so much has happened. How do you keep it together? You have no reason to apologize. I understand."

I thought then of my own losses and the fate of Sleep, but up against the tragedies in her life, mine seemed trivial.

"Somewhere out there in the jungles, my best friend from childhood is struggling to survive. I think he's still alive, but it's been nearly two weeks and no one really knows."

The depth of her sincerity shone for this was her night, her moment to be heard, held and consoled. I was unaware of Montagnard or Vietnamese cultural practices concerning mourning. I imagined she was yet to obtain closure, have her grievance facilitated, and for a moment, someone that shared her losses.

"It is good that you have not given up. You have seen this friend since coming to Vietnam?" Xûan asked.

"Two weeks ago, before the attack on Pleiku, I went to see him."

Suddenly, I sat upright and leaned against the cool, stone, wall and pained collectively, for childhood friends having died in war. For Packy, Leo and Beenie; for Tommy and now, Sleep.

"Mel, what is wrong?" she asked, alarmed at my sudden move.

I looked at Xûan, her face etched with questions and empathy. How would I explain to her that the loss of my friend, Sleep, in part meant a loss of my childhood? The sum total of secrets and dreams rested now with me alone, never to be acknowledged. How would I explain the mourning bench, its role, and substance in the Baptist Church or convey the small town flavor of summer revival as we came of age spiritually, the union of fellowship and the covenant for life?

In an attempt to assuage my fears, Xûan cleverly placed herself between me and my dread. She gathered my attention as she whispered and pulled her warm body close to mine. She spoke again, in her Montagnard dialect, and used words she knew I did not understand. Her rhythmic language and her seductive moves spoke for themselves. It was a language I understood after all, that of a woman when there was something she wanted and she said it as only a woman could say it. Later, she partially opened the shutters to the sound of wind through the trees. Upon that wind, rode a wisp of bovine and the rustle of dried sunflowers planted beneath the window. Moonbeams reflected from the rice paddy like a mountain lake, then a shaft of moonlight struck her face and exposed a shiny, teary cheek.

"I may not understand, but tell me, please. I want to know, Mel."

A litany of memories became my Albatross, my solitaire rhyme. Without contrast or perspective, I presented random childhood memories that popped into my head.

"In grade school, our walks to and from school were long leisurely walks. We'd tarry, chase the girls. We were courting. Little girls with bows in their hair, wore dresses with a sash, tied in a bow at the back. The boys would carry their books, it was the grown-up thing to do. At Miss Sangal's Store, we bought Mary-Jane candy, BB Bats and a penny's worth of cookies.

In our free time, we flew June Bugs tied to a string, hunted brown eggs and baby rabbits. We climbed trees, ate muscadine grapes and boiled peanuts. After high school, some hired-on at the mill…, then the war came. I mentioned some simple pleasures in our lives that now seemed far removed and never again recalled.

"My condolences, Xuan. I'm sorry for the loss of your family. I'm sorry for the pain and disruption the war has caused you."

Then she told me of her people and their struggles. she said, the name Montagnard (Mountain-yard) or Mountain People, was a general term given by the French in their occupation of Vietnam. It described the primitive tribes of the highlands. Ethnically, there lived pioneers and descendants of the Hmong tribes, Khmer, and Cham that occupied the Indo-China Peninsula long, long before the ethnic Vietnamese migrated from Southern China and took away agriculturally rich delta land and pushed tribe after tribe deeper into the highlands. Those struggles developed a hard and fast malice, because in spite of aggressions, the Vietnamese Natives referred to Montagnard tribes as Moi, for savage, Aborigines, or wild men. Vietnam, known for centuries of wars and invasion, quickly rendered Montagnards as minorities, one constantly ignored and disposed.

"As a people, history has been a struggle, Mel. Throughout the years, land has been taken away from us," she said.

Their greatest advances came when France colonized the country, re-established schools and promoted the teaching of French as well as tribal languages. Tribal authorities negotiated with Saigon governments for land protection, equal rights, preservation of tribal customs and government representation. French rule included a segregated military, where the Montagnard, as did the Negro soldiers during the American Civil War, First and Second World Wars, fought in segregated units.

As Xûan and I talked, there emerged an increasing number of historical similarities in cultural experiences with our respective governments.

They were at home in the jungle hills farming, among other crops, tobacco, and rice. They suffered as pawns in the military efforts of the French, Japanese, Vietnamese, and the Viet Minh, for control of the country. Their history and experiences became the foundation for a greater sense of ethnocentrism. The American military intervention in Vietnam, initially trained Montagnards who had superior acumen and were fierce in combat.

The Negro, as did the Montagnard, developed a sense of self-emergence, and having done so, sought himself. Both lacked recognition and clothed in the negative projections of the "other," the Negro, too, was repulsive. Everything was for the "other," and in constant comparison, the Negro wished he was the other. Xûan and I compared the two minorities. The Montagnard fared tremendously better, because their tribal customs had been preserved and practiced. Endowed with land and values of their own, they as a people remained intact. The Negro, on the other hand searched for validation. His native past and customs as a way of life was once forbidden and far less than a memory. To some extent the Negro was out of touch in a broad spectrum and unaided by the cohesiveness of (African) culture. The result was an increased state of self-consciousness that placed at the center of his being a desired recognition. Since he lacked reinforced props of his past, the Negro proceeded to imitate rather than flourish as a contented true being.

Burdened, then relieved, famished, then fulfilled, we each contemplated our understanding. From that perspective, the night had been kind and borne unto it was a stronger sense of kinship and connectedness.

When morning came, still full of the thoughts of the night before, while saddened by the plight of the Montagnard people and the continued plight of my own, I conceded the death of Sleep. As with Tommy and Packy, Leo and Beenie, again, the old church received one of their own and Reverend Lucas found ample stories to tell. Peg-leg Sim and Emma Gibson, assumed the place of the bereaved, my mother sung the solo and in the cold of February, the air was stiff through leafless hardwood and perchance a cloudless sky.

Mothers, too, bore the burdens of youth. She strained, as did their sons. Mothers knew. At birth, she labored, for the river of life ran through her. In death, she labored no less, for like that river, his passing was again through her. Painfully, mothers prepared themselves and accepted his memory.

A tiny courtyard next to Xûan's house surrounded a well from which she had drawn water and bathed. She then prepared water for me. I walked into an adjoining room where she dressed and asked by which cultural standards she lived; Vietnamese values or that of the Montagnard? Among many Montagnard Tribes, the women took the men in marriage, and the two resided in the woman's house. The eldest female in residence was head of the household and owned all family goods, the house, the harvest, animals, and land.

"Your friend is coming, yes?" she asked about Habrasham.

"Soon," I answered, then looked at my watch. "About your cultural beliefs, my being here, will it cause problems?"

"No," she answered.

"You tell me when you can stay. My mother will know."

SLEEP

"An LRRP unit has spotted your grunt friend, the dog handler," Major Campbell said to me.

I rose to my feet, anticipated a chance to fly a rescue mission.

"Sit down, Navy. Now listen!" Major Campbell continued. "You have a mission, but you listen carefully because this mission is your primary concern. You got that!"

"Yes, Sir," I answered.

On a wall between two area maps hung an insert of the border region of Cambodia. Area maps were permanent and familiar to all the pilots, but the insert changed from one brief to another and emphasized mission specifics. The new commander, Follett and staff joined the briefing. My mission was an extraction of a Special Forces LRRP patrol, from across the border in Cambodia, just west of Kontum. Pins on the map, flagged my call sign and radio FM frequency for the patrol, along with primary coordinates for pick up. If for some reason, the patrol failed to make the initial rendezvous, the map insert offered alternate coordinates. I copied the instructions and notes onto my map.

"Once the extraction is done and you cross again that border, an escort will meet you here." By escort, Campbell meant a gunship. "You clear that border, Navy, and it's a go for that M.I.A." Sleep was seen two days earlier, still in the vicinity where last sited. "The LRRP team will direct you as best they can," the major concluded.

Recon patrols were small detachments, sometimes as few as three men whose primary mission was to gather information rather than engage the enemy. From forward base camps, they often walked into the bush, but often the distance dictated being ferried and later extracted. Only the operations unit could terminate or alter mission objectives. In spite of the go-ahead search for Sleep, I was cautious and feared the effort was inadequate. Although grateful and anxious to have the mission, Sleep's fate, hanged from the tender hooks of chance. However close and promising, mercy was the extent of our efforts.

I collected the gear given to me and changed clothes. Over-the-head earphones replaced military helmets, a few survival tools and flash cards with common phrases in Cambodian and Vietnamese language, and pertinent rights under the Geneva Convention. Officially speaking, border crossings never occurred. U.S. protocol didn't include Cambodia or Laos. On such missions, the pilots dressed in civvies and posed as members of an international peace organization, which was neutral to the conflict and flew tan, unmarked, and unarmed aircraft. My only civvies were a pair of khakis and a white, V-neck pull-over shirt, with red, white and blue piping around the neck, sleeve and waist-band. I pulled on my Chuck Taylor All-Star sneakers, and headed for the helipad.

Belk, my co-pilot and I prepped, cranked, and flew north, northwest out of Pleiku on a course of three-five-zero. Our first course change to two-six-five, took us west, across Ho Chi Mien trail toward the border. A mountain range, bathed in morning sunlight and purple in color, slid beneath us. Belk peered through the windshield, and checked reference points. Within minutes, we closed in on the border, just south of the point where the borders of Laos, Cambodia, and South Vietnam converged. I made mental notes of flight time, distance, and fuel consumption. Available fuel to some extent would determine the depth and flexibility of the search for Sleep. When Belk noted we had crossed the border, little more than the distance changed. The territory was identical: valleys and dense, green jungle with an occasional sparkle of a stream or river. We flew deeper into Cambodia, with the sun at our rear, and unconnected to anything friendly except the radio frequency of "Tin Spike," the patrol's call sign. Ten more minutes passed before the crackle of radio interference garbled an English-spoken voice.

"...Six..."

"Could that be them," Belk asked, then he answered himself, "....gotta be."

122

"Tin Spike to Bravo Six. Do you copy?" the voice said clearly.

"That's it," I signaled Belk, then answered the transmission.

"Bravo Six to Tin Spike, we got you clear. Can you make a visual?" I responded, asked if the patrol could see the helicopter.

"Negative, Bravo Six, stay on course." The thud of the Huey rotors, a distinctive sound was very deceptive. One moment it appeared miles away and invisible and another moment, it was on top of you.

Another ninety seconds of eternity passed as the patrol searched the sky for a visual on the Huey. On first sight, they popped a smoke grenade. Belk and I sat eyes on the jungle below. To our left, at a distance, at the 10 o'clock position, rose a cloud of purple smoke.

"Tin Spike to Bravo Six, do you copy smoke?"

"Roger purple smoke, Tin Spike," I confirmed the marker.

"Purple smoke affirmative." Upon confirmation, I banked the Huey against the western horizon and sat up my approach to a small clearing adrift in purple smoke.

The LRRP team of four had an injured man that hopped on one leg between two soldiers that assisted him. An injury potentially complicated issues, but as the team scurried aboard, I lifted and climbed swiftly above the treetops as altitude was our only assurance. Belk pointed and requested someone put on the auxiliary headset.

"Sergeant, what's the status of his injuries?" I asked.

"Took a bamboo stake in the knee, but nothing serious," said a burly man with sleeves rolled above his elbows. "Once we cross the border sergeant, we're going after that MIA, that dog handler. Get us as close as you can to your last sighting."

"Roger that," the sergeant replied.

We flew east into the remaining morning sun as I gave the controls to Belk while I compared map coordinates to that of the LRRP leader. The zero-nine-zero heading brought us again to the mountain range and we crossed back into South Vietnam. Belk changed course to one-seven-zero southeast, when Sanderson's voice, our escort, blared on the radio, then a visual as Sanderson reversed his course to join us. Belk allowed Sanderson to set the pace and locate the LZ where the initial extraction failed weeks earlier.

"I got it," I said to Belk, then took the controls as Sanderson and I sat up the "hunter, killer" mode of attack. Belk and I became the eyeballs while Sanderson covered us. I swooped in close among the treetops. Scattered among the trees and canopy below were boulders, rock outcroppings and the reflection of water of an undetermined depth. Where possible, I flew below the treetops, and cruised the lanes and openings among the dense growth. The powerful rotors broke tree branches, something I learned from Odine. The rotor blades were 48 feet long with a twenty-one-inch cord or width and fitted at the tips with metal weights as a counter balance. The leading edge of each rotor was stainless steel. Sparse limbs and trees to four inches in diameter, posed little danger for the force and construction of the rotors. My heart raced and my eyes darted among the surrounding foliage. I feared a sane voice suggest we break off the search. Having covered a large area, I flew slower passes, but if prolonged, I asked for trouble.

It was a typical day. The sun burned bright and hot as the mechanical roar of helicopters invaded the deadly depths of jungle steam. For once, that familiar slap of the rotors, came to arouse one set of ears and pierced the monotony of the steamy, green places able to disorient a man. We peeped into the many hidden places, into the bosom of perdition that seldom gave up its captives.

Bamboo rose to the height of 50 feet and so dense it denied any primary or grassy growth. The green of Kapok trees, the green of Asian Pine, the yellow bamboo and the darker green bamboo, stared back.

"Navy, I think we got something over here!" Sanderson radioed. "Is that him…?"

"It's a G.I.," I heard the copilot say.

"There!" the co-pilot again yelled into his headset.

Sanderson and his copilot also spotted what they thought was a dog that ran among the thicket. Although the trees were enormous, there were no vines, but the depth of the water was unknown and bamboo was everywhere. A hundred yards away, Sanderson pointed to a hole in the canopy of bamboo. We both orbited the hole and inspected the ground below. Air rescue were better suited, I thought, but knew another hour was too long. The rotor wash from both ships caused the opening to dilate, open, and then close. The size of the hole was unknown until both ships pulled away and the nimble tops of the bamboo settled. The opening was twice the width of the rotors, but offered no immediate escape. I pondered the prospects and flew again over the area where I discovered a cathedral like opening near Sleep's location. The opening resembled an outdoor orchestra's shell. Huge yellow bamboo drooped at the top, created an overhang that shaded the water and ground.

"Navy, you're not thinking about going in there are you?" Sanderson asked. It was the only way.

"I know I can get in," I murmured. "I'm looking for a way out."

As much as the helicopter could fly vertically, like up some giant chimney or elevator shaft, it was not a safe maneuver. A loss of power in the process left no reserve or potential power for autorotation. The helicopter needed running room, a brief taxi to develop in training terms, translational lift, before it transitioned into a vertical posture.

"I'm going in," I informed Sanderson. I whispered as if no one aboard understood my intentions.

"I didn't come here to die, Navy! Keep those RPMs high, you dumb shit." It was Belk's curt but amiable warning to me.

I increased throttle and a gentle pull on the cyclic lever for a nose-high attitude, and settled below the treetops. Just above the water and a sparse outcropping of six to eight foot trees, I weaved a crescent shaped entrance, burst limbs in a gentle arch and arrived at the over-hang of giant bamboo. Members of the LRRP team rushed to the slumped, mud-caked figure and carried Sleep to the deck of the helicopter. One dog sat in the turbulence created by the rotors and they took him, too.

"Coming up!" I said as I twisted in power and pulled up on the collective.

The Huey became light on the skids then rose to a shallow hover. Slowly, in a petal turn, I looked for the path I cut. I inched left, then right on directions from the LRRP team. The process was cumbersome. LRRP members balanced themselves on the skids and relayed clearances through the cargo bay. Branches of trees and the dense bamboo flailed in the rotor wash obscured the path flown in. The helicopter was enveloped by foliage and seemingly sealed beneath the cavernous canopy. Above, we saw the silhouette of Sanderson's gunship as it drifted over the canopy and awaited some reply from me. Initially the terrain offered adequate space to climb out.

Belk contemplated our predicament as well. "There's your path of least resistance," he said, then drew his hand across the instrument panel.

I nodded in agreement. We needed to see the opening upon approach and lastly, pray I hit a soft spot.

"Bravo Six to Viper One," I called to Sanderson.

"Go ahead, Six."

"Viper One, your rotor wash is destroying the opening. I need you to hover out of effect of those bamboo tops."

"Roger, Six," said Sanderson, then lumbered toward the east and away from the hole in the jungle, just far enough for visual assistance.

As if jogging in a phone booth, I drifted toward the opening now marked by a huge shaft of sunlight. I sized up the task, and again radioed Sanderson.

"Bravo Six to Viper One."

"Copy, Bravo Six," the gunship answered. "What's your status? Navy, I can't sit here forever and beat-up the air." The 'B' model gunship required a great deal of in-put and effort to hover for extended periods.

"Viper One, situation is under control," I answered. "I need to be sure you're not staring down the throat of that opening once I blast out of here, bringing it up!"

For a maximum performance takeoff, I crabbed carefully to the farthest side of the overhang, maxed the RPMs, then nosed-over and headed into the crescent shape arch. With sufficient airspeed into a light wind, I applied maximum collective, nudged the cyclic and the Huey rose into a turning climb.

"RPMs! We're going in the red!" Belk shouted above the scream of the RPM warning siren.

With barely enough power, the Huey cleared the treetops. I bottomed the pitch immediately and went into a dive to gain airspeed, flew into a crooked, but wide ally among the trees, then roared once again to altitude as the gauges settled back to normal.

"Not much left of him," I heard via the auxiliary headset.

"Is he conscious?" I asked.

"He knows he's alive," the voice answered.

Once we regained altitude, Sanderson flew alongside and shouted angrily into the radio headset, "By the grace of God, Navy, you pulled it off! I think you're out of your frigging mind! You damn crazy! You are crazy, you know that? Any idiot pilot that does that has to be out of his mind!" Sanderson leveled a biting but serious critique of me. I took a chance and it worked.

"Be cool, Sanderson, and let's get out of here," I said to the escort. "Better notify med-evac, we're inbound."

We flew to the 71st Med-Evac hospital in Pleiku and landed. I wanted, needed to be aware of Sleep's condition. I lingered, then walked through the

MASH tent unintentionally into graves registration or the morgue, where I saw individuals using ID tags to reconstruct bodies from body parts. That sickening scene sent me reeling toward the door and sunlight where I came upon a stack of bodies awaiting processing. I wandered back to the pad, the helicopter and MASH tent and learned, upon stabilization, Sleep would be flown-out to a hospital. For me, Sleep left a sapphire ring and instructions with whom to barter for a prized AK47 assault rifle.

LIEUTENANT THOMPSON

As the monsoon season approached, Habrasham and I flew an infantry soldier to Saigon and Long Binh Jail. Recently court-martialed, the soldier was sentenced to prison, at Long Binh. The jail was affectionately called LBJ, President Johnson's initials were an oft used handle. A thirty-minute drive northeast of the Vietnamese City of Saigon and center of American Military Operations, stood Long Bin Jail, an American internment and holding facility. The jail's construction and amenities were subpar to any third world effort. Among indiscretions of the Vietnam War, corruption and profiteering were endemic and in terms of current vernacular and monetary values, the likes never before seen.

Once Habrasham and I passed through the detention yard and the office buildings, having seen the worst of it, I was ashamed, seethed with anger, then quickly concluded such shame was misplaced. Of those who proffered from the wars' vast sums of crime and corruption, few if any would end up in LBJ. Instead, the presence of an inordinate number of black soldiers, meant the system of unequal justice was just as effective in war as peace. War created the same inequities among the same ethnicity at a similar or greater frequency as in peacetime. My thoughts churned among the scenes I witnessed.

A conex was a steel storage cube with dimensions similar to 8'X8'X16' and ¼ in. They served as shipping containers and equipment storage. Long Binh Jail had a string of those containers with vertical strips cut from the four sides that simulated jail cell bars and provided ventilation, light, and surveillance of its occupants. Habrasham and I saw soldiers, confined to a steel box, some half naked in the heat of the day. They laid in a drunken or depressed stupor, one without his boots, another one without a shirt, canned like wild animals in a zoo. Their spirits were broken and their liberties revoked. In a war of wrongs and unpardonable sins, there in the red dirt and dust of the open plains, stood a miserable and dehumanizing facility built with the imagination of a pre-schooler. What crimes of war warranted such treatment? My shame was a result of being human and having watched this happen to other humans. Habrasham and I flew back to Pleiku in a silence unchallenged. We sped away as if a plague ensued, as if the on-rush of air cleansed and stilled such anger.

Back at Camp Holloway, I watched the sun fade against the day, heard the twang of steel guitar strings played to the whine of a broken heart. The sound of recorded country music, George Jones or Hank Williams; sad tales matched my feelings, mingled with the good smell of fresh bread from the ovens in the baker's tent. As darkness fell, I shared the LBJ experience with Lieutenant Thompson.

The new battalion commander, unlike the previous one, authorized the painting of nose art on the helicopters. Thompson became the resident artist. Much like the names, feminine figures and menacing grins of animals that adorned World War II air craft, a few ships were personalized.

A sudden surge of the main generator, briefly distorted the beat of a Lou Rawls album that played on Thompson's stereo. We shared many similar experiences surrounding our dreams and efforts to fly airplanes. Uniquely, Thompson developed a particular impatience with anything slower than himself or having the slightest imperfection. Such items he characterized jovially, as "raggedy." With Thompson, something was always raggedy. At the air base, new asphalt basketball courts with shiny, orange baskets and white cotton nets were raggedy when his and my team lost repeatedly to Air Force pilots. The Army's living quarters were surely raggedy and had no comparison to Airforce concrete barracks having windows and glossy floors.

The next day, dark clouds, and torrents of early monsoon rain, committed all aircraft to the ground. Nothing flew from Holloway, so Thompson and I hooked a ride into Pleiku. To escape the mundane, we hung-out in the bars, cavorted with bar girls and momma sans (madams). A few brothers from the 4th Infantry Division sat together in the first bar we entered. Lopez, an aircraft mechanic for helicopters and a colleague, pulled two bar girls to a corner table. Thompson and I sat with the brothers. The rest were country music lovers who serenaded the ladies and guzzled beer. It was a slow day for business.

Surreptitiously, I watched as one bar girl humorously imitated mannerisms of the three Americas, the Blacks, the whites and Hispanics. Quietly and for their own interest and entertainment, the girls enlisted an array of body language, voice inflections, and vocal slang that indicated major differences in the three groups. It fascinated me to see their wonder about such diversity and how it must coexist in the American Republic. However, the ability of the bar girls to communicate minutely, in English, made for a lively exchange.

Later, Thompson and I thumbed a ride back to base aboard a vehicle headed for Dragon Mountain. Thompson reminded the driver we'd get off at the fork that led to Holloway. It rained throughout the afternoon with no end intended. The driver drove through the checkpoint and sped toward Dragon Mountain, when Thompson reached through the canvas rear-view opening and grabbed the driver by the collar,

"Holloway! Stop this raggedy truck. I'm getting off at Holloway!"

Once on the ground, in eight inches of mud and the smell of beer on his breath, Thompson paused and restrained me for a moment then said, "Now look at that…, will you?"

We considered a panoramic view of Camp Holloway and compound.

"Is that any way to live? Does the Air Force know something we don't? Are we leaving any time soon? You'd think they'd at least pave the driveways. Surely, they could have left a few trees. Not one bleeping tree and hootches as raggedy and moldy as a forward base camp. Rats, big rats, live better than we do."

Having traversed as best we could, the mud and mud holes, we arrived at Thompson's hootch.

"I hear you did some pretty nifty flying to rescue that MIA a few weeks back?" Thompson said.

"Where did you hear that?" I asked.

"I've heard several versions, here and there and from your co-pilot."

"Nothing unordinary, a bit desperate perhaps. I expected some repercussions, from the brass, some comment, but no word so far."

"Follett, may recommend a medal. He's big on that," Thompson chimed.

"Naw, not for that. We were never there. It never happened. You know what I mean?"

"Tell me, Navy, what do you think of Captain Taylor?"

"I'm new to his platoon," I answered. "Transferred when you guys arrived. Until then, I flew guns. Taylor is no different from the rest of you hard-asses."

"He keeps volunteering me for recon. Why is that?" Thompson asked.

"Taylor's got aspirations to be a commander. Once he's matched personnel with performance, he's impressed his superiors. Make sure you know the area of operation like your living room. Know every LZ, every hill, and tree line associated with it, apply your skills correctly and with some luck you can handle any mission they throw at you."

Thompson spoke fondly of the new Cobra gunship already operational in some units. He hoped to stay in Vietnam long enough to fly guns and that new gunship.

"Which do you prefer, 'guns,' or 'slicks'?" he asked me.

"Guns are exciting, the aggressor, but they don't get their hands dirty except in dire circumstances. They both go into the LZs but it's the slicks that are committed to the ground."

"Ah, come on, Navy! Every viper pilot that goes to slicks, says that. Tell me what you really think."

It was a common reply, however true or trite.

"It takes some guys two or three tours to get sick of the killing. Then those same people point to other reasons for having enough. Gunships are for suppression, killing at a high rate. The fact that Charlie shoots back or first, justifies the act, but hardly the results."

For Xûan's village, I had plans that improved the quality of life providing I scrounged some useful materials in abandoned surplus throughout Camp Holloway, the air base and Dragon Mountain. I could only imagine the layout of the village. I envisioned such grandiose plans as a pumping station and a school building with traditional flooring integrated with the use of bamboo.

The balance of the week, milk runs of supply and re-supply from one nondescript hole in the jungle to another filled our days. The next time Habrasham and I were off, I took to Xuan's house, the building plans and sketches of a water delivery system.

"I hope you don't mind, there are things here I thought you might like. They're of little value, so you need not feel indebted to me."

It was a Vietnamese custom to devalue gifts. Xûan wanted to laugh, but covered her mouth with a hand. She knew I did so deliberately. Flashes of lightning pierced the cracks in the shutters. The lightning blinked like a neon sign, then, it was dark again.

"It has been two weeks since I last saw you, Mel. I worry."

Xûan had little interest in security, or possessiveness. Although she understood harmony and character, she didn't subscribe to feminine wiles. The Vietnamese in general, were great believers in character and placed little emphasis on the physical body. She didn't know why I gazed upon her, and she didn't seem to know she was a beautiful woman. Neither Xûan nor Rachel understood the power and dominance of womanhood, not fecund power or seductive power, but neither understood the cosmic and feminine connection of rhythms, order, and reformation.

In the quiet, unlit morning that followed, Xûan and I went over the plans for the village. My efforts were modest and applied to almost any location near a water source, but I could do little more until I knew the physical dimensions of the place, its grade and elevation. She was concerned about an obvious invasion of equipment and machinery. I had organized the work in stages that required the services of one additional pilot, Habrasham. The pumping station employed a common reciprocating pump and needed virtually no maintenance or spare parts. Xûan agreed the system would be an advantage, one that created no debilitating dependencies.

"Why do you want to do this, Mel?"

"If this is where you're going once the war is over..."

"After you leave," she corrected me.

"Okay, after I leave. It's for you and for Tram, all the people. I'll enjoy doing it."

"Mel, it takes all day. You can do this on your day off?"

"You said it's 70 miles from here, correct?"

"The roads, Mel. The roads are maybe seventy miles, then no roads, no buses, we walk."

I invited her to relax. I had it all worked out.

"No sweat. I hadn't planned to drive. I don't have access to trucks."

Xûan then nodded her head, understood my plan was to use the helicopter.

"Minutes, my lady, just minutes away. In a couple of weeks or fewer, it's done."

I had choreographed every move in my head over a hundred times and located many of the items that included pipe and pump for the initial stages.

"You are a smart man. You can build these houses, how many are here?"

"Those (I pointed toward a grand lay-out and elevation) show how they could look. It will depend on the quantity of materials secured, but you and your people will decide where and in what configuration. This shows how each building can be divided within or added to another."

Montagnards favored elevated, living spaces, long houses built on short stilts. In yet another drawing were common areas for a school, gatherings or the main pumping station. "You said you wanted to establish a school and teach, right?"

"Yes, I do. A real school," she pointed to a series of buildings.

"Will this help you help your people?"

"Yes, I thank you very much."

In a humane gesture, I said. "Good, maybe in a few years the war will be over and I can come to visit, and see how you're doing."

"Someday, you come back?" Her smile drifted into a long, wishful look.

"Who knows? I'd love to."

"Maybe you be married by then," she suggested.

"Maybe you'll be married too," I said.

"When you come back, for how long will you stay?" Wishfully, she hoped and considered such.

"I don't know. Not long, I suppose. There's a lot of work to be done in my country, too. There are pressures to succeed and make things better for others like me. To be realistic, I don't think I'll ever come back, but we will write, you and I, and I'll always think of you."

Xûan had no problem with realism. She understood I, too, had a village and a people that I must lend support. Up against the enormous needs of each culture, a love affair and the individual desires of two people did not amount to very much. We knew our lives pointed in different directions, similar means to similar ends, but in different directions. She told me so.

"How long will you think of me, Mel?"

I put away the papers and plans then pulled her close. "I shall always remember you, forever."

"Forever is only a moment. Eternity is but a little while," she said softly as if disappointed in the brevity of such memory.

"And you are very wise in that respect, but where I come from, that's a lot of planting and weeding, years you'd rather not think about. There won't be enough time to forget you, Xûan."

Dawn crept over Pleiku and like my home, roosters celebrated its arrival. A flight of fast-movers, F-4 Phantoms, departed the air base in a thunderous roar, their afterburners glowed like tiny moons in morning's twilight. I heard a series of sniffles and knew Xûan was crying, so I pried her away from me, saw her weeping face and huge, wet eyes.

Habrasham arrived and we drove Xûan to MAC-V, then he and I headed for Camp Holloway. Helicopter crews sustained attacks at an increased rate as the Viet Cong became more aggressive. A combat assault into a cold LZ, one without resistance, became a rare event. About mid-morning that same day, Habrasham and I mulled about on stand-by as flights returned from an assault southwest of Pleiku. Several ships had been downed and resulted in a number of casualties. As the pilots spilled into company area, Reljac ranted and raved at another pilot. In Reljac's opinion, the other pilot demonstrated poor flying skills, in and out of hot LZs. A fight ensued and it quickly escalated into a brawl, as Reljac was livid. The pilot in error failed repeatedly to wait for a signal from the flight leader before lift-off. Entrance and exit of a tight LZ meant everyone followed cue.

The problems created by an accident, a midair collision in this case, were enormously grave. If a pilot who flew in the second, third or fourth flight position, lifted prematurely over other ships unaware of his launch, it caused a mass entanglement of rotors, with multiple crashes. Flights already departed had only the crews aboard, but helicopters in descent mode were stacked up in the air, stair stepped above the LZ, unable to land and loaded with troops. Instantly, they became sitting ducks. Reljac's tantrum and provocation were small compared to the enquiry that followed. Both pilots faced disciplinary charges. Command suspended the errant pilot's flight-status.

In spite of our losses, the officer's club became a rowdy cavern that evening. The day marked the end of six months in country. It was a time to be jubilant, when we considered the trials already completed and the plight of those less fortunate.

Men with names like Crazy Hoss, Deadeye, and Big White, told jokes. Reljac drank to near unconsciousness. Belk looked steady, but alcohol only added to the lack of clarity in his Kentucky accent. He, too, was drunk. Habrasham, chased bourbon with beer, laughed at Big White's lies. Anything that deserved a thought, Thompson found something raggedy about it. The reel-to-reel tape of prerecorded music played a homey ballad, Tom Jones' "The

Green, Green, Grass of Home." A sad song, full of recollection, where growing old was still part of the scheme of things. The song extolled the virtues of home, where evening soothed and nighttime embraced, where mornings had no memory and good times grew like trees of summer.

Between tables, two pilots danced obtusely, arm in arm, drunk beyond the acuity to stand alone. To the hoots and howls of the crowd, they staggered to the uncertainty of tomorrow. Among such fervor and festivities, the month of February had no further promise.

Song of Summer

"Well, are you coming out? Come on, please?" I pleaded rhetorically.

Xuan smiled broadly from her kitchen window as we both looked at one another through the magnification of binoculars. Habrasham and I hovered at a distance near the stand of banana trees. I took the controls, leaned the Huey over and encircled the banana trees, then back to an abrupt hover. I repeated the move in the opposite direction as I made smaller and tighter the turns, over and over again. I tried to dart, drop, and rise with the grace of a dragonfly, the ones I chased as a child. I tried to orchestrate the message, "Come on out," when finally, I saw Xuan, bolt from the rear door of the house with the bounce of a little girl and headed along the dike. I settled the Huey adjacent to the trees and shut it down as Habrasham headed past Xûan to his woman's house.

"You are crazy, Mel. Why you play that way?"

Then, as if I, too, were Montagnard, she spoke to me in her native dialect. There existed no comprehensive written language to translate their speech, so her efforts to teach me common terms challenged us both. Xûan's voice reminded me of our first talk in December at the New Year's party. If only I could meet her, I then thought. That memory would have lasted forever. Someday far into the future, I would tell the story to Rachel over and again, of the woman who looked like her.

"Am I still such a young boy, too young to be a pilot?"

137

She beamed at me and, still winded from her run along the dike, said, "That was long ago. You are a crazy young man who can do many things. You are very wonderful."

"And you?"

"What about me? What is it you wish to know?" she asked, her face camped at my shoulder. The moan of wind through the banana trees, the rustle and wave of their huge leaves, mingled with the low crackle of voices from the radio headsets.

"I wonder about your safety, if it's better you stayed here in Pleiku instead."

"Many hope the war will change Vietnam, but for Montagnards, it is not certain. I need to go back, be part of whatever changes that come."

The Government, she thought, governed the Vietnamese one way and the Montagnards another. Saigon created reforms and programs that in essence, tied them to the system, created a dependency, before punishing them through criticism and funding cutbacks for being dependent. I understood the concept all too well. Montagnards wanted what was already theirs, and controls to their own development. Xûan rolled the sleeve of her blouse, placed her exposed skin next to mine, compared our skin tones, our likeness. "Same, same," she chuckled. She was proud of our association, her young vulnerable lover with strong, but sensitive ties to a simple life. Now and then in her bouts of wisdom, came a separation of unselfishness and possessiveness as she wished I had no reason to leave Vietnam. The war once destroyed her life, then presented solitary alternatives with no conventional escape.

"My mother thanks you for the cigarettes, and Tram, too, for the things you gave to him. I explained to my mother your plans for the village."

"And what does she think?"

"She said, 'Ceux qui sont noirs.'"

"I remember, she used that term once before, the first time I met her. It's French for something black, right?"

"It means literally, 'the black ones' or 'those that are black.' Occasionally, my mother spoke of French Soldiers; among them were black soldiers with strange, beautiful eyes and kind hearts."

She meant the French Moroccan soldiers who fought as allies and subjects of France, against the Viet-Minh in the early 1950s. Moroccan and Algerian soldiers, like American Negro soldiers, shared historical similarities. They also shared a great deal of empathy.

"When can we visit your village?" I asked.

"My mother will go again next month. She will talk for you. Then we will go."

We sat in the silence of dusk and early evening, long past the time Habrasham usually arrived.

"What is the name of your village, Xûan?"

"What do you mean? My village has no name. It is in the mountains near another village that has no name."

"So, someday if I come looking for you, how do I find you?" I continued my line of questions.

"There is no name. You come, and I will find you."

"I'll ask for the Village of Xûan Yun, and somebody will know."

We both laughed at its improbability. Habrasham arrived and we lifted for MAC-V.

The next morning, he and I flew the colonel to Dalat and to our surprise, the colonel didn't detain us, instead instructed us to return to Camp Holloway. That afternoon, having kicked off my boots, Habrasham came into my hootch.

"Wanna go into Pleiku?" he asked me.

"Oh, man, Hab, I'm sick of 'C's, and who knows where the colonel will have us tomorrow?" He and I kept a stash of choice 'C' ration selections on-board and too often ate on the deck of the Huey.

"You'll be on standby tomorrow, you jive farmer! I have a Jeep and I'm on my way to the showers."

"Wait a minute, Hab. Her folks are back, that might change things. I don't know."

"You kidding me? You dipstick! The only way you're going to find out is to be there!"

He liked me, liked being around me, but often reminded himself, I was less than half his age and didn't know spit about life. I slipped into my sandals, grabbed a towel, and we left for the showers.

Later, we dressed and drove into Pleiku. At Xûan's house, she guided me through the door and into the house where we paused briefly, greeted the mother then headed out the rear door. We continued to the backyard and onto the dike that pointed to the stand of banana trees and a mountainous horizon, many miles away. The dikes were an earthen mound above the waterline, linear, and only as wide as a footpath. They intersected at right angles, formed huge squares and rectangles that loomed for miles and held water for moisture dependent rice plants.

Xûan and I took a slow stroll along that dike, amid mutual glares that spelled our feelings. No agenda or special wish framed that day, no boundary or written script confined any whim that sprouted wings. We touched politely, playfully in our venture towards evening and the edges of an endless, flat world. We walked beyond the war, beyond its many restrictions and jagged edges, to a place neither had gone before. Since November, we lived in the small spaces between the horizons, between doom and desolation, promise and deliverance. In the long afternoon shadows, occasionally we peered back at the rear edges of Pleiku, awash in an evening breeze. Dwarfed as we were against the vastness of the open rice fields, sheltered by the sky and only a wisp of clouds adrift, came a look that said my feelings were just as exposed. Xûan's mood was unfettered, her smile beamed, punctuated by laughter around her huge, beautiful eyes.

Finally we came upon the growth of banana trees where Now, and present, became the only measure of significance, the only cup from which we'd drank. There where evening stood, was a place of our own, our moment of moments and we called it home. We stood akin to seasons changed, ripened in our golden years and faces stamped on tomorrow. There in the cool, long shadows of the banana trees, we preferred the stayed, eternal security of yesterday. Our yesterdays, forever clasped upon a memory. And when now, and present, could no longer compete, we turned reluctantly and again, strolled toward the strict and imposed order of reality.

At Xûan's house, we sat silently in the rear doorway. Two people dangled at the edges of war and asked for our sakes, a war that was kind and merciful, that unlike the masses, we avoided its toils and uncertainty.

"My mother and Tram went to visit. I will go after them later," she said as we moved into the house where she removed her shoes and waved me over to a seat.

I sat as she stood and faced me. With my chin cradled against her body, she explored my face, touched the tiny scars from my childhood, and named each from my recounted stories. In an ultimate intimacy, she shared in my yesterdays.

"Why do you look at me sometimes and do not smile? What is it that you see, Mel?"

"I'm smiling. I'm smiling inside," I answered. Flippantly, I chose to deflect the question.

Again, she laid down her words one at a time.

"Your smiles that you keep hidden, are you ashamed of something? Are you not happy, Mel?"

"Ashamed, what am I ashamed of? How can you speak of happiness in times such as these? I'm more inclined to put happy on hold, as I do what's necessary to survive."

Immediately, I understood the tragedy of my remark. Mine was the luxury to delay or put aside some time for the roughage in life, before I went on to a level of living more familiar. For Xûan, the Montagnards and the Vietnamese people, life was a tent pitched among the ruins of war, with all a tent's semblance of permanency.

I buried my face in her bosom, and searched for words to explain the months of probing stares. I sought kind words that said she was much more than the memory of someone else.

"I wish I were as much comfort and support to you as you are to me. My love for you can only be painful in its obvious limitations. I fear taking too much. I see you as someone I've known all my life, someone I lost, but through you I've regained."

I tried but wasn't ready, couldn't say the words. I knew the need to explain my actions would arrive, but the words wouldn't talk for me, wouldn't spell the grind in my guts, or summon fate to explain this terrible joke played on me. Xûan gently pressed my head against her, held me, and contemplated my remarks.

"My days with you are not many, Mel. The Buddhists say, 'All is pain.' Nothing we do will escape it. The further we venture into consciousness, the keener our perceptions, the more vulnerable we are to pain. Our sensitivities are the result of our growth and understanding. Pain is the price we pay, Mel, for our joys and our understanding. Share with me your thoughts that look back at me, but never speak."

I pulled Xuan into my lap and kissed her. In that embrace, I praised the courage she displayed, her will to accept the fate of our existence. I held her there, waded deeply into the currents of our wishes, while flogged ever so gently by the brown of her, the black of her, her tan and bronze.

The mission briefing the following morning outlined intelligence reports on VC activity in and around Pleiku. Red alert orders for Camp Holloway and the Air Force Base became the frenzy that hailed the first week of March. Days later, in the predawn hours, explosions in bold splashes of orange and red, again engulfed the town of Pleiku. I flew among three flights of helicopters dispatched to pick up a quick reaction force at Dragon Mountain. We lifted and headed south along the row of houses that bordered the rice paddy. At 300 feet, hostile fire from the ground lashed the fuselage. Return fire was prohibited due to residents that fled communist forces. Ahead, the first platoon descended. I came around like so many times before, peered down at the last row of faded, pastel houses to my left and the blackened area to my right that marked the stand of banana trees.

The enormous expanse of the rice paddy, its placid sheen of water and network of dikes like so many windows darkened for the night. I concentrated on the blackness below and assisted Gallagher, my co-pilot as we picked a spot for landing. In a flash, the number two ship sustained several direct hits before it descended rapidly in crash mode. Suddenly, a tremendous explosion rocked our Huey, sent it out of control. Gallagher froze with an unconscious grip on the cyclic control lever as thick smoke billowed through the cabin.

"I got it!" I yelled.

Having lost all power, I checked the airspeed indicator and bottomed the collective pitch. With the remaining power, I used the cyclic and turned into the wind. Within 100 feet off the ground, I yanked up on the collective, channeling all remaining power to reverse our descent and cushion the inevitable crash. The skids smacked into the mud and water of the rice paddy. The grunts were off and running as the door gunners snatched open the pilot's doors. As I turned to bail the seat harness, a second explosion propelled me into muddy water. Everyone aboard escaped as I pulled myself to my feet. While the first light of dawn lit the rice paddy, I ran toward the dike that led to Xûan's house, saw the water buffalo tied to a stake. I untangled the mud-caked com cord and chicken plate, ditched the helmet and looked back at the smoldering rubble that was Baker One Three, my helicopter, its hiss and groan of burning metal kissed by the stagnant paddy. Another ship landed nearby and my crew scrambled aboard. With my .45 automatic drawn, I worked my way toward the rear door of Xûan's house.

I heard the cries of a child and angry shouts of someone out of view. Somehow I resisted the temptation to rush in, but saw a weeping Xuan, who held her son, Tram. A bead of saliva connected Xuan's lower lip and her wrist, glistened in the twilight like a string of jewels. A lone enemy soldier held them in terror as Xuan continued to cry. His threatened expression peered back at her, made her part of his threat. With the enemy's focus on Xuan, I stepped through the curtain doorway and fired one round into his chest, then another. Xuan covered her face with one hand and wailed against the scene of her mother who laid dead before her.

"We have to leave here, now!" I said.

Xûan was hysterical and wore only a gown. I held Tram in my right arm and the .45 automatic in my right hand, then, placed my left arm around Xûan. As morning crept upon the day, we dashed into the soft bog of the rice paddy.

Blinded by her tears, Xuan found it difficult to keep pace with my long strides. Among the buzz of live rounds came a loud, whump! I reached, took a firm hold of Xûan, and pulled her alongside me. Then another whump! The explosion lifted us all into the air, the echo of it and the pungent smell of cordite, enveloped each of us. In an instant I saw one or more helicopters circled us. When everything seemed cast in silence and slow motion, she screamed, but no sound reached my ears. Her eyes were ablaze and her mouth agape, as if she saw in me a monster. Suddenly a vail of blood closed her eyes and pulled her away. Silently, she sang for me the song of summer. Upon the song without sound, rode summer's end. In life's harvest of youth, last was its sound.

The ground came up and the sky rushed past my head. The child, slipped from my grasp, from an arm numb beyond response. I felt the mud and water against my face, smelled the sweet scent of jet fuel from the crash. As my senses faded, life leaked from my wounds. There at the edge of life, in the mud and water tinted iridescent by spilled jet fuel, I yearned for things of yesterday and times untested by desperation. I yearned to hear the lonely whistle of a bobwhite bird across the quiet sunshine of a Saturday morning, for the taste of dewberries in spring. I yearned for the smell of fresh sawdust warm against my body and the look of a scarecrow as it strained to see over summer corn. There at the edge of life came a moment's peace for a troubled soul.

Summers come and go. Each offered no clue or secret to its endless repetitions, but young men weren't so resilient, they faltered, they paled against permanence. Young men lived but twice, once in themselves and once in their dreams, then summer is fled.

A Banging of Drums, Slowly

March 1968

From far away came unintelligible sounds. Imageless, translucent light sparkled from an unknown source as I floated on a void, shoreless sea of foam. And long it was, before those sounds and images made sense, allowed me to grasp the fix I was in, and showed me the dark on which I'd impaled myself. Sounds of a machine paced my breathing. A rigid clasp like the jaws of a vise, pointed my head towards a blur in the ceiling and nothing suggested anything existed below my shoulders.

"Hello, Mister Streeter. How do you feel today? How are you? Can you hear me? You have a visitor again, today, Mr. Streeter. Someone has come to see you."

A female face looked down at me, seemingly at the bottom of a well. Her voice was distant, almost an echo. When her face disappeared, Habrasham's face filled my view. My heartrate increased at the sight of him and the machine strained to keep pace. I braved the thought: Were my legs and arms attached and what did my parents know?

"You've suffered a severe concussion, Mister Streeter, along with multiple shrapnel wounds to your legs, neck, and larynx," the woman said.

Then his face came back.

"You're in Na Trang and everything is going to be alright, Navy. Don't worry, you did nothing wrong. Charlie (the Vietcong) was waiting for us."

Habrasham knew my first concern was my use of judgment, but said the VC was better that day and my actions were above reproach.

145

One day, I heard a new set of voices and the ceiling had a different texture. "Hi! My name is Nurse Shaw, welcome to Okinawa, Mister Streeter! You're doing just fine. I'll raise your head, broaden your view a little."

When my head pointed upright slightly, I saw but the head and shoulders of Lieutenant Shaw and the grin on her face. Then a small contingent of males appeared, pulled my chart and talked amongst themselves, before saying, "Mister Streeter, you look fine today. You've had surgery twice in different areas and I've got good news for you. You're going home."

"I'm happy for you, Mister Streeter, you're going home! And everything's going to be all right. You rest now and I'll come back later," Nurse Shaw said.

I considered the fate of things left undone, an unfinished letter, perishables, in my locker, and who now, flew my missions? Interred unto myself, unable to communicate, I recalled my fantasies of becoming a naval fighter pilot and later, those of becoming a helicopter pilot. When reality presented itself, the price one paid for grandeur, its means seemed tainted by the end and no longer worthy. I made the grade, but only in the height of vengeance did I belong to that killer class of individuals who looked their enemy in the eye, then wiped them from the planet.

To my left, was an elevated, seemingly unoccupied bed. Where one's legs would lie, the bed was flat and unruffled. I wondered about the individual who presented only half of self, physically. I wondered if I shared a similar loss. Dying ain't so bad, I thought. Left alone in one's injuries is what's unacceptable.

MEMPHIS

MARCH 1968

Home is where evening goes, where my dreams come to rest, where I laid my burden down, but I'm told, the day my family received notification of my injuries, the olive drab sedan cruised along Mulberry Street, among smiling dogwood trees in bloom. Unlike the mailman, the milkman, or geese that flew south, the driver didn't know his way, but circled the blocks, backed, turned, and frightened everyone in view. The courier presented a telegram. His remarks included a brief scripted message with the look of apology for his presence. The telegram read as follows:

"The Secretary of the Army has asked me to inform you that your son, Warrant Officer 1, Melvin R. Streeter, was wounded in action on 8 March 1968 after the helicopter he piloted was shot down over South Vietnam. He received a fragment wound to the neck and several penetrating wounds to the lower extremities. The extent of any permanent damage is undetermined at this time."

I'm told that momma screamed, stumbled in her darkness of clinched eyes, then bellowed toward the heavens, a plea for mercy. Absence of the word "death" gave some temporary reprieve to the thought of a permanent loss, a reassuring gasp to repel the choke of death. It gave back their son, however broken and maimed.

A new pattern in the ceiling tiles signaled another change in location, but little else in a world that passed above me and resonated from a machine that paced my breathing, indicated where I might be. In my drug-induced drift between consciousness and sleep, I tried to make sense of a staccato of commercial ads on TV. The telecast suggested I was stateside in Memphis, Tennessee, an eight-hour drive from home.

Once while attended by a nurse, my left hand attacked me. The hand and arm were numb, and, seemingly unattached, as if it belonged to another. It moved, it groped and flopped in and out of my line of vision. Before leaving, the nurse restrained the hand, retied it to the bed rail. Like a dumb animal that might wonder off or befall some mischief, the hand required restraints. The hospital smelled of new construction, sterile and hollow. In an area for recent arrivals, members of the staff prepared us for visitations. The staff drew curtains that separated me from my neighbors, gave me a pep talk on my medical progress.

In an hour, figures in heavy clothing crowded into the doorway and the curtain walls. My grandfather, then my mother entered. A nurse insisted I remain stationary, explained the breathing apparatus, and told them to stand at the foot of the bed for my benefit. Then, the nurse left us alone. Someone cried, but I did not want them to cry. My mother, moved to my side with tears in her eyes. She kissed the cast that covered my head and face. That was especially painful for me. I remembered too well their concerns and fears. I squeezed mom's hand and held back my own tears. Maurice had grown, but he, too, wiped his eyes. Grandma turned, bent with grief, then, left the enclosure. I did not want it that way. 'I must be a mess,' I said to myself. My grandfather followed grandma out the door and I heard my mother's sobs, and those of Ellen. When the grandparents rejoined us, the family gathered at the foot of the bed while my grandfather, the country preacher, offered a prayer. Suddenly, what they feared most as parents and siblings laid prone before them. My father spoke first.

"Son, you've had a tough time, but the worst is over. The doctors said, in three weeks, a month, you'll be ready to go home. That's a blessing. We'll have you home, knowing you're alright." The stable voice came from out of view.

Drugged beyond the reach of pain, I couldn't imagine what I looked like as I laid there with a stainless steel brace about my shoulder and steel rods that held rigid my head. Recent pains in my lower extremities signaled the presence of legs or a leg. But as my eyes swept from one side of the room to the other, I studied their faces, their stares, which suggested I was missing something. I closed my eyes to see what they saw. Surely, someone would have told me by now. After everyone's initial statement, it was apparent a one-way conversation was the best it would get. I saw them hampered by the same silence I dreaded. It was a silence I endured, imprisoned as I was at the end of dream. Someday I'd tell them about Rachel, the Rachel they didn't know, and about Xûan and her family, and Sandra. It wouldn't be a war story, but one of compassion and learning; a fitting conclusion, after all. To date, the people, the war, and the circumstances that surrounded Xûan, became a story I wished to tell, one that longed to be told as I accepted whatever physical deformities I had. Hours passed, it seemed, until Ellen moved and stood next to mom and the hand formerly tied to the bed rail. She held my swollen hand as tears streamed down her face. I winked my eye and moved my index finger like a pencil, tried to make her understand the word "day."

"He wants to write something!" Ellen said.

At once, the hunt for pencils and paper, that the man child might speak his pain. I raised my left hand, while a pad slid under my wrist and a pen from mom. Crudely, but gloriously in everyone's strained eyes, I wrote the word "Hi," then the letters "Ok" and eventually, "no pain." A collective sigh and everyone felt somewhat at ease. I tried to ask how long had I been there, but couldn't convey it, so I tried to write the word "date" on the pad.

"Today is the 15th, March 15," my mother said, "and you're in the city of Memphis, Tennessee, in a wonderful, brand-new V.A. hospital."

I dropped the pen as tears filled my eyes. Two weeks and no word from Habrasham. My family was puzzled by my teary reaction when told the date. I reached again for the pen and wrote the words "shot down 8."

"Yes...," my mother said "...it happened on the 8th."

I then wrote, "I ok, love U."

"We love you, too, baby." She squeezed the words through lips that trembled.

"I want to write something," Maurice said, wanted to be part of the conversation.

In a rush of words and tears that lacked composure, mom said, "He can hear you, baby... Melvin can't speak..., he has to write. Ask what you want and he will try and answer you."

Maurice pointed to the bed beyond the curtain at my right and asked, "What's wrong with the man over there?"

"Oh, Maurice, he might not know that." My parents explained to my kid brother that I could not see around the room.

A TV news cast mentioned The Reverend Dr. Martin Luther King Jr. and his purported arrival in Memphis. Sandra had developed a manuscript concerning King. Many viewed him as a potential political threat and some power brokers anticipated the impact of such a move. Dr. King's unpopular alliance with the Anti-Vietnam War movement and his Poor People's Campaign, were risky, but profound political moves. Sandra subscribed to a school of thought that believed in the "New Man Theory," one that said history every so often produced a new man in terms of his emergence above all else, leadership, political savvy, and the championing of human rights. To Sandra, Dr. King was that new man in a very late stage of transformation, ready to burst upon the scene. Immersed in thoughts of Sandra and Dr. King, that night I dreamed he came to the hospital.

In a very vivid dream, I wanted to remind Dr. King of our previous encounter in Atlanta, years ago. In a trio of men, he walked the ward, but before I could get the trio's attention, they had spoken to my neighbors, waved, and wished speedy recoveries. I raised my hand, my left hand and attempted to call him over. I waved vigorously, but the trio only waved in return as I strained in pain against the attached machine and the trachea tube lodged in my mouth and throat. I trembled and floundered like a newborn, unable to articulate my wishes. The dream offered me an opportunity to explain to Dr. King my new-found dedication to cause and community, instead, I awakened in its heightened excitement.

The week passed amid the boredom and stillness of my injuries, but lying in wait, I feared, was the revelation I was incomplete. The evening news reported the approach of a very heavy snowstorm and its promise of inconveniences, which prompted the family to re-evaluate their intended stay. Physically, my body responded well and by the third week, the 21st of March, I quietly rejoiced and acknowledged the presence of all my extremities. I also began the oral intake of foods, but the faculties of speech would take a while longer.

On a later visit, my dad gave me a haircut, my mother fed me and I still wrote with my left hand. My head and neck, still stiff from immobility, insisted I turn my entire body rather than my head alone. On Saturday, everyone went out to eat, and left my mom and me alone.

"Melvin, an old friend of yours, Sandra, has been very persistent about you and your recovery. I took the liberty and invited her up to see you. You don't mind, do you?" Mom asked, as she sat close to my bed, held my hand, filed and shaped my nails.

"No," I motioned.

Then my mom continued.

"Sandra and I exchanged letters these past weeks. I'd like to meet her." Mom studied my eyes for any reply whenever she paused. "She sounds like a nice girl. Pretty, too. She sent some photos of you two when you were in school. Now that your sister is taking company, your dad and I see how much you missed over the years. You skipped your junior and senior proms, the high school experience in general, then you rushed through college in two and a half years, abbreviated that experience. What plans do you have now? Soon it'll be time to join the real world, get married..., and raise a family. We've pushed you at times, did what stimulated your interest to work at a level near your potential. Now we risk sounding selfish, asking that you come back to us and relive the years we've lost. Is that so terrible as it sounds?"

I scribbled a note as a nurse came in to check the remaining bandages.

"Try and talk, Mister Streeter. Put away your pen and exercise those vocal cords," she said.

Barely above a whisper came my voice. "Now that Ellen is dating, don't you have enough of that?"

"Enough?" my mother asked. "Is not an issue. It's having you home again and participating, sharing with us. I would like to be a grandmother someday, and you'd make a great father."

"You and dad shouldn't blame yourselves. I might have taken some things a little slower, but I'm fine, I've learned a lot, wouldn't have, otherwise." I caught my breath, struggled, then tried to continue. "What are you and Sandra talking about?"

My mother smiled and removed the cardigan sweater she wore.

"She's a heady one. You better look out for her," mom said, laughed lightly.

Although my mother approved, she was not sure of my experiences in dealing with the antics of cunning women.

"I know what ... Rachel thought of you, but Sandra's different. She comes right at you." Mom hesitated when she mentioned Rachel, not sure how I dealt with Rachel's death.

My plans were not so different from what she wished, but I would not rush things anymore, not even to settle down.

"I'll be glad when I get you home, put some meat on those bones, and hear you talking again. Thank God you're going to be all right," she said, gleefully reassured.

"Ma, this is not the little boy that left home six years ago. I'm much older now, much, much older. I've seen things and known people that helped me understand myself relative to the rest of the world. I've taken a long look, listened, tasted and touched the grief of others. I'm not bitter, but I'll never be the same." I labored in my efforts to speak, so I paused, then started again.

"Sandra's gotten to you. She impresses you, doesn't she?"

"She, like me, spoke of lost opportunities," my mom said. "Sandra's a lively one. I hope you invite her home sometime. She was ready to come as soon as she learned you were in Memphis. It so happens, she has business here next week, so I'm not so sure I could keep her away after all."

Later, when the family left for their hotel, I laid awake, afraid to sleep for fear of haunted dreams, but before long, they, the sleep, and dreams descended upon me.

At Xûan's house the water buffalo was tied to a stake. It was her signal to me of danger. One explosion, then another and the rice field rose fast to engulf the helicopter, my crew, and the grunts aboard.

I awakened to pains in my neck, struggled to scream and reached to free myself from the fiery confines of the cockpit. Instead, I felt the strong grip of aides at my side. Once awakened, they left me in the relative comfort of reality. Wet with perspiration, I breathed heavily, then above the den of silence, heard a sympathetic voice beyond the curtain.

"There's them that die, and them that live, and them that live the dying over and over again. Hang on, soul."

Unable to reply, I listened to the howl of the winter wind. A few days later, around noon, I felt a disturbance in the air. A pleasant feminine voice, different from that of my mother or sister, spoke. It was Sandra. Her presence said, "Not all is dead." Sandra approached me, placed a kiss on my lips, and handed me a greeting card and a small wrapped gift. She wore a dark gray business suit with a white blouse, tied in a bow at the neck, and leather boots. I introduced my parents, then my sister and brother. Mom and dad stood, and the women embraced. My raspy whisper and the single bandage on my throat, again brought Sandra's attention to me.

"Your voice, what has happened to you?" She was confused as how best to embrace me.

Ellen took Sandra's things and placed them on a vacant chair. Sandra still wore no make-up and looked out of character dressed in business attire—not at all like the rough, baggy styles of our college days. Sandra turned, winked then again approached the bed.

"I'll be in town all week, and if I may, I'll come see you every day. When my letter to you in Vietnam came back, I was so afraid." She started crying, but talked through the tears, told me of the ordeal of repeated calls to my home with no answer. Mom stood and went to Sandra's side.

"My dear, you would have been crushed to see him those first weeks."

Mom tried to comfort Sandra. She placed her arm around her shoulder and the two turned and walked out of the room. Ellen rushed to the bedside and raved about Sandra's exceptional, good looks and figure.

"She's pretty! Even prettier than the pictures she sent! She's really pretty."

When mom and Sandra returned, Sandra related the convenience of her visit.

"I work with SCLC. A week ago, a protest demonstration led by Dr. King in support of the City's Sanitation Union went awry. Some blamed planning but there was violence, too."

Sandra continued, "Dr. King is disappointed with the outcome, particularly the way it played out in the press. So, I'm among an advance party to organize and plan another protest march, one that is orderly and peaceful." She then looked at me and said, "I'm going to be here for a while. We'll be seeing a lot of one another."

"Good, someone here to see you on weekdays," mom said.

The family gathered their things and prepared to leave. In the family's exit, they all embraced and promised to keep in-touch, then, Sandra and I were alone.

Sandra stared for a moment, then asked that I explain what happened to me. I picked through the scenario as best I could, not at all sure now, if some dream version invaded my memory.

"How long have you been talking?"

"Four days, and Sandra, you haven't changed one bit. You haven't aged one hour."

She took a long look at me. "Tell me when you're tired or don't feel well. There's a lot we need to talk about, okay…? You have a wonderful family, so

153

warm. I bet they're that nice to everybody." She paused, sighed before saying, "I'm sure your being away from all that action, the flying and excitement, is breaking your heart. I hope you've had enough."

Only Sandra could say that without being insensitive or cruel. In fact, only Sandra could call attention to my selfish endeavors.

"I'm sorry I wasn't here earlier." She started to cry again, searched her purse for a napkin then said, "So you think I haven't changed. Well, I have. I'm very different. I'm not as brave as I used to be and not as 'anti' everything. I mentioned the book I'm writing, still working on." She stopped and again, looked at me. "Do you feel like listening to all this? I hope I'm not boring you."

"No, nonsense," I said, "keep talking."

"Did you miss me, Melvin? You didn't write very much. We've really got to talk, seriously. I wanted to bring the last letter I sent you, the one that came back, but I don't have the nerve to read it to you. I didn't think I'd see you so soon."

"Why don't you just say what you wrote?"

"Not now." Again, she sighed, looked me in the eye. "I've missed you. It's almost two years now and many things I thought could wait, I've reconsidered. My goals, my wishes, I thought best be done alone lest I be sidetracked. My biggest change is knowing what I really want, that I want to be with you, wherever that might be, and I'm not saying this to sound good because you're recuperating, either. I really mean it, Mel."

It would take more than talk and want of change to convince me, but I could imagine what that change would look like on her. Yet, I had no idea what my needs were, going forward.

"I want to hear you, know where your head is and what plans you have. I don't mean right now, considering—I mean what were you thinking a month ago, two months and where do I fit? It probably sounds like I'm rushing things, but these are my changes, where I'd like to be."

I measured my words, wanted to be fair with her and my confused conscience. In terms of her place among that of Xûan and Rachel, Sandra, for all her good looks, intentions and straightforward pursuits, was just another face in the crowd.

"Sandra, I was always flattered by your attention. I could never say no to you, not even now, but you must understand, I've gone through some changes also. As for where my head is, I've just discovered I still have a head. From where I was to where I am now, amounts to a metamorphosis, not merely a change in fashions and falling in love; if that's what you're saying. Between circumstances and a couple of individuals, there's been some bold impacts on my life and a great deal for me to consider. Much of what you and I have is like you said, things, feelings we've held and waited for some proper moment to express."

In my pause, we exchanged thoughtful looks, then, Sandra said, "You mean you're seeing someone?"

"No," I answered. "Those people no longer exist."

"Gone?" she asked.

"Yes. They're gone."

"We're going to work through your injuries, I understand that, but what has two people who have nothing more to do with you, have to say about you and me?"

"Calm down. Before I'm well again, we'll have a better understanding of what we both are going through."

"Melvin," she said softly, "I hope you're right. Somehow, I thought you'd always be there. I've always had things my way, but now I'm willing to compromise. I accept a challenge, but don't make it impossible for me."

"Your challenge is me and the baggage I've accumulated. There's no one else," I said.

She wiped her nose, more tears before saying, "Okay. You'll love my new-found selfishness. I want to be spoiled and loved, by the person of my choosing. You're right, I've waited a little long to say this, but in all my letters of late, I tried to share those feelings. Yes, I am in love with you, have been for some time now—hoped it wouldn't come to this, but I can handle it if at the moment you're not in love with me."

She stood and looked down at me, a pointed, piercing, stare, but I was not her focus. Her eyes glazed-over in bubbled tears that didn't fall. She did not blink, but unconsciously, stumbled now among posits and her place among them.

"Remember, I asked you, not to make me come after you, come looking for you, yet, here I am? I won't lose you again." Her gentle embrace said the same.

Although touched by Sandra's poured revelation, in all honesty, it was Xûan I thought of in that embrace. The memory of Xûan's touch, her needs, and the uncertainty of her fate, insulated my feelings. As night fell and visiting hours concluded, Sandra left with puffy eyes, claimed she'd restore me. Against a roar of rain and wind outside, my throat, dry and sore from the long day of strained speech, I lapsed into a deep and dreamless sleep.

The next day Sandra returned with an endless spat of wishes. "With you, Mel, I can be myself. I don't have to worry about being in control. Get well, Melvin. I want to go ice-skating and bike riding; I want to go for long walks and movies, and vacations together. Now I understand what flying has meant to you, and I want to share in that, too."

I wanted to say how relationships had not worked out for me, and how tragedy awaited. I wanted to warn her to stand at a distance, to observe my development before she made a choice, but already she knew she'd stood too long on the sidelines, and wouldn't be discouraged. On April 4th, Sandra arrived with an armload of magazines, newspapers, and chocolates. she said progress for the new protest march improved. We were about to have dinner from the employee's cafeteria when someone said Dr. King had been shot.

"What did you just say?" Sandra asked.

The woman repeated the remark, said she heard the news on her car radio in route to work. Sandra and I skipped the meal and went to the nearest television set where a news flash announced Dr. King was dead. Among other startled faces, we watched several bulletins before Sandra left. The evening before, in spite of a driving rainstorm, she left to attend a rally at a local church, Mason Temple. News that Dr. King would say a few words prompted a hasty departure. Sandra had a habit of taping whenever possible his statements, sermons, and his speeches.

A day later, Sandra tried to sound positive, but with little to say. She displayed a different persona, one that mourned the losses of the movement as much as she cheered its progress. The evening, prior to my scheduled release, Sandra returned. It had been a day full of meetings, and she revealed the second protest march would occur as scheduled the following Monday. Memphis, among many cities around the country, experienced some civil strife after the death of Dr. King.

"After the march on Monday, why don't you drive down to Rain Seed, stay a few days. Considering the circumstances, no one at your job is expecting you back so soon," I suggested.

Inspired, she left with that in mind, and promised to return the next day and see me off.

Late morning, Sandra met my folks at the hospital and awaited my discharge. She affirmed her promise to visit, and tugged at my bulky new clothing. As the family sedan moved away from the curb, I stared back at Sandra who wore a soft overcoat tied at the waist, with the collar pulled up around her ears and her hands buried in the pockets. The crowded look in her eyes was the pall shared by Memphis and the entire world, coupled with her wishes to launch a new beginning.

The Haunt of Homecoming

As a late morning sun rose above the pines, my family and I drove south into Mississippi, into the promise of spring, south, toward the rolling, red hills and Florida's Panhandle. Thick was the wind, yellowed with pine pollen amid early blooming azaleas.

At home, hand painted banners, placards, and balloons welcomed me.

"Come on in, baby, you're home now," my mom said.

Among my things from Vietnam were letters from newly promoted, Captain Thompson, but nothing from Habrasham; no message, no story, or news on the condition or fate of Xûan and Tram. My family watched befuddled as I opened first the mail and packages from Vietnam. Having noticed that, I stopped, opened their gifts and proceeded to offer thanks for their help and prayers.

Amid the muffled roar of gunship fire, I screamed at scenes of bodies ripped apart, tumbling in the brush then awakened in the reassuring clutches of my mother's arms.

An alarm sounded and cautioned the family that although the physical structure neared repair, some mental or subconscious aspects of my injuries hung on. I hoped they would condone it in its utter harmlessness, but I knew, too, the questions would come. I was prepared to generalize the incident in an effort to save the family further agony.

That morning, Sunday morning, amid the quiet of the house, I heard sounds of my mother singing to a worship service broadcasted on the radio.

"Good morning," I said in a hoarse voice. In my presence, others felt a contagious need to clear their throats, to aide my speech.

"Well, good morning, handsome. Feel like having some breakfast?"

"Oh, yes," I answered.

She dried her hands on her apron among pots of food and the roaster ready for the oven.

"There, and with a cold glass of milk, sit down and enjoy it."

Mom joined me with a cup of coffee. With a smile she studied my presence, watched me take small portions as I made favorable gestures. When asked why she didn't go to church, she said no one wanted to leave me alone after last night's arousal.

"How long has that been going on, the nightmares?" she asked.

"Oh, since I was a child, actually," I joked.

"You're still my child," she said as she brought the cup to her mouth.

"And still having bad dreams, obviously," I answered.

"Now, let's try again," she said, patiently. "Melvin, when did you begin having those nightmares?"

"Can't sleep very long," I said.

"Are these nightmares in general or about the crash?"

"Different dreams, some about the crash," I answered.

For my mother, I managed a pale smile. My eyes had a lazy, mechanical blink as I remembered those last moments in the quagmire of the rice paddy. I remembered the end approaching, felt its presence like the weight of a shadow but present, nonetheless.

"There's a funny feeling near death," I slowly stated. "It's not really funny, but a different energy, a strange clarity of the senses exists in that desperation. The soul is eternally optimistic. Instantly, I accepted the extent of my wounds and praised the parts of me still useful, those parts that said I was still alive. I was half expecting to be in hysteria and incoherent while dying, as I imagined dying."

"Enough about dying, that's all behind you now. Your throat, does it hurt? Your scream was loud. I didn't think your voice was that strong?"

"My throat is sore, but that'll go away."

"A number of relatives, friends, and church members will come by today, Melvin. Don't overdo things."

The first of those well-wishers was the Reverend and Mrs. Lucas, on their way to Memphis and the march on Monday. The minister talked candidly for a spell, joked some, then, fell silent.

"Do what you can for Sleep. You, more than anyone can relate to him. He seems normal, but stays to himself. All of you boys were on the mourning bench together, drafted about the same time, Son!" said the burly man, as he brought himself to a standing position. "Take care of yourself, and let's see you in church next Sunday."

It was suppertime on Tuesday when Sandra arrived. The family gathered around to hear her talk of the march and her unique insight into the probable direction of the Civil Rights Movement without Dr. King. After supper, I took Sandra for a walk on that cool April evening. Sandra's sporadic cheer and near nervous moves appeared restless and preoccupied. Sandra was like a sailing ship on a placid sea having no wind. Her ship awaited some assistance for movement, direction, and motivation. She spoke of the effects the assassination had on her attitude lately.

"Last week we talked in terms of our personal needs, and change," she began. "I'm not sure how, or what reaction I'm to assume. Considering my stress and your recovery, if it means my stepping away, I'll do that too. My priority is to be with you. I hope it doesn't get to that, but that's where my head is."

Above, in the northern sky, a full moon watched over us through a thin layer of clouds. The sound of wind through the trees, the tumble of dried leaves crossed the hardened clay road, joined us in the night.

"You're not going to give up your work for me. You're dedicated, I know that, so don't even think about walking away. I've always admired your devotion. You've inspired me and I'm ready to do what I can."

I thought, too, of Xûan and her inspiration, how she insisted we both were obligated to our people.

Unenthused, she said, "Mel, you don't know how long I've waited to hear that. Not merely for you to come along, but be a force with your opinions, your energy, and anger. Hey, I'm glad you feel that way, but in the weeks ahead, whatever happens, we have to keep in touch, Mel, okay? No more than a few days should pass and I not hear from you. Now is that a promise?"

"Yeah, that's a promise."

That was unusual, our promises.

Our huddled walk in the evening fell silent again except for the sounds of our footsteps when I asked, "You were right about Dr. King, so you have to finish your book. But tell me this, how do you suppose he'd lay the groundwork for this new militancy without compromising his non-violent stance?"

"Sounds like you've been reading my notes. Has his death changed anything for you?" she asked.

"In college, I saw him as a gifted preacher, and a great humanitarian. Now, I understand what you've been saying. His wasn't simply a ministry of souls, but a ministry of issues as well."

That confession amounted to a major victory for Sandra.

"Let me hear it!" she said. "I need to hear you say it! All these years you complained of slow, ineffective tactics, wasted optimism and a lack of political realism. Now, finally, you're coming around."

I informed her earlier of that painful but liberating dream encounter with Dr. King.

"I disagreed in a tactical sense," I said. "Which brings me back to my question, how would he deploy his new radicalism without compromising his stand on non-violence?"

In stride and without missing a beat, Sandra answered, "I believe he had arrived at a conclusion within himself..., my thoughts here," Sandra threw up her hands, made, quotes with her fingers before saying, "concerning some waning practicalities on non-violence, private and largely unexpressed were his views that America didn't have the capacity to be consistent and comprehensive in fighting racism. To answer your question, I think that within his philosophy, was room for compromise. Had he weathered the more dissident personalities, saw no change in the political climate and was still suspect of America's conscious effort, I sense a shift in strategy away from purely political, social, and economic, rights, to a broadened spectrum of human rights and a revolution in values." Sandra's studies and opinions had been tempered in a crucible of years of involvement and came with confidence.

Sandra was like the Nation in general, forced onto a new course. Sewn already were the seeds of tumult. In my opinion, The Vietnam War, the assassination of President John F. Kennedy and now Martin Luther King Jr. marked the end of innocence for our generation. What once was perceived as good for all, became the privilege of a few, while the extent one went to achieve it, redefined an era, its values and temperaments.

The next morning, laughter from the kitchen awakened me. Later, I joined the family and Sandra for breakfast where the conversation centered on my health and strengthening voice.

"Did you rest well?" Sandra asked.

An odd remark, I thought, considering she was the guest.

"Did I... rest? Did you rest well, I should ask!"

"Okay... you both are welcome here," my mom laughed.

Sandra spoke of Ellen for a while. She liked Ellen, who benefited most from Sandra's visit. Ellen found Sandra intriguing, considered her smarts, good looks, and utter freedom. Alone unto ourselves that day, I told Sandra about Rachel. I explained my love for Rachel as opportunistic, a chance to live what for years I longed to have. I had no idea how to explain Xûan. Rachel and Xûan were like merging streams of water, each became indistinguishable. Xûan and her story remained a secret, secrets that bound only from the shackles of dreams. At that moment, I found no need to involve Sandra.

After nightfall, a series of knocks at the rear door brought me face to face with my friend, Sleep. I begged him in, but Sleep declined in a raspy, hoarseness of his own.

"Hold on, Sleep. I'll come outside," I said.

Hair and facial hair was an expression of the "counter culture." His hair grew phenomenally long, his cheeks were sunken, and his eyes loomed large in their sockets. Sleep and I embraced, then sat on the rear steps.

"I heard you were home, and I knew something must have happened. Either you were sick or injured."

There was wind in Sleep's voice. He lacked patience and some of his sentences did not connect. It was Sleep of old, his loyal friendship made him come by that night, made him plunder for words sincere. But it was also Sleep, the victim that arrived cautiously, and lurked feverishly like uninvited guest.

"I've been in the hospital, in Memphis for the past month," I said.

"Man, them doctors crazy as hell," Sleep fired back. "All they got is pills and talk."

I remembered him as a child, then compared that child to the man next to me and saw the casualties we both had become.

"I have a lady friend here from Atlanta and I want her to meet you."

I stood and called Sandra to join us. Sleep stood also, wanted to pass on the introduction.

"It's, okay, Sleep, she's like you and me. She reads you from the inside."

Sleep paused, but was not inclined to do so.

"Sleep, this is Sandra. I'm sure I've mentioned her over the years, especially while in college. And Sandra, this is Carl, we call him Sleep."

"How you doing, my sister?"

"Hello, Carl. I'm pleased to meet you."

"I'm pleased to meet Melvin's lady."

"Is that the way he said it, I'm his lady?" Sandra asked with a grin.

"Sure did—his woman from the big city of Atlanta. She's a fine sister, Melvin," he said, then released her hand. "I'll come back to see you, Mel."

The light at the rear of the house came on. Mom stood inside the door, opened it to catch Sleep about to turn and leave.

"How you doing, Sleep?"

"I'm feeling alright, Miss Claudia."

"How's your mother?" Mom continued.

"She's doing fine too, Miss Claudia."

Mom stepped onto the back steps and closed the screen door behind her.

"Sleep, you're welcome here, any time, day or night. Please come by sometime and through the front door. We feel awful, you coming around like you're a stranger."

"Yes, ma'am. Good night, now," he said, gave a parting nod to Sandra.

Sleep weathered the moment in spite of his angst, resigned himself to a sense of polite patience amid its discomfort. The shadowy figure disappeared into the dark of the yard. He once slept with the passions of a bear in hibernation. Now his eyes would not close against the night, would not shut out the demons, nor shade the light of memories that screamed in his head. As a child, Sleep's mother once said of him;

"Once that boy's asleep, it takes a heard of wild animals to wake him up."

On Saturday morning, Sandra reluctantly ended her stay in Rain Seed County and returned to Atlanta.

I delayed visits to my neighbors out of fear I reminded them of their losses. Like a pariah, I hobbled solitarily in the restrictions of my injuries and like Sleep, I, too, emerged in the evening under the cover of darkness to visit boyhood haunts. Unaware of the seriousness and depth of my medical condition, I struggled alone in its effects. My nocturnal prowl reminded me how fleet and carefree our childhood was. I stood beneath the trees, the majestic oaks, and graceful magnolias that still bore our initials in the bark. Conversations on where I'd been, the things that happened to me, and my healing were hard to avoid. A talk with Tommy Pratt's mom became a typical jerky conversation.

"That Northlee boy didn't get drafted. The Harpers, none of their boys went to war. Billy Northlee ain't no more in college than I am. He works up there at his daddy's store from time to time, but his name's on the books up at the state college just the same." Miss Pratt stood from the wooden rocker that held her elderly frame. She was older than my parents and Tommy was the youngest of her children. She moaned lightly, brought the weight to her feet then stood against the doorframe that led into the house.

"These old legs gets real stiff, Melvin. Have to stand up from time to time or they aches me something awful. Phyllis was talking about you last night. She said you looked good, and you do, Melvin. I'm glad somebody from around here made it back home from over yonder. It looks like Rain Seed County paid for the sins of that war all by itself. It don't make sense all them boys going over there and dying that way. People's a-marching, protesting, and talking 'bout peace and love and the dead bodies kept a-coming. I don't know what the world's coming to. Around here, you didn't want to stay at home or leave home, scared the guv'ment car be waiting for you with a telegram. Some white folks, too. They had theirs, too. And for a spell there, Melvin, when you didn't write home, it nearly drove you poor mother crazy. Please, don't ever do that to your family again."

The sentiment of Tommy's mom reflected the negative discourse the war caused in many communities.

A few days later I bumped into Sleep at a neighborhood store. On Sleep's insistence, I bought two six-packs of beer. I wanted to spend time with him, and hear what he had to say. We took an old path into the woods toward our old hideout and settled for a spot that overlooked the saw mill.

"Billy Northlee will tell you he's registered in college," Sleep said. "You'd think he'd want to be cool about something like that, but he don't care."

I listened, as Sleep appeared more coherent under the influence of alcohol.

"We should get together more often, Sleep, find some girls or play a bruising game of basketball," I said.

I reminded Sleep we both were casualties of the same circumstances. We found things to laugh about and cursed jovially. Beer ran down my chin, as I focused on the points I wanted to make.

"Sleep, remember when we met in Pleiku, man, it was good to see you? Both reminded of our yesterdays, and a reason to get back to the good life."

"I don't care much for my yesterdays..., the war that is," Sleep said. "Now is now, yesterday is gone. My yesterdays, keep me awake at night. I can do without that yesterday," Sleep growled back.

"You're right, Sleep, but I meant our yesterdays, here in Rain Seed. No one can take that away from us. It's all we have. I wouldn't take anything for my yesterdays. It's the only realness in life other than the present. The future is full of uncertainty, but the past is concrete. Hold onto the past, Sleep, yesterday wasn't so bad for us. I'm a child of yesterday, sad times and all the memories of what we wanted to be; you a veterinarian, and me a pilot."

Amid assurances and gilded past of yesterday, be it but the grace of God that surpassed that.

Sleep, unfazed by the beer, thought out his replies. "My memories, my good memories are locked in by those yesterdays, you're talking about. I know that you know what it's like to look over the sights of your weapon and see what happens to a man when you pull the trigger. One night, I wrestled blindly with a VC." Sleep's diction was as clear as a bell and his memory seemed as fresh as yesterday. Then he continued,

"... in a pouring rain, I held in one hand a fist full of his shirt, while flailing a machete in the other. I felt the muzzle of his weapon pressed against me and knew any moment, it would explode in my guts—so I hurried my swing with the machete, prayed my strike was first. I struck him..., I didn't know where... , but I felt his body twitch and snatch against me. How faint his shriek, and the spew of his blood. My hand, still tangled in his clothing, we staggered a second, or two, exhausted, before I tripped over what turned out to be his head. I know that's the way it happened, but in my dreams, my swing with the machete is late and I'm blown away."

"I have those dreams, too, that come in the dark," I told Sleep. I reached for words to inspire my friend to want, wish, and live again. "We have to get on with our lives, Sleep, make new memories."

Frequent notes from Sandra spoke of a coverup and complicity among the government concerning Dr. King's death. That view took away the driving force of energy that I liked about Sandra. In a blue mood, I played recordings of Billie Holiday. Like Billie Holiday, my life had become tragic, one of losses and shortcomings, setbacks and take-ways. Now, I sought to define my own blues and how it held me.

Days into my continued depression, angered and ashamed, I suffocated in silence and pity. My physical condition worsened and the world closed in on me. I avoided others for their lack of understanding and avoided going to bed, for my sleep was crowded and infested with bad dreams. Before long, unable to see beyond the day, beyond the moment, and without rational faculties on which to lean, I sought to end it all. My thoughts represented the end of the good, the end of the dream, and the end of my struggle. I had lived my life, taken some lives, and saw too many of those close to me pass away due to the war. I lived my dream, squeezed it for all the goodness there was, and paid the price for having soared so grandly. On the other hand, I became a poison unto myself, as Rachel, Xûan, and now Sandra, perished as result of my presence.

Alone in the house, my decision was to end it all, immediately. I reached for the pistol, the .45 automatic I shipped home months ago. I placed the barrel under my chin and angled it so the round would pass through my brain, forced a round into the chamber, then closed my eyes and pulled the trigger. I heard the distinct snap as the hammer fell harmlessly against the firing pin and empty chamber. My tense body relaxed for a moment as I snatched the clip from the hollowed grip and wondered what happened to the bullets I loaded the evening before. About that time, the sound of automobile tires on the gravel driveway signaled my family had returned.

Hastily, I hid the weapon in the overhead compartment of the closet. Ironically, my dad later came into the room and gave me a stern lecture about loaded guns around the house.

"You know how Maurice gets into everything around here, Melvin. We can't leave loaded guns around. I took the bullets out. We have to be careful," he said.

I answered with an affirmative headshake, not at all pleased to be alive. Before he left the room, dad handed me the handful of bullets. Moments later, I reloaded the clip and sat mindlessly when the phone rang. It was Sandra. Her conversation began slowly, but soon became reminiscent of her old self, vibrant, full of life and advice. She asked had I missed her, wanted to hear me talk and laugh, be romantic. I tried to say how depressed I'd been.

"Melvin, I haven't been myself either, disappointed, and disillusioned."

Sandra rambled on and on, brought tears to my eyes as I heard her come to life again. My trooper fought off death and the long tentacles of war.

"Mel, I called home and talked to my parents, talked a lot about you. I admit the images of your family stayed with me, how kind they were to me. Those few evenings at your home reminded me of what I always imagined families should be. I know now my parents wanted the same and to some degree, our fortunes became our misfortune. I told them how you insisted I owed them an apology. Mel, you still there? Say something."

"You're talking, go ahead," I growled.

Spontaneous contact with either parent was rare for Sandra. Her apologies spoke largely of her desire to mend their differences. I needed little to camouflage my voice for my sobs resembled a mute attempt to laugh, but I was encouraged by her talk, my spirits lifted.

"I want to see you, Mel. I've been praying for the two of us. I don't want to be alone anymore. I want to see you every day. I want to be with you."

My mom came into the room and found me crying as I clutched my throat. I made no effort to disguise the discomfort. I handed her the phone without notifying Sandra.

"Melvin, what's wrong?" my distraught mom asked.

"It's hurting. My throat, it's in pain," I whispered.

My mom informed Sandra of my condition, and concluded the call. My parents drove me to the county hospital where I received treatment for pain and sent home. Sandra remained in touch and contacted several clinics in the Atlanta area for advice. Early the next morning, dad and mom made the four-hour drive to Atlanta and had me admitted to a hospital.

"...Burden Down, Lord, Burden Down..."

April 1968

Again, I regained consciousness in a hospital, in bandages, but the face before me belonged to Sandra. My parents stood in the background with what seemed a re-play of Memphis. It was scary in that respect, then the doctor came into the room.

"Hey, how is our man today? Come on, you can talk. Talk to us," he said.

"I can talk?" an unrecognized voice emerged half-hoarse and with some pain, but my best effort since Memphis.

"We'll keep you here a day or more for observation, then you can go home," the doctor stated.

Sandra leaned over the bed and held my hand.

"When you go back to the service, I'm going with you. I don't care where they send you. Some hole in the wall place I've never heard of won't change my mind, I'm going," she said.

"What about your job, your career, for heaven's sake?" I asked Sandra under the puritanical stares of my parents.

"The doctors say you'll be fine. We believe that. That's all we have and you're all I have," Sandra said.

"What about your work at S.C.L.C.?" I asked again.

"I'm going to take a breather. Think of myself for a while, and take care of you. Soon, we both will have a go at it. There's much to be done, no doubt about that. And, you always told me how smart I am. I know I can find a job, but I'm talking about us now, you and me. I've spoken to your parents about my feelings and my wishes. They have the usual reservations and concerns, but will wait to hear from you before they bless any intentions." With tongue-in-cheek, she rolled her eyes.

"Sounds like a proposal to me!" Dad said.

I caught a wink of an eye from mom to Sandra.

"My son, you have your hands full. Once her mind is made up, there's no stopping her," Mom happily concluded.

I admired Sandra's commitment and her plans. Now came the wonder, the questions. I considered if such a commitment had the capacity to effectively eliminate deep, emotional feelings for Rachel and Xûan. That I grossly underestimated the depth of those relationships, meant a monumental task awaited Sandra, her patience, understanding and ability to erase such feelings.

That the earth had tilted was a certainty. The "world" was once again restored and no facsimile need present itself. Each new beginning had its form and texture—that Sandra led the way for me, softened that approach, added to my willingness to begin anew.

There in my stillness, stood a crowd of reasons and wishes to live again. The wisdom of Xûan, its clarity, its warmth, once again penetrated. Relative to my recovery, I never once understood the complexity of that transition. Of grace and mercy, God still loved me.

Weeks later, in late afternoon, the family gathered fallen limbs, and raked leaves from the yard for burning. Ellen watched the clock for she had a date who, when he arrived, joined the family in an outside supper off the grill.

When I spoke of dating in college, mom's attention hung on every word, with frequent inquires. I was a stranger in that respect and perhaps, that was a good time to share the stories of Sandra, Xûan and Rachel. As Ellen and her date departed, I went inside the house, into my gear from Vietnam and removed a series of envelopes.

"I need your help with this," I said. My parents, even Maurice sat in anticipation. "Literally, she was just another person, but figuratively, it encompasses everything I've ever been."

I placed a handful of glossy color photos of Xûan on the table. I watched their reactions as they glanced my way in differing degrees of puzzlement. Maurice spoke first.

"That's not Rachel!"

I smiled. If anyone could explain this enigma, it would be my family. They knew my vulnerabilities, my passions, and would understand the parallels and coincidences I presented. I spoke of the anxiety I experienced the day I first met Xûan, which was the same day Rachel died, I later learned.

"The look in Xûan's eyes was that of Rachel's when she was troubled and wished to avoid others," I said, then presented the typed written letter that informed me of Rachel's death almost a month after the fact. "Here's the chronology of events, the way things unfolded. Three times this woman appeared before I received news of Rachel's death. Each appearance was full of pain and anxiety, but subsided once I received that news."

"Who is she?" my Mother asked.

"Her name is Xûan." I spelled it for them, and wrote it out so they could see it. "I met her in early November and lost her the day of my crash. Something has suggested there's a profound reason for her presence and timing in my life."

Before long, evening and darkness descended and we moved into the light of the house and resumed our discussion. The subtle smell of smoke from the remaining embers, and pine straw drifted through the screens as I told the story how Habrasham recruited me to fly for MAC-V, my early meetings with Xûan, her story and that of her people.

"So, what do you think?" I asked them. "Please, say something."

"I can hardly believe my eyes," mom said. "But son, what's your problem with her and Rachel. She's very lovely, too, but to suggest something out of this world, well, I don't know. If you accept that Rachel is dead and this person is real, what then is the conflict?"

Strangely, I asked my younger brother for his opinion.

"I don't know! Why she look like Rachel?"

Surprised, my jaw dropped.

"That, and the timing of it all, is what got to me, I think. And that, my man, is the question of the hour! Why does she look like Rachel? Why did she happen to me? Why put me through these changes with her twin-like resemblance? Not only did her appearance mirror that of Rachel, but our relationship mirrored anything Rachel and I could have."

The gritty truth and candor of my experiences with Xûan, I conveyed with a language I never imagined before my parents. So many nights in spite of its danger, I felt compelled to be with Xuan, nothing compared to my need for her presence. Mom pulled Maurice into her lap and covered his ears against my graphic details. I tried to explain the calming effect Xûan provided; sultry and alluring, beautiful and enchanting, and how with her losses and my loss of childhood friends, we served as inspiration to one another. I mentioned that Xûan and Rachel were the same age and how unavoidable it seemed the tangled webs of fate that descended upon us. Somehow, I felt the correlation in our respective cultures, magnified and created a stronger bond. I explained, too, my feelings against the war long before I met Xûan, how even in war and under the auspices of war, someday I'd have to atone for the lives I took.

"I've spent my entire life wanting to fly, dreaming of it, chasing its experiences and preparing for that and that alone. Few things other than flying have held my attention. It's been a single driving force, a single end for the gratification of a single individual."

My dad stood, having heard, and seen enough of my negative tirade. "Melvin, don't be so critical of yourself. I'm happy you're sharing this with us, but your answer may not be so simple!"

Still on a roll, I paced the floor. A tightly wound coil of emotions slowly unwound.

"Perhaps you're right, dad, but the war took everything and gave back to me this self. It gave me a sense of perspective, reminded me of what I am and where I belong, as well as where my loyalties lie. I could have spent a year in Vietnam, escaped injury while never having met Xûan. I could have returned in either of two ways, the way I left or the man standing before you. The former I'd consider a loss, for he had no goals beyond flying and proving his prowess as a pilot. A week ago, I was reminded how detrimental a return to that singularity and inability to see beyond one's self and the depths one sunk trying to shoulder it all."

That reply aroused no comment for I referred to my attempt at suicide. The hours passed swiftly in that discussion when Ellen and her date returned, then quickly retreated to the front porch. Minutes later, Ellen entered the house and approached the dining room, where everyone sat.

"Who is this?" she asked, referred to the photos.

No one answered, but awaited her baited response.

"She looks just like Rachel, except the hair. Look at this one, ma. She's just like Rachel! Who is she?"

"Ellie, Melvin had a girlfriend in Vietnam...," Maurice chuckled.

"Have a seat. We're talking about some of your brother's experiences in Vietnam. Tell us what happened to Xûan? Why do you think she's dead?" Mom asked.

I explained as best I could the shoot-down and the actions that followed, but it was a healing conscience in need of closure that said Xûan was dead. It appeared at lease mom understood the burden I carried, then offered words in defense of my tirade.

"My..., my..., how we sometimes allow our dreams to be bigger than ourselves. But you've got lots of time to be whatever you wish. You wanted to fly airplanes, I wanted to be a dancer. I'm still not sure if it was the dancer in me I tried to satisfy, or vengeance, because papa never allowed it. But I'm happy. I've had a good life and I'm still dreaming. The difference now is I know what makes me happy."

Mom rounded the table to where I sat, draped her arms around me, and continued her motherly advice.

"About Xûan, she was real. Draw whatever conclusions you wish concerning the resemblance to Rachel. Life is wonderfully mysterious, but true love isn't so plentiful we should explain it away through rationalizations. Don't be afraid to remember Xûan for what she was to you and what the two of you shared. Rachel was able to fill some holes in her life, and she loved you, too. Remember her for that."

"Things are difficult right now," my dad began, "a little confusing, and you're still healing." He smiled faintly, then continued. "Someday, you'll look back on those experiences and see things differently. Maybe they'll not seem so dire, so explicit, only, your lesson on how you fit in this world. There's lots of living and learning still ahead of you."

Now, nine weeks following my shoot down, I reported for my final medical checkup, at Fort Binning, GA. There I was given a clean bill of health and fourteen days of additional convalescence.

Once at home, I settled in with a copy of the driver's handbook as Ellen boasted of her success with the driving test. That afternoon, Ellen took me for a few minutes of driving practice near the high school. I went through the tedious maneuvers of parallel parking that required more skill than I imagined.

"Are you doing that on purpose? You can't knock over the post, Melvin, they'll make you retake the test and pay the fees again, too!"

"You sure it's supposed to be that close?" I asked. The Desoto was huge and cumbersome.

"I don't believe this," Ellen moaned. "Mom and dad give you the car, you drive without a license, and can't even park!" She was surprised I didn't master the most rudimentary functions of the automobile. The sparks of an old rivalry were reborn.

"Come on, Ellie, get out of the car, and tell me what I'm doing wrong. No one parks this way anymore, anyway!"

"They do, too. You get out and watch me. I'll show you how it's done!" she boasted.

"No, if I'm to learn, I need to be at the wheel."

Ellen reluctantly stepped from the car, watched, then shook her head in disbelief. Things got better when I applied principles used in everyday flying. I used visual reference points other than the markers and the car slid into the parallel slot.

"For a first timer, you stank, but I'll get you ready," she stated in a matter-of-fact voice.

"I'm sure you will," I replied.

My little sister basked in my presence, my limited success, but wouldn't let pass, an opportunity to boast of her skills. We took the long way home, happily bickered as the rivalry rose to new heights.

"I used to say I'd never get in an airplane you were flying. But, I guess you're a pretty good pilot, huh?"

"I'm okay when no one is shooting at me."

"Are you and Sandra really going to live together?" she asked.

"Where I'll be in two weeks is anybody's guess, and who knows what Sandra's going to do next? You think she's serious about going with me?"

"I know she's serious! What I don't know is why she's stuck on you. If I had her looks I wouldn't be waiting for a knucklehead, Melvin."

"That low, huh? By the way, Sandra thinks you're very pretty."

"I hope y'all make up your minds before I begin applying for college."

"What does college have to do with Sandra and me?"

Ellen slinked her shoulders. "I want to go away to school. I don't want to go up to state."

"You mean be close to the knucklehead Melvin?"

"Yes, my knucklehead brother and his girlfriend or wife. For my sake, y'all better get married. Otherwise, I can kiss that idea goodbye. I don't see what the big deal is. You went away to a school of your choice, why do I have to go to state?"

"Change your approach, tie the reasons for a particular school to your field of study, rather than just getting away."

"Melvin," Ellen sighed. "You don't understand! We've talked about this for a long time and it ain't got no better."

"Attending state is that bad, huh?'

Once at home, our dad asked, "How did he do, Ellie?"

"I know why they have no wheels on those helicopters he flies."

"Now, why is that?" Mom asked, half-expecting Ellen to poke fun at her brother.

"He wouldn't be able to park 'em. Can't parallel-park a bit and can't drive much better either."

Ellen then wove a tale that supported her wishes.

"Melvin and Sandra are going to get married and live in Ohio. I have a choice of Ohio State or Central State, and on weekends, I can visit, maybe babysit."

"I see she's been working on you, Melvin," dad said.

"Melvin said it was okay," Ellie continued. "I can live with them or visit. Didn't you, Melvin?"

Although I steered clear of the debate, dad made clear his intentions.

"Maybe your brother would like to send you to college?" Dad said.

The next day, a noise from the bedroom caught my attention. In the silence that followed, I called through the door.

"Maurice, what are you doing?"

I then heard the distinct sound of a round being chambered in the .45 automatic. Suddenly, I remembered reloading the gun. I rushed into the bedroom to find Maurice atop a stack of books, on a chair, with the weapon in his hand. I approached him calmly, maintained eye contact.

"Give me that. Don't play around, give it to me."

Maurice panicked, attempted to replace the pistol. His sudden move shifted the books and tilted the chair off balance. I leaped toward him and reached for the pistol as he descended toward the floor. In one arm, I caught the child like a sack of feed and harmlessly grasped the gun with the other as our bodies crashed to the floor. Just as quickly, I was on my feet, hid the pistol for fear dad had been aroused. No one came, so, I gave Maurice a firm and teary lecture, hugged him and tried to emphasize the luck of the tragedy avoided.

Two weeks after the incident with Maurice and the gun, Sandra and I relaxed in her apartment in Atlanta. Fayetteville, North Carolina, and Fort Bragg was my new duty station. Together she and I went as planned and found an apartment.

On a sweltering day in June, we packed and prepared to move most of Sandra's things. She wore one of my shirts, rolled above her wrist and was strikingly beautiful as the afternoon sunlight filtered the curtains at her back. Her study, bore a peculiar interest in the war, one that surprised me. I found a small bundle of letters I'd written, neatly bound with a ribbon, and a map of Vietnam hung on a wall. I moved quietly and found many references to myself, even photos from my stint in the Navy, those I'd sent from Vietnam and news clippings of helicopters she'd gathered. She leaned against the doorframe behind me, watched my silent browse when slowly she approached me, pointed to the map and places like Dak To, Qui Nhon and Pleiku, among others I'd mentioned in letters. It was not clear if her silent gaze was about me or the chilling moments I dared to resurrect. Without a sound, she held me, conceded that those terrible days were behind us, and symbolically closed that chapter.

In September, we made plans to visit Sandra's parents. Just outside Washington, at the edge of the district and sewn into one of Maryland's well-to-do neighborhoods, lived the Petersons. In a drama, no less than given the prodigal son, Sandra's parents welcomed the newness that was their daughter; repentant, mature, and happy to be home again. Recent phone conversations made easy, their teary embraces as I watched, uncertain if my presence was a distraction.

"Mom, dad, this is Melvin. Melvin, my mom, Cybil, and my dad, Stanley."

"It's my pleasure to meet you both," I said as I shook both their hands.

"Likewise," said her father as her mother gave an approved nod and nursed more tears.

"Well, come on in," her mother said. "Never mind the bags, we'll get those later."

We walked into an outer room, a family room bathed in sunlight with an array of live plants and sat.

"Can I get you something, anything?" the mother said to me. "And you, Sandra?"

"I'm fine, thanks," I answered.

"You still make the ginger beer? I'll have some of that," Sandra asked.

"Oh, no, your dad can't drink it anymore, his ulcers, and all. I made some frozen custards for you," her mom offered.

Sandra once loved her mom's custards and Cybil hoped it was something on which they could still connect.

"Yes, but only if you made it," Sandra answered.

"I said I made it, now come on. Excuse us," Cybil said as the women left for the kitchen.

Her father stood and approached me. Again, he extended his hand and said, "Time can cure almost anything, but you've helped in bringing this along. My wife and I appreciate that."

"Sandra's done a lot of growing-up, Mr. Peterson, and needed this for a long time. I can't take the credit," I said.

"Just the same, you must have shown her something," Stanley said.

Sandra and her mother emerged holding a tray of frozen custards.

"Melvin, how are your injuries? I trust you're okay?" the mother asked and handed me a small bowl.

"I'm doing very well," I assured her.

"You're such a young man to have been through so much. Sandra has told us a great deal about you and your family."

Full of smiles, a light chuckle and a little coy, Cybil continued.

"Do we need to take a little walk, you and me, Melvin? My husband and I have been wondering if there's more to this visit than bringing my daughter home. Ever since she left for college, I wondered what kind of fellow would slow her down, get her attention—and look at you," Cybil said, as she turned her attention to Sandra. "Glowing and blushing like a preppy."

The father then said to the mother, "We've got a few days, Cybil. They'll tell us what they want us to know."

Sandra's parents were young, as young as my own but professionals, very cosmopolitan, and entertained, a great deal.

"Melvin, this is good," Sandra referred to the custard. "Enjoy it because, this and ginger beer is about all mom does in the kitchen."

"Melvin, that's not true," Cybil chided, although we all laughed at that remark. A healthy dig at what Sandra considered her mother's shortcoming.

I didn't imagine the reunion and conversations would go so well. I didn't think Sandra had the capacity or desire to let go the past.

"From day-one until Junior High School, you had the benefit of countless meals that I cooked, long before someone else cooked for you. By the way, how is your cooking?" the mother asked Sandra.

"I'm good. I surprise myself. You're looking at the full package, mom," Sandra bragged.

"Melvin?" her mother asked, invited my input.

"Yeah, she makes great sandwiches," I joked.

Another round of laughter, then I cleaned-up my remark. "She can cook," I said.

"Melvin, you intend to make the Army a career?" her father asked. "What plans have you got?"

"I still owe Uncle Sam another year. I have a degree in engineering, but in a real sense, I've never worked a day in my life."

"So you haven't any goals, nor thought much about your future? And you, Sandra? I suppose you'll go back into journalism, providing you find such a job in North Carolina?" Sandra's father probed, offered his assessment of what seemed our cavalier approach to life.

Calmly, Sandra said, "I'll be fine, dad. We'll be fine."

"What are your intentions for my daughter, if I may ask?" the father continued.

"Mr. Peterson…, I'm in love with your daughter. Your wife was correct in supposing an arterial motive in the timing of our visit. Generally, I choose carefully my moments, but since we're on the subject, my request is permission to marry your daughter. Her wellbeing will always be central in whatever we decide."

Sandra bit her lip, stretched her eyes, as she was surprised at what I said. Marriage was a reference for us, not something we planned or planned to mention. Cybil, having listened, feared at one point her husband was a bit too invasive, now risked that same depth of inquiry.

"Congratulations, to the two of you!" Cybil said and embraced her daughter. "I had a hint this was the case and Sandra tried her best to avoid the subject these past weeks. Tell me, are you going to live on an Army base for the next year?"

"Dad, mom," Sandra began, she spoke firmly, "I'm burned-out. I need some time, off. Melvin is well again, we have minimal overhead expenses, no debt or issues, and we've given this a lot of thought. I moved to Carolina to be with Melvin. Where he is, is where I want to be. We have a year which allows us flexibilities to save and choose well our future. I promise you, what we do in the end, will make you happy. Melvin's parents are just as concerned. They've asked the same questions."

"I'm truly happy for the two of you and I'm convinced that what I've been hearing these past months is something very special," Cybil said.

"Thank you, my dear, for sharing this with us, however cursory. Frankly, I was afraid we'd never see it," her father replied.

I lauded the courage that Sandra displayed, her capacity and compassion through revisits of my torrential dreams and cries in my sleep. She stayed close to slay those demons, to counter the mysteries and memories of Rachel.

At a New Year's Eve party in Atlanta, Sandra and I stole away from the gathering like courting teens avoiding the eyes of a chaperon. Sandra pulled from her neck a set of I.D. tags—my Naval Dog Tags.

"A long time ago, a young man gave these to me and said, 'I'm going to be somebody, and when I am, I'll come for you.'" Grinning, I remembered those words. Like the items found in her former study, I never imagined she was such a fan of sentiment.

"He didn't know an awful lot, that guy," I said. "He was different, you showed him that, but he couldn't define that difference except to say it was a good difference or there was no reason for you to choose him. To be somebody, was a search for tangibles."

"And now, has he found those tangibles? Are you somebody?" she asked.

"You made me somebody…, Sandra."

"You made that promise to me and I hoped you meant it. Time passed and I didn't interfere. I knew your dream was bigger than the two of us and no moment was big enough for the three of us. I waited at the expense you'd remember that promise, and although I always feared for you in the war, I shudder when forced to consider how close your demise. It has always been you, Melvin."

"So…you going to marry me?" I proposed.

"I've been telling you that for months, now. Besides, our folks are expecting it."

Sandra's immense strokes of composure had become invaluable. She knew how and when to apply them in my sleep, she knew how to "Shhhhh." Like an extended hand or beacon in the night, skillfully she guided me through troubled episodes.

Her voice was full of reassurance and surrender. Our sighs and giggles echoed in the vertical shaft as we staggered in a close embrace.

In the spring of that New Year, 1969, among a blush of cherry blossoms in her hometown of Washington, D.C., Sandra and I were married.

DESTINY'S CALL

SIX YEARS LATER, MARCH 1975

The blues is also a color. It's how I talk to myself when the pains done gone, but the healing ain't come yet. It's the color of my separateness and where I've been, and it forms the shadows of uncertainty in where I'm going.

Sandra Streeter stood at the front window. Outside, a gray overcast sky and low temperatures preserved a rare snowfall. Beyond the front steps, the wrought iron fence and sidewalk, she watched an Army Jeep approached the house. A meeting at the local Army Reserve Center requested my presence. Near noon, I drove to Reston, Virginia and thought more of domestic concerns, than the impromptu meeting.

The Reserve Center at Reston sat at the edge of town. Only the commander was present who presented me a communique and orders that summoned me to San Diego, California, by 1600 hours Sunday. Travel arrangements included a flight to depart Dulles at 0600 the following morning.

Our family recently returned from a mountain retreat owned by Sandra's parents. Joint trips were common in recent years as our marriage solidified relations between Sandra and her folks. We had one child, Tillie, four years old and Sandra was presently five-months pregnant.

Somewhat excited, I hurried home concerned only about the ambiguity and lack of detail contained in the communiqué. I was discharged from the military in 1969, and assigned to the active Army Reserve. With help from the in-laws, I signed on with a defense contractor.

Whereas I found refuge in the official authority of military business, Sandra was ambivalent, more realistic about its intrusion. Maneuvers between Reserve units were common, even partial participation caused no stir, but each generally came well announced. The next morning, dressed in fatigues, boots, and a field jacket, I packed a few personal items. My mother-in-law would stay with Sandra and Tillie until my return. In the dark of the morning, in a brisk winter wind, Sandra drove south, a short distance to Dulles Airport. Still a bit uneasy about the timing of my training, Sandra complained and now in the enclosed quiet and darkness of the car, she continued.

"What would they do if you didn't go? It's not like we need this. Of all the families and pilots between here and San Diego, someone has crossed a lot of names to get to Streeter."

I reached for her hand, pressed it gently in my palm.

"You'll know what I know, When I know it," I said. "Besides, we promised we wouldn't worry about this. It'll pass." With a loud sigh, she punched me playfully with her elbow.

Military transports, unlike commercial facilities were austere. Having to park at a distance, I spared Sandra the long walk, and kissed her goodbye in the open expanse of the parking lot. The flight included a stop in Houston, then on to the sprawling Marine Base at San Diego, CA. where once again, I stepped into Sunday morning.

Two others joined me and piled aboard a Jeep idling on the tarmac, then sped to a tactical air wing. In the office, a middle-aged sergeant and a young Private sat at work. The sound of someone playing billiards echoed from an adjoining room.

"Where's the latrine?" I asked, clutching my flight bag.

"The head's down the hall to your right," the private answered from the desk nearest the counter.

The billiard player was a child, aged nine or ten. As if tired of using the cue stick, he shoved balls toward a pocket with his hand. The boredom of the child typified the mood of that Sunday morning. I again approached the counter, requested information, and the likelihood of a meal.

"My orders say maneuvers for delta south are mobilizing here. Does that come with a meal?" I half joked.

"Yes, Sir. I'll have someone here in just a moment."

"What is delta south?" I asked.

"Meek?" the Private called to the sergeant, who sat at the rear desk. "You got anything on delta south?"

The child that played at the billiard table came into the room. "Dad, how much longer?" He asked the older of the two clerks, the sergeant.

"Come sit down, Scott, we'll be out of here in a minute."

"Sergeant Meek," the private repeated, "you know anything about delta south?"

"They fly training missions along the Yucatan, in and around Honduras," the sergeant said, pulled on his jacket, and headed toward the front counter and me. He presented a matching set of orders, compared them, and applied his initials.

"Captain," he addressed me, "here's your itinerary and I.D. The crews will assemble this afternoon. If you'll come with me, I'll point you toward the mess hall. Hold onto that I.D., you'll need it for meals and you can leave your bag here with Private Brody." My rank was CW-3, still a warrant officer, yet, Sergeant Meek addressed me as captain. His copy of the orders also stated captain.

I ate breakfast again, and waited for Army flight crews to join me. My Army greens and insignia stood out like a cabbage in a flower shop. Aside from conversations with a curious few, it was a solitary vigil that overwhelmed me in its lack of disclosure. The itinerary listed an initial meeting at 1200 hours, then lunch, followed by quarter's assignments and equipment check. When it neared 1:00 P.M. eastern time, I phoned home.

As Sandra and I approached our sixth anniversary, our marriage retained the air of a steamy courtship. In addition to a graduate degree, she matched my enthusiasm for flying and obtained several flight ratings. I developed a passion for political activism and found plenty challenge in the shifting interest of civil rights.

At 0600 the following morning, I joined three dozen pilots in a small crowded auditorium within the complex. A Hispanic officer, in the uniform of a Central American Republic, approached the podium and sat up a projector. The lights dimmed as the flicker of images splashed against the screen. The officer narrated aerial photos of helicopter air assaults in mountainous, jungle terrain and simulated attacks that showed the progression of training techniques. It was similar to training films shown in the J.A.A.T. operations. It got interesting until someone tapped me on the shoulder. It was Sergeant Meek, the marine clerk.

"May I speak to you a moment, Sir?" I stumbled slightly past men and their knees to the single aisle that divided the theater.

"Sir, your estimated time of departure has been moved up considerably."

A little confused, I made reference to the presentation in progress. With a casual glint in his eyes and the sudden flash of a smile, the sergeant said, "They'll catch up."

The pace of events changed as pieces of a puzzle came together. The few details included an intense and concentrated review of aircraft position and movement signals, weapon system capabilities and review of survival, evasion, and escape techniques. Several faces became consistent with mine as we moved from one brief to another. Finally, a room bedecked with flags and tables arranged in conference style displayed seven neat stacks of gear and clothing. I joined six others who shared the various briefings.

"A-t-t-e-n-t-i-o-n!" was the loud rang of a voice within the room. An Army colonel walked in and quickly eye-balled us, then said, "Stand at ease."

Finally, we got to the teeth of a quagmire that begun almost 55 hours earlier.

"You're here on orders to participate in a joint military operation. One condition necessary to execute those orders terminates your current military status. This operation elevates you to active duty. With it comes a promotion in rank and the opportunity to serve your country at one of the highest classified levels. The assignment may last four to eight weeks. Upon completion, your status will revert to the former, the rank you will keep. No one is obligated to participate, but such a mission permits me to continue only in the presence of those wishing to do so." The eyes of the colonel crept slowly across each man's face as he awaited a response.

Seven abreast we stood. The gravity and perceived significance of the occasion voluntarily drew us stiffly into a position of attention. Mildly stunned by our selection and the colonel's revelation, no one moved. The colonel then spoke in a slower, relaxed manner.

"You may sit. When you walk through that door, The Sergeant of Arms, will issue weapons and ammo. Afterwards, you'll be driven to the flight line and remain under escort until you board your transport. In the meantime, you're not to contact anyone concerning your status or departure. Specifics of the mission will occur in a final briefing at the flight line."

I was excited, cautious not to give more than I could afford, but anxious to know it all. What could be so sensitive about Honduras? I asked myself. Issued M-16s and .45 caliber side arms, we snapped and buckled our gear under the watchful eye of a staunchly clad M.P. None of us knew how to react, what we could or could not say even among ourselves. Individually, each had a history relative to the events about to unfold.

The warrant officers were promoted to CW2s. By 1100 hours, we were in route to the flight line. A long drive brought us to a series of hangers and Quonset huts at the edge of the base. At an adjoining hangar stood the three dozen warrants and officers who shared the auditorium presentation, the Honduran connection. Dressed and geared, they, too, stood ready for departure, but noticeably separate from our seven. The M.P. driver invited us to wait in whatever comfort we could produce. We slumped on our bags, made small talk, lit cigarettes yet avoided introductions.

We waited in the open, away from the hangars, pounded by the roar and heated air as aircraft departed. In a silence full of questions and uncertainty, each tried to fathom the sudden change of events, but was unable to look ahead, unable to find refuge in the present, and unable to go back.

"There's your colonel," the marine M.P. said, nodded toward a figure that crossed the tarmac between planes. Everyone stood, adjusted their gear, and prepared to render a salute.

"Morning, Colonel!" the M.P. said and joined the seven, flipped a salute. The M.P. presented a satchel of documents then posted himself as sentry. At a distance, the Honduran connection formed a single line and filed onto an old DC3.

"All right, let's get inside," the colonel said, as he pointed toward the adjacent Quonset hut. I strained to hold back impulses to react differently than the others. There was a flash of fear in my guts, chilled and waxed; I did not know how I should react. The colonel was none other than Jake Habrasham, from my unit in Vietnam and helicopter flight school. In an instant, the presence of him brought new highs of ambivalence. With him, came a new playing field and a new set of rules. For me, the sight of Habrasham brought feelings of anger and joy. I was happy to see him, yet remembered a bitter taste of disappointment and abandonment.

As we entered the building, Habrasham and I avoided eye contact as if intentional, as if first to look acknowledged an explanation. Once settled, he introduced himself, then from memory or having studied each man's personnel jacket, he introduced the team.

"We have a great deal to cover in the next 32 hours. I'll get right to the point. We're going to Vietnam." He paused and allowed the comment to take hold, then focused for the first time on me, as if to say, 'Where else.' "Now listen up!" he said, then proceeded to tack photos and maps to the burlap-covered wall behind him. They were huge exposures in black and white.

He unfolded a sectional map of South Vietnam and hung it above the photos. "Let's gather around here," he called us forward. "American troops were withdrawn from Vietnam two years ago. Those that remain are primarily embassy staff and communications specialists. More importantly, last month Vietnamese President Thieu, declared the central highlands a military liability. In doing so, the South Vietnamese military has withdrawn their forces to the extreme south, forming a line of defense from Na Trang, to Tay Ninh Province. They're being beaten, to say the least. We don't know how long they can hold that line." Habrasham pointed to the map and the city of Dalat, just below the imaginary line of defense. "Our interest lies here, at the city of Dalat." Our eyes followed the pointer to the first photo of a building and surroundings.

"This building is of strategic value," he continued. "Perhaps the highest priority at this stage of the war lies with this team, this mission. The contents of this building is our mission." The pointer skipped back to the map. "Cargo vessels, anchored two miles off shore, will serve as depository. Each trip, a fifteen to twenty minute flight, the worst of which is the flight pattern we establish, since time is essential and origin and destination remains a constant."

"My hopes are we truly control every inch south of Na Trang," he concluded.

Habrasham paused briefly before continuing.

"You've all been chosen based on experience and flight capabilities. Many particulars involving this mission won't be apparent until we're in country. Unit structure is as follows." He assigned Wahl and Giroux to fly Delta four, a gunship. Chastain and Joiner would fly Delta three, another gunship. Lagos and me in Delta two. He would fly lead with Oldfield in Delta one. Two Huey slicks with two cobra gunship escorts spelled the gravity of the mission.

"Our call sign is Delta. Any questions?" He pointed again to the chairs as he stood before us and lit a cigarette.

"What aircraft are we flying?" asked Wahl.

186

"Huey H's with cobra gunships," Habrasham replied. "Everyone here is rated for both aircraft. Often, we'll rotate assignments, therefore, pilot, copilot designations are arbitrary, day to day."

"How long will this take, and what part of this can we share?" asked Lagos.

Habrasham laid it out for us. "Official language …, we're on maneuvers, all else is classified. Communication lines are still open and once in country, we'll arrange connections on a weekly basis. Embassy forces and cease-fire monitors number nearly 200 Americans, while another 800 marines are on stand-by to provide security for evacuation if that need arises. Ultimately, weather, equipment, and security will determine our stay."

"When do we depart?" asked Giroux.

"Within the hour," he said, amid some mild disgruntled shuffling.

"We could be gone as long as two months, to Vietnam, and this is all the heads-up we get?" Joiner asked.

"These operations are born from extreme measures, they're never easy, cordial, or convenient," Habrasham answered. "That's all I can give you."

"We have to pack this stuff, load it?" asked Lagos.

Habrasham smiled before he answered. Somehow avoided his patented laugh.

"For six months, technicians have been crating that equipment. Those crates will be sling-loaded to the underside of the two slicks."

Oldfield asked the next big question. "What's in there? What are we transporting?"

Habrasham inhaled deeply from his cigarette and dropped his head. As he exhaled, it appeared he was prepared to give a reply, but uncertain as what to say.

"The termination of American presence in this war left Vietnam a stockpile of weaponry virtually unmatched in the free world. The most sensitive of those munitions will be the subject of our efforts."

He answered the question, but I didn't buy it. Again, we gathered our gear and headed into the brilliance of sunshine near 1400 hours, then driven across the tarmac to a waiting plane.

I wondered what the other pilots knew of the concrete building, and how long had Habrasham been a lieutenant colonel.

Confined as we were to the cargo bay of the huge C 141 transport, the team settled quickly to thoughts of themselves, thoughts of those things left behind and how quickly the present had changed. We each tried via memory to measure the horrors and sacrifices of a previous tour of duty in Vietnam, with what laid ahead.

West, toward the east we flew, toward the international dateline, as the sun sat and quickly rose again. A new crew and plane waited on the island of Guam, along with meals. We again reviewed the codes and frequencies for communications and intelligence reports on improved enemy air defenses. Included were passive countermeasures against enemy jet aircraft now prominent in South Vietnam air space. Ten hours later, in pouring rain, we landed in Cam Ranh Bay, marked by a single row of lights along the runway.

FORTY-ONE DELTA RED

MARCH 1975

A native Vietnamese drove a three-quarter ton truck to the rear of the plane. His Asian features, and quaint smile peered from the truck as a staunch reminder of what we may have forgotten. We climbed aboard and he drove down the runway to a sliver of light, a partially opened hangar door that closed quickly behind us. Several crews worked on two Cobra Gunships and four Huey Slicks. Immediately, we assumed quarters far from the flicker of the welding torch and sounds of a grinding tool.

"It'll be light in an hour. I suggest you get some sleep. Find a bay and make it comfortable, but no one leaves this location. There's a briefing at noon," he said.

The departing plane left behind only the quiet, hiss of rain as I thought of Sandra and Tillie, and wondered where I'd hide this bit of trivia and any horrors born from it. Only in my tumultuous dreams did I truly consider a return to Vietnam. Too excited to sleep, I lingered in thought, and wondered how the past seven years culminated into another dusty, bunk in Vietnam.

Marriage had been good for Sandra and me. When we thought our love and companionship was the elixir of life, our daughter, Tillie was born. Tillie quickly became the most exciting package of moving parts I ever saw.

Again, I awakened in the heat and glare of the eternal summer. Daylight brought a particular clarity to the surroundings, the smell of neglect and dust of abandonment. My attention turned to Habrasham, to questions amassed over the years. He would know the fates of Xuan and Tram.

Around 01100 hours, his booming voice rang out, "This way, gentlemen, and watch your language, other individuals here probably speak English."

The photos once displayed at San Diego now hung in place as part of a larger photo of Dalat and the coast. An equally large, color-enhanced map of South Vietnam hung next to it, and called attention to prominent landmarks and radar towers. Plans included an emergency evacuation route and coordinates to a naval vessel offshore in the South China Sea, in addition to the two mentioned as depositories.

"In a moment you'll meet General Stretch. It's the general's style to work closely with his men, including meals. Be cool. Throughout this operation, he may frequently be your passenger without notice. Another thing, in all cases except when you communicate with one another, Vietnamese personnel will serve you, direct you, and inform you. Radio communications will be in the Vietnamese language until they know you are American. Don't be insulted and don't insult them!"

A mild commotion down the hall announced the arrival of the general. "Carry on, please!" he said, and asked us to be seated.

"I'll brief you in-depth after lunch but, before we go, I need to share something with you. Our area of operation is a small one. Our task is gigantic, laborious, and repetitive. Men, you gotta stay sharp. Now listen carefully, there's a war going on and in some respects more intense than any to date. Our base of operation will be right here as long as it's safe to be so. There's tremendous fear among the Vietnamese military in general that the Americans have abandoned them. Funding cuts in Congress and suspension of future appropriations have created conditions you must be aware of and mindful not to become a victim of. As the Vietnamese Army move south, the populations follow. Don't be distracted, drawn off-course by any situation, no matter how grave it may seem. That's a snapshot; be alert!"

The general, had not changed much in seven years. The concrete structure at Dalat was still his baby. Disturbing emotions filled the years since my abbreviated tour of duty. The tension of secrets combined with an anxiety ridden initial meeting with Xûan, and the death of Rachel, formed the bedrock of my insecurity. Somehow, the concrete structure in Dalat was my baby, too.

"Get' em over to the mess hall," the general said to Habrasham.

The dining hall resonated to the rhythmic cadence of the Vietnamese language. Although filled to capacity, our entrance went unnoticed. Service of American food was of great relief and the lingering scent of powdered eggs from breakfast was poignant. The officers' mess was an elevated room, not a second floor, but a platform, reached by two shallow steps. Windows provided a partial view of the harbor and an endless string of conex storage containers. A balcony on the rear with wooden patio furniture afforded a view of the bay that was traversed by a pontoon bridge made of hundreds of reticulated floating units strung together.

Forgotten memories hung on the wind; the smell of rain as summer dragged slowly over its deposits of rot and renewal, its molds, fungi, algae and its smells, odors, fumes and fragrances. After lunch, I walked onto the balcony, rested my elbows on the wood railing, and gazed across the bay.

"What cha say, Navy?" The voice came from behind me, adjacent to the open, double doors. I turned as Habrasham sat quietly with a cigarette, before he stood and approached me with an extended hand.

"I remember the first time someone called me Navy. It was you." He exhaled smoke from his nostrils, looked carefully at the floor, then dropped the cigarette butt and ground it out with the toe of his boot, then again focused on me.

"You remember, do you?" Habrasham asked. I looked hard and long at him, not sure, if I should celebrate or complain.

"It's been a long time, colonel."

"Seven years, to be exact," he said rather proudly, then continued. "Married man, huh? And you've got a little girl, is it?"

"Why, yes. How did you know that?" I asked him.

"Relax, I know all about you. I know where you've been stationed, for whom you have worked. And, once or twice a month, you and the little wife, log time in a twin engine Bonanza. You've maintained your helicopter ratings through reserve training."

"Well," I wiped my face with my hand. "Guess there's nothing I can tell you." I was not at all surprised or impressed.

"I know that you still love to fly, and like most of us, the agenda matters little. And, perhaps more than you care to admit, there's something personal at stake here."

"What am I doing here, Hab?"

"You asked me that once before."

"And once before, you lied to me, Hab. Why are there secrets between you and me? Who do you work for and why are we really here?"

"Careful, captain. I out-rank you, and since when did relationships supersede orders?"

"You've always out-ranked me, Hab. That never kept you from being honest."

"Listen, son!" he said. "You and I had the same choices. I chose to come back, and face the hard questions. Yours was to stay at home and heal. I had no problem with that. Have a seat, Navy." He lit another cigarette, tried to appear inconspicuous. I wondered if his reference to me as "son" was one of admiration or was it condescending? Never had there been such a divide or sense of difference between us.

For any commander I would have simply flown the missions, but Habrasham was part of the fabric that patronized and exploited my youth. We once shared the passions and the anger that created a loyal bond.

"Why am I here, Hab?" With steely eyes and without conscience, I probed for answers and called in my markers.

"You're not listening, are you?"

I saw muscles tightened around his mouth and jaw.

"We're talking sensitive crap here! Everyone who's ever been in contact with that place in Dalat, has a file." He paused and searched for a way to avoid further inquiry. "I formed this team from a short list drawn up by the general."

"How long have you been in-country, relative to this operation?" I asked him.

"I've been in and out of here for the past two years."

We looked at one another—one wanted to ask more, the other knew he'd already said too much.

"What's in the building, Hab?"

"You don't give up, do you? Look, in my opinion, there's no rhyme or reason for it, but that's my opinion and limited understanding of the scope of that war! It was a nuclear reactor, full-blown and functioned. You didn't hear it from me, nor will you repeat it, ever!"

The revelation erased every guess, every idea, I ever imagined. For so long, I internalized secrets I never knew, hidden well among the pain of my own struggles.

Conex containers bled with rust in the salt air, and rotting canvas ripped by the wind, flapped now in the wind-blown rain. The American presence seemed long, long ago.

The afternoon briefing consisted of the six warrants, myself, Habrasham and General Stretch.

"Welcome to Forty-one Delta Red," the general began. "This is a classified mission in which highly sensitive munitions are being prepared for shipping." The general was first a scientist and secondly a soldier. His loyalties were to science, to the discipline and respect inherently essential while employing it. A veteran of such operations as the Manhattan Project, General Stretch remained a man of precision with an enormous capacity for detail. One would think such talents were a waste in the military, but the war in Vietnam was contrary to then Colonel Stretch's mission. His influence over operational policy in the central highlands was unprecedented, covert and largely unchallenged throughout the war. The best kept secret of the war lay veiled in gossamer, scientific, professorial, authority; tucked away in a sleepy little farming province that came to no one's attention.

The general stressed patience and conscientiousness to thwart accidents. An invisible corridor, a quarter-mile wide, extended from Dalat to the coast of the South China Sea. A crack Vietnamese Army unit, precariously protected the area, but repeated flights along the same routes always attracted attention. Slow flights flown with sling-loaded cargo was alarming. Slow flights flown along the same routes carrying sensitive munitions was suicidal. Besides the transport efforts, the naval vessel offshore housed a trained recovery team poised in case of a spill or aircraft failure that led to a spill.

"Don't underestimate the dangers of this mission," the general said. There were two Hueys, held in reserve. Their primary purpose was to dispatch the recovery team, but since the plan was "zero defects," meaning any catastrophe was forbidden, the extra Hueys would support a rotation schedule for maintenance.

That afternoon, we made our first mistake and flew over the terrain we'd occupy for the next month or two. Enemy observers on the ground were sure to organize. However, in a mix of light rain and sunshine, we boarded our respective aircraft and re-conned the corridor that pointed to the ships offshore. Afterwards, Habrasham and I flew north, northwest towards Ban Me Thout and up the valley until the twin peaks of the Hodrung Mountain came into view. The roads below looked like a trail of strewn debris, a solid flow of human desperation. Once over Pleiku, we circled the remnants of Camp Holloway, the Air Force base, then turned towards Anh Kha and Route 19.

"How long has it been that way?" I asked about the migration of people.

"For the past three months it's gotten heavier each day."

"I often thought of her when it rained, especially at night. For a long time I couldn't stand being alone when it rained. How is she doing, Hab?"

Without warning, pretext, or provocation, I spoke of Xûan and he knew.

"She's okay. Give it a few days, feel your way around. Once we establish some measurements in terms of schedule, I'll take you to her. It's a different world down there, Navy. Without our forces, there's no comfort level. We don't own the skies anymore."

The following morning was a throwback to any of the war years. Briefing included intelligence reports, and morning weather. In Vietnam, the higher temperatures and thin air affected the operational limits of helicopters. The air density index was posted each day and informed pilots the lift capacity and performance expectations of the helicopter. Throughout the war, the air density index was a briefing essential. Last was the general's quota for deliveries. Intelligence reports that predicted how long ARVN troops could hold the line of defense became the basis for schedules and completion. Given the enemy's estimated strengths, the team had but a week's margin for error. Door gunners arrived and the team, two slicks and two cobra gunships lifted for Dalat.

The city of Dalat sat west from the port at Cam Ranh Bay, a brief flight as we approached the northeast edge of the town. Only during the 1968 Tet Offensive was Dalat attacked.

Adjacent to the concrete building sat a string of 4x4x4 wood crates strapped with steel banding, evenly spaced, and rested on steel nets. The four corners of each net, when brought together, enveloped the wood crate, then attached to a clevis hook at the end of the tether line. Once secured, well, rehearsed spotters at the edge of the drop zone operated PRC radios and gave both a physical and an audible signal for the helicopters to lift.

Habrasham lifted with a stiff tether. I hovered above the next crate and awaited my signal from the spotter. Upon signal, I cleared the ground with the crate, then lifted slowly to altitude. I felt the tug of the cargo and settled into a flight posture a hundred yards behind Habrasham. Minutes passed before the jungle horizon faded to the watery blue of the coast, and then the horizontal white ribbon of sand and surf. Once at the coast, I reduced speed to arrive at the vessels only after Habrasham departed. Once above the ship, I hovered until the tether was perpendicular to the deck. With signals from shipboard spotters, I lowered the cargo below deck.

The routine continued through the first ten days with steady flights that stopped only for refueling. By the end of the second week, we understood the enormity of the task and the third week seemed bogged in days unwilling to pass. They were long, grilling days where breakfast and dinner were sometimes hot meals, but lunch was always C rations consumed without a pause in flight. The incessant pace became unforgiving and nights weren't long enough to recover from the effects of prolonged siting. Whether we flew left seat or right seat, Huey or gunship, we withered under the pressure of precision flying.

Satisfied with the progress, the general promised the crews a steak dinner in Saigon. A reward for three weeks of near perfect deployment. Rejuvenated by the thought of a grilled piece of beef, we boarded the Huey at the drop zone, near 1500 hours in the afternoon. In the flash of a moment, mortars rained on the compound and exploded randomly, two and three at a time.

"Get those choppers in the air," screamed the general.

I was at the controls of the dinner-bound Huey with my RPMs high and about to lift-off. When the four ships gained altitude, the general, aboard my Huey, radioed for status of each helicopter. The general quickly asked for the FM frequency and set up communications with ARVN Commanders to access the scope of the attack. When Cam Ranh reported no such incident, all aircraft headed back to base operations.

"Ain't this a bleep! All dressed up and nowhere to go," someone said.

After chow, we gathered at communications, for weekly calls home. By now, everyone understood the lingo, but memories of our first attempt ranged from comical to downright frustrating. Many of the chats sounded like my first call.

"After I speak, my signal for you to speak is my saying, 'over.' So... do you miss me, over?" I spoke to my wife.

"Of course I miss you. Are you having fun? Over."

"Um..., not much, but it beats working, over."

More serious now, she sighed. "We really do miss you..., Oh, over."

"You said that already. Where's Tillie? Let me talk to Tillie, over?"

"Talk to me, It's been over a week. We sound like kids on walkie-talkies, over."

"I'm in Honduras. I'll call every weekend so forget writing. Now get Tillie, over."

Habrasham sat at the console with his finger on the panic button. There was a brief delay implanted in the transmitted calls that assured time to thwart a misspeak. Everyone happily accepted those conditions. Such communications were popular throughout the war.

Tillie got on the phone. At age 4, we talked adult talk about taking care of mommy and helping around the house. Then Sandra was on again.

"Hey, guy, I bet you're flying every day and having so much fun you're ashamed to say. You hurry and get your butt back here. We miss you. Mel, you still there? Mel, ah over."

"I'm here. I gotta go. Say hello for me and kiss Tillie. Tell Tillie to kiss her mother for me. Over."

"Okay, baby. Mel…, heads up, now. Goodbye. Over."

"Goodbye."

THE VILLAGE OF XÛAN YUN

I was last to exit the Comm. shack the day of the attacks. Some pilots made no connection but tried again later.

Once again, the concrete structure avoided harm, but sniper fire began the next day and in a two-day stretch, two door gunners were hit. It was seven years since I rinsed blood and human flesh from my aircraft. To minimize the effects of monotony and exhaustion, General Stretch frequently rotated pilots and aircraft assignments and flew part of each day on one of the Hueys, monitored all communications, and allowed no one the opportunity of complacency. At the end of the fourth week, the intensity of the monsoon season increased. High surf and strong winds made turbulent and unsafe the waters off-shore. Bad weather became a blessing and the first real break to rest and mend sore joints. Habrasham phoned the tower for a weather report and updates of conditions further north, then he and I made flight plans for Kontum and flew out in late morning.

Sounding like his old self, he asked, "You sure you're ready for this, Navy? Married man and all?"

We climbed to 4000 feet, high above the clouds, above the beautiful patchwork of rice fields and terraced farms: above a nation in panic, and far beyond our own fears of sure death if forced down. Habrasham informed me of Xuan's injuries suffered in 1968, mentioned, too, how Colonel Stretch fed her updates on my progress. As promised, once she recovered, she retired to her village.

The Province of Kontum slid silently beneath us. Ahead, came the border and the Ho Chi Minh Trail. Habrasham flew without his usual confidence, made audible references to landmarks, and used them as navigational aids. In a high 15-degree bank, he turned south before beginning his descent. Towards the peaks and clearings came faint trails of smoke and clusters of settlements.

"You'll recognize it, Navy. Keep your eyes open."

"How's that? I've never been here."

"Keep looking," he said. Gently, he flared the helicopter for landing among jagged rocks.

Three buildings came into view that shared a combination of bamboo and steel substructure. I recognized the arrangement and looked over at the redhead.

"You did it! You built the school from the plans I left...Alright!"

People gathered in the shade of huts and pointed quizzically. I peered among the figures that stared back, but did not see Xûan. As Habrasham shut down the Huey, I stepped from the cockpit.

"This is your show, Navy. Stay as long as you like. I'll keep it hot."

I walked toward the group while my eyes darted among their faces and among the speculative conversation that wondered what would happen next. A gauntlet formed ahead of me, one that led to the village entrance where I heard the sound of animals and the smell of smoke. When someone spoke directly to me, I pronounced Xûan's name, and immediately a child dashed into the village with Xûan's name on his lips. The murmur rose sharply in the crowd as the sound of her name echoed around me. Before long, a head wrapped in a colorful cloth made its way and the crowd closed in behind it. The child sent into the village, pulled the woman toward me, but pointed first to the helicopter, then to me. It was Xûan, in a burgundy top, tapered along the sides and black, silk like pants, generously large in the leg, and sandals. She ambled toward me in a half-smile, more a stare, then gently grasped my forearm in disbelief. She spoke excitedly, first to those around her, introduced me to no one in particular, but to the entire crowd. Then she paused and in English, said to me, "You came back." Still in a stare that said she didn't know how to react, she spoke to those around her, amazed at my presence after having restrained her reaction to a polite squeeze of my forearm. She directed me through the gate as we neared a long house, centrally located and flanked by several leathery-skinned, muscular elders. After a formal introduction to the village leaders, Xûan and I, behind the elders, quickly toured the three structures built from materials scrounged around the bases at Pleiku.

Xûan translated as the elders spoke. They walked among the huts and small fires, the vibrant colors of fruits and vegetables gathered in intricately woven baskets. A wisp of smoke, perhaps to repel insects permeated the village. They talked continuously, the three elders, pointed along the village boundaries, pointed toward the sky, and made reference to their clothing. Surely, Xûan ignored portions of their speech, still stunned by my presence. She then explained the humor the Elders displayed long ago when told of my building proposals. The elders were told of the American that longed to meet the people of Xûan's village and things he wanted to do for them and how, in an effort to save her life, nearly lost his own. She explained her feelings for him, the American, whose looks and life were so similar to their own. The elders were impressed when told that others indebted to this man, who revered him, wanted to construct the buildings in his stead. Although the elders appreciated such sincerity, they had little faith in those who would do his good deeds, until that day the helicopter arrived with supplies.

In a shaded area, sunlight glistened through the trees as I sat among village leaders and sipped a potent alcohol brew from large ceremonial jars.

"You are welcome among our people, welcome to our food and to our small village," Xûan translated. They pointed again to the shaded edge of the village, toward shadows from large trees and a row of connected huts, then left Xûan and I alone.

"It is a place you may stay if you wish," she said wishfully.

Finally alone and adjacent to Xûan's home, neither of us knew what or how to say words too long committed to thought. Once inside, I looked Xûan squarely in the face as memories rushed back, frames of Rachel and pains of anxiety reminded me of the fragile youth we once were. Short of silken fabrics, body oils, perfumes and non-demanding clerical duties, Xûan had succumbed to the harshness of her surroundings. Though still beautiful and petite she, too, seemed aware of a fading luster, and if just for a moment, showed signs of sheer vanity. Xûan removed the colorful fabric from her head. With slow, circular motions, she revealed a presence unique and sovereign. Her hair pulled backwards, formed a neat and attractive bun at the back of her head. She looked not at all like Rachel. Xuan's huge eyes, brown skin, and shapely body, belonged to her in spite of its cultural insignificance. She was vibrant, yet conserved in her display. Finally, all that I knew of her, belonged to the face before me. Within it I would not look for Rachel, would not allow Rachel's mannerisms to cloud my view or the transfer of Rachel's wishes, and misfortunes. The native Xûan, in all her brown, her black, her tan and bronze, existed in a setting of her own.

"I suppose I should have called first," I joked.

She smiled, put away the colorful cloth, but did not answer. In fleet glances, she stroked my face ever so softly. The room in which we stood was small, with a low ceiling considering my height. The shadows from the corners framed her regal stature.

"Hello, Mel," she finally said as she looked back at me, full of wonder, full of questions an eternity could not answer. She held me in a stare reminiscent of looks once reserved for her. Perhaps she saw subtle changes the years had brought to me, or like me, was simply overwhelmed. Scenarios that depicted how this meeting might occur, now paled in comparison. I scanned the dwelling and the bamboo matting that covered the floor, woven as it was into a similar straw that covered the walls. It was pristine, airy, and comfortable.

"How have you been, Xûan? I hope you're well."

Reminiscent of her whisper, her softly spaced wording, she said, "Are you well, Mel? I worried about you for a long time, until the colonel told me you were no longer in the hospital."

I approached her, not certain if I was to hold her and kiss her or try. I wanted once again to wallow in the fiery passions that once enslaved us, but tactfully and without emotion, Xûan extended a hand instead and led me onto an extended outer area similar to a tiny porch. There she patted with her hand the bamboo flooring, and asked that I sit while she unfolded a piece of fabric that contained a batch of photos. Not once was I certain where this turn of events would take us nor what it would cost. Bare feet passed nearby and the strange sounds of tropical birds called from the trees. The photos showed how happy and beautiful she was, and the few times she publicly expressed her affection.

Overcome by her own memories, Xûan stood sharply and walked inside. I followed her back into the shadows and coolness of her home and into her open arms as we clung to one another, while her huge eyes bubbled with tears, but did not look away. I kissed her there, once more summoned by her black, her brown, her tan, and bronze. And she again said things softly in her dialect that I could never be, then wiped away her tears. The wounds of want, once healed were again reopened. Softly and slowly, she spoke with words long since assembled and stored away, words she once stumbled over in the long nights and years gone by; words otherwise unspoken, but preserved for a wishful presentation.

"I still love you, Mel. I love you very much. In the early days when you went away, I wished, hoped you would be okay and come back to Vietnam, come back to me. Months became years, many long years, only my nights were longer. Eventually, I stopped wishing, stopped waiting and tried to close that part of my life, but only the hope and waiting went away. I have learned to live with my memories without the disappointment of promise or expectation. Now, you have come again and I am afraid to ask for what reason, afraid to know for how long. The many stories you once told me of your town, stories when you were a boy. Now, you have come back to me, brought again ripples to water once stilled, water that once reflected clearly, now tremble with uncertainty. We talked many days about this place," she said. "I have much to show you." The soft voice, the quiet wisdom, the gentle spirit, came from the colossal giant within her.

Then I spoke. "I will always love you, Xûan, always. In the saddest of days, I thought of you, and in my moments of joy, I wished you well. The fates have been kind to us, for the years were filled with memories that smiled as each of our faces were painted on the days."

Then Xûan said, "For those few days we shared, we have paid so much. I knew of your troubles, but I knew those around you would care for you. I asked Habrasham not to mention me ever again. Now, in your presence, words are powerless to express how glad I am to see you."

Then I said, "Just seeing you again, knowing you're alright, I have so much to tell you." I held her there, an embrace familiar—in a dance of ripened wishes and a momentary peace.

"Come," she said, "and I will show you the places I once spoke of and things I have saved for you."

Within the village, the grounds beneath the trees were bald and swept, having no primary growth. The shaded earth was cool. Toward the trees on the western boundary, the ground rose gently around the mountain to the edge of the forest. There, huge trees and rock stood tightly together, guiding a shaded river having large, gray rocks that slowed and softened the river's flow of water. A series of steps upon a rock ledge led to a limb that reached toward extended limbs from similar trees on the other side of the river. Cool, mist-filled air clung to my skin as we crossed and stepped from one shaded limb onto another and continued to a point that overlooked a bend in the river, then we sat. Above the roar of rushing water came voices of children that played in the surf. The place had a magical presence of Shangri la, with breath-taking views of an aquatic and jungle paradise. A thin scar that extended from my ear to my throat came to her attention.

"I remember this! I remember when it happened!" she said, then dropped her eyes, recalled that far-off moment. She parted her hair and showed me a scar that stretched just beyond the hairline at the center of her forehead, then explained her brief stay in the hospital and the funerals of Tram and her mother. She said the colonel came to her home in Pleiku and asked that she remain on his staff, and discovered the plans I left behind. Only Habrasham knew of my equipment stashes around the base. With his help, the colonel fa-cilitated construction of three building. Xûan toyed with my wedding band, not at all surprised, somehow she knew of my marriage.

"Is she the one that was in love with you?" Xûan asked and referred to Sandra.

"Yes, she is the one."

"She is a good wife, yes?" Xûan asked.

"Yes, she is."

"I am glad. I am sure I would like her also."

With both hands, she reached and pulled from her hair a tiny clip fash-ioned from bamboo. Her bosom rose and fell in that motion, then settled back into place. The way her hair framed her face, the splash of her huge eyes in the shaded light, matched the splendor of Shangri-La.

"Is there someone for you, Xûan, a man in your life?"

"Maybe, yes, there is a man."

"Maybe?" I asked. "You love this man? Is he good to you?"

"I did not say there is a man for me. You asked and I said, maybe." She looked into my eyes, her face inches from mine and I wondered if she ever un-derstood the lure, the enchantment in her beauty. Somehow, the shaded light, and muted greens of the forest, brought a gloss to her eyes and a lovely contrast of her brown skin and shiny black hair.

"Yes, there is a man," she added. "And he reminds me of you. I do love him. I love him for what he is and what I remember of you. Now you are going to ask, how can I love this man, when thoughts of you fill my dreams? My answer is, what exactly attracted you to me in spite of your feelings for someone else?"

Caught in the splendor of her looks, seduced by a memory and feelings I knew would never die, I missed the point of her statement, unaware she now knew about Rachel.

"I never thought problems between Montagnards and Vietnamese would have an impact on my return to this village. My marriage to a Vietnamese, and Tram, my Vietnamese son were potential problems had they lived. I would have been an outsider to my village, a visitor. With Tram's death and my mother's death, I was alone for the first time."

Xûan paused, looked up at me with a curious smile then touched softly my lips with her fingers before she continued.

"Once I met a man from far, far away. You were that man and you reminded me of what I was—reminded me that I was no anomaly cut-off from the world, but prominent throughout the land. I must be crazy," she chuckled ever so slightly, then continued. "I fall in love with the wrong men. You were an outsider, but full of flames, burning for someone else. Somehow, I wanted to believe you forgot that someone and that fire went away—I wanted to believe that for a little while, I was for you and you were for me. Then," she paused again and buried her face in her palms, only she did not cry.

"And then what?" I prompted.

"Then you went away. Later, when I came back to my village, knowing you were alive was all I had. Then, Lon came into my life. I needed someone. His presence helped in my transition from hope and wishes to molding memories."

"This Lon, is he the one, your man?"

"Yes, Lon is his name," she answered.

"Does he live with you? Does he know about us, about me?"

"He does not live with me, but yes, I have told him of you…, knew I had to let go."

"Would he be upset, if he saw me here with you?"

"Maybe, yes. He has to understand. You will meet him, yes?"

"Do I have to? I mean, men aren't as meek about this as women." I felt uneasy about such a request.

"Before you were never afraid," she said. "You were a brave young man. Now you are a little older and too cautious. You have big muscles, your pimples are gone, and hair grows on your face. What we had was long ago, Mel. Lon respects that. Do not be afraid."

Nearly lulled into a sense of surety by her calm and halting speech, but to meet her man was no wish I encouraged. She then stood and stepped out on the limb in front of us. As if painted upon a canvas, among pinstripes of sunlight, her eyes still glistened in the cool shaded air, her pose suggested offers already considered, but now highly improbable. The cruelty of the Gods, now seemed poetic.

"Take off your shoes and come with me," she said.

"Why must I remove my boots?"

"You cannot walk here in those shoes."

I followed her advice, rolled up my trouser legs, and left the boots behind. We walked from limb to linear limb, one of many virtual walkways in the trees. I looked across, up and down the river, saw a maze of limbs more than 30 inches in diameter and high above the ground. Like walking on rafters in a construction site, there was no interior growth or leaves to obstruct ones view or prohibit movement. They were African Kapok trees, like Banyan Trees, having huge trunks with secondary roots that grew like tentacles of a jellyfish and formed long, vertical, rope-like limbs to the ground. Older tentacles appeared as support columns as they grew perpendicular to out-stretched limbs, six and eight inches in diameter.

"This is where I come when I want to be a child again. This is where I came when I wished to be alone with my thoughts of you," Xûan said.

The fact she had a man dampened my excitement. Suddenly the depth of my blessed return would not grant the wishes that brewed inside me. Short of heartfelt condolences and clarifications concerning Rachel, fear of a domestic confrontation said it was time to go. But Xûan literally ran ahead of me and challenged me to keep pace. She was correct about the boots, for my bare feet smacked and gripped the contours of the limbs. Soon the sound of falling water and laughter of children intensified when I paused for a moment and looked up to see a group of children that laughed at me. The children played on a narrow, sandy shore at the bend of the river. There an out-cropping of rock stilled the flow of water and individuals washed clothes. I looked back for my boots, but had no idea where to find them among the maze of limbs. A few steps away, another rocky ledge formed steps to the ground below.

The children stared, pointed, and laughed at my lack of coordination. Their faces were like my face years ago as a child. Xûan talked of the children and their rapidly changing world. In such change, their choices were seldom ideal. The spine of mountains that created the country's western border had long been a communist supply route and haven for quick strikes and evasion. The children, aware they were the subject of conversation, again plunged into the surf.

Xûan and I climbed onto the gray rocks that stair-stepped to the ground.

"Mel, do you see the boy wearing the bracelet?"

I looked and saw the child preoccupied with my presence. Just above the bicep of his left arm was a bronze ring.

"Yes, I see him," I acknowledged.

"Mel, the boy with the bracelet is named Lon. He is our son—your son and my son. He was born in October, 1968. I imagined many ways for you two to meet, but was never sure it would occur. I am glad it is now. He means a great deal to me and I hope you are not disappointed."

LON

APRIL 1975

"Come with me. Lon will follow," Xûan asked, then turned and ascended the rocks to the first of the limbs.

The child followed and negotiated the limbs as skillfully as his mother. When we reached our starting place, I rejoiced and slumped next to Xûan and my boots. Lon sat to the other side of Xûan with darting, curious eyes as huge locks of curly hair released steady droplets of water.

"Does he know that I am... his father?"

"I think he knows," Xûan answered confidently.

"Does he know what little I know of him, and how frightened I am? What do I say?"

"Talk to your son. He has waited a long time to meet you."

I stood before Lon, perhaps a grand and imposing figure unlike any man he'd ever seen although, he didn't appear frightened or uncomfortable in my presence.

"Hello, Lon. Please, excuse my near-nervousness or lack of excitement ... I had no idea. Frightened as I am ...I'm glad to meet you." I extended my hand and as evident of my shock, I lacked composure. Of course, my fears had little to do with his presence, but more to do with a life-changing perspective.

"How are you, tee-day?" Lon said, in plain English. The words, long-since compiled, sprang from his throat.

Already overcome and stymied with a mixture of emotions, added to my surprise was the boy apparently spoke English. I choked. Amid sounds of strange birds, I looked around me at the many sidewalks of limbs, the afternoon shade cast by the mountainside and the rolling river below. I felt tears welled-up in my head, tears of fear, guilt, and excitement, were suddenly ready for pouring. I fought back those tears as best I could, stepped forward, and placed my arms around the child, held him close with a feeling of indebtedness for the years gone by. Many years would pass before I understood my feelings in that moment. Like the river below, the churned flow of events, the years and probabilities never once suggested such a turn of events.

"I'm fine, Lon, surprised, excited, and a little scared, too. I never imagined..."

The sudden knowledge of a son, a child, presented far-reaching ramifications. Many thoughts and considerations begged for attention.

"My mother talks of you many times. Much things about you. I am happy to meet you," Lon said. Quietly, as he juggled his words, Xûan instructively coached his English. In his conclusion, he grinned and gasped for air.

The three of us sat and reviewed the photos, as Lon was very familiar with them. Xûan failed to suppress the glee in her voice, but displayed a restless and flashing brilliance. Her long relieving sighs, childish laughter and hands that would not be still. As the son of the village schoolteacher, Lon spoke well, English and Vietnamese.

"How do you feel, Mel?" Xûan asked, then said, "Once I thought it best you not know. I feared it be a burden for you."

"...It's too soon. Please don't hold it against me, but give me a moment to grasp this. He's you and he's me, and there's nothing about us I dislike. I'm not, as happy as I'm surprised and somewhat disappointed having no time to consider it. It'll take some time, but I'll get there. And that may be the easy part."

My marriage to Sandra only tamed the beast that suggested Xûan and Tram died as result of my actions or inactions. For seven long years their memory haunted me. Now there was Lon. Just when I thought the nightmare had ended, it took on a new life. Surely, Lon hadn't suddenly sprung from his mother's loins seven years earlier. Certainly, he wasn't an afterthought or the result of some promiscuous fling. Suddenly, along with Lon came a need for clarity, some construct that explained the profundity of his presence. Perhaps Lon was always a part of me, the part that spelled and predestined my return to Vietnam. Or, was he born in the fertile dreams of my childhood, among the toy airplanes and play beneath ancient oaks and shaded sand? Perhaps, Lon was result of things imagined, things offered up by dreams of manhood. Xûan and he stood among the days, the endless string of summers and Saturdays I forever craved.

From that perspective, perhaps Rachel was no more than a surrogate for Xûan, a metaphor. Rachel's face and likeness called me forth—a true love tempered in my youth, but merely the means to an end that was Xûan. Rachel's flaws, how she understood her shortcomings became Xûan's resolve. Rachel's agony and search for redemption amounted to Xûan's strength, wisdom, and confidence in the future. What Rachel could only imagine, Xûan lived it and prospered. Perhaps Lon was destined to be, as surely as I was destined to fly.

Suddenly deflated, I exhaled in a sense of composure, one not necessarily for that moment, but for those years of haunting. The lives of Xûan, Lon, and me seemed intricately woven long before the sickly feeling that came upon me when first I saw Xûan.

Now, shortly past 5 P.M., I thought of Habrasham waiting in the Huey.

Lon removed the bracelet from his arm and presented it to me. For years, every shop from Saigon to Hue sold knock-offs. Prior to its commercialization, early significance of such a bracelet came from having worked in league with Montagnard tribes and having that item presented as a token of acceptance and appreciation.

"Thank you, Lon," I said. "Take this, my gift to you." I gave him my watch, however inadequate compared to what seven years had deprived each of us.

Xûan informed me she learned of her pregnancy while hospitalized following the attacks on Pleiku in March 1968. When finally I relaxed, I shared photos of Sandra and Tillie.

"... your sister," I said to Lon. "And she would be proud of you."

As the sun descended beyond the mountain, the afternoon became more unsettling for brewing inside me was the question of disclosure. We left the walkway in the trees, the muted greens, and Shangri-La, then headed back toward the village, pushed gently by the sloping hillside. I walked barefoot in the dirt, my pants rolled, and we each held hands.

Xûan wanted to prepare a meal, for me to sit and share their presence; wanted to extend that unbelievable opportunity, but she also knew of the nocturnal excursions of communist troops and the supply route nearby. I briefed them on the state of the Vietnamese Government and made her understand the lack of stability in the entire region. Xuan wished not to invite the gloom of such circumstances, so our thoughts ran ahead as hopes and plans of many such meetings took form. Xûan asked if she and Lon could go to Cam Ranh Bay to visit me.

"I'll return, for sure this time," I informed them. "I'll visit often in the coming weeks. We'll do some things together."

I held her there in the afternoon light as Lon looked on, saw his mother as never before. In that embrace, I remembered the nights we shared and how much I wanted her then. Now as she pressed against me, her tremble said she remembered the same. She held me, too, remembered when we belonged to one another and the war was our sanctuary. Not since those days had Xûan translated her silent screams and offered up the whisper of passion and the need for surrender. She then pulled Lon into the embrace, and held the two of us in a fusion of desires, wishes, dreams, and belonging. What sorrow and secrets laid fallow in my doings? Xûan and Lon escorted me across the village to the south gate, toward the Huey that sat in the grass like a giant dragonfly. At the sight of us, Habrasham hit the breakers, and I boarded reluctantly.

Habrasham flew high above the jungle-covered ridge, banked right and headed down the valley. At one point I adjusted my helmet and turned to him, thanked him for his help with Xûan, for his role with the colonel as he looked out for Xûan. I didn't say much during the flight, didn't talk about Xûan or Lon, or what it was like being with them. I didn't talk of the fury that grew inside me, nor my need for answers and explanations.

A smile lit her face and she whispered all night. The day had begun like all of Xûan's days since she stopped listening for the sounds of approaching helicopters. Now, due to a magical turn of events, she babbled phrases, wondered if there was something she forgot to say.

"Did I mention how much you two look alike?" she asked Lon, rhetorically. "He will stay longer the next time," she said wishfully. "Then I can show him the school; ask about his work, cook something to eat and listen to the two of you talk. You think we should go to Cam Ranh?" Xûan continued in her random delivery. For much of that evening, she talked softly through her thoughts, had her arms draped around Lon and stared off into the night. Lon listened to his mother's listless whispers and responded as if she actually spoke to him. And when Lon summed up his thoughts about that day, having simmered in the same excitement, he asked his mother to tell him more about his father. A smile lit her face and she whispered all night.

THE FALL OF SAIGON

APRIL 1975

ARVN forces suffered as did the general population in a form of mental aggression, bullied, and intimidated through communist propaganda about the eminent fall of the Democratic Republic of South Vietnam. Only in the well-equipped, well-manned ARVN units, did the fighting resemble anything but an all-out surrender. The impact of deteriorated moral, depleted supplies and lack of effective leadership among ARVN personnel made for longer hours in the air for the team.

Three weeks after I visited Xûan, the team completed its primary mission. The weather remained marginal in what was largely mop-up work. Isolated attacks became daily occurrences and Cam Ranh became hot or unsafe.

"I don't envy the position you're in, Navy," Habrasham said. "Since I don't know what your plans are, I'm not sure if I can help. Yes, I've kept things from you at the insistence of Xûan. Whatever differences exist between you and me, let's settle them now, pronto! Whatever you decide to do about Xûan and the boy, the next 48 hours are going to be crucial."

Laced in that plea of solidarity was the latest intelligence report.

"I depended on you, Hab and in spite of your promise to Xûan, I expected some contact, some clue."

We schemed every hour of each day, looking for an opening in the schedule, for some excuse to dash off into the hills, but the work plan would not allow lt. Fears I'd never again see Xûan and Lon impaired my concentration as each day ended in disappointment. The following week, General Stretch had us prepare for evacuation. "We're going home," the general said, but in the silence of my duties, I saw flashes of that afternoon in Shangri-La, searched for some meaning for such a brief visit and that new revelation.

Days later, factions of South Vietnamese troops exchanged shouts and taunts like families feuding. Amid those heated exchanges, several explosions ripped the complex, caught everyone off guard. Wahl and Lagos had slight injuries and Oldfield was missing. Spared were the aircraft, because each was stored inside to avoid sabotage. By noon, removal of enough torn tin and twisted beams allowed access and removal of one Huey and a grinning Oldfield crawled from the rubble. In a final exit, we used thermite grenades to destroy the remaining ships, then flew off the coastline, south to Saigon.

All of Saigon was a magnet, an island amid a population seeking asylum or some assurances in view of advanced columns of communist troops. The pace of activity created chaos from failed communication exchanges via radio and telephone. Evacuation notices for embassy and American personnel signaled 24 hours to complete all business. No protocol, agendas or schedules, official or non-official received recognition beyond the next 24 hours. In a terse meeting, General Stretch called to me.

"I did what I could for Xûan," said the general. "The Montagnards are the true indigenous people here and that may explain their feelings of being the least threatened; however, for those like Xuan with military affiliations, there will be reprisals. For reasons obvious to the two of us, she and the child deserves safe passage out of country. Colonel Habrasham has orders to assist you in any way possible."

"Thank you, General," I said, took one-step backwards and rendered a salute.

"The colonel is waiting," the general reminded me.

We flew east over the harbor, above loaded sampans, pleasure boats and rafts full of individuals headed for the *U.S.S. Blue Ridge* and other transports offshore. I climbed high above the countryside, across the interior toward the valley and Kontum, At any rate, it was an intense two hour flight before I descended and used the hillside to buffer the sound.

Once more, Xûan's attention laid in the grasp of the skies, drawn to the sound of helicopters and to her many wishes and memories of the man that often came with those sounds. I met Xûan, turned her in her tracks, and headed for her house. I explained the military situation and eminent danger, but she shrugged off such gloom, smiled and invited me in.

"Please, sit, Mel. Something has happened and now it is time for you to go."

"Xûan!" I began. "You don't have to stay here. I've come for you and Lon, the two of you can come with me to the states." I spoke with the promise of a savior, thought she'd be excited and appreciative, "I know this is short notice," I continued, "but I don't have time to explain how serious things are."

Xûan ignored my desperate plea and offer of asylum. She approached me as if seven years had not passed, as if the war that raged was but a storm in the night, and we need only close our eyes until the night had passed. She held my cheeks in her tiny hands, then said.

"What am I to do, Mel, go away with you and live in your town? What will I be? Whom will I be besides always in waiting, always reminding you of someone you once loved? I would still want you long after I stopped seeing you, long after I stopped saying it to myself, and long after I regret having gone there with you. All these years I have waited for you, felt you inside me and somehow, I knew you would come. Now, except for Lon, we must put away those years, wrap them gently in memories, and occasionally look back, but softly as not to stare or disturb the present. Without an end, I would never have the courage to start anew. I want to grow old around the things and places I know. I want to be free to love and remember you without interfering. I promised to never leave my home again."

Her words came slowly, all full of sorrow, full of courage, and full of resignation. In an effort to rebuild, Xuan had moved from reflecting to fabricating a new beginning. Now I'd say the things I didn't say long ago, I'd explain the juxtaposition of her and Rachel. I put aside urgent thoughts, that of an idling Huey and the menaced danger of the hill country.

"Long ago, as a child, I loved you and your name was Rachel."

I looked up into her eyes to be sure she heard me that she understood. If not, I would begin again.

"The years that grew up around Rachel and me passed like words in a love song. Years, coated in rhyme and full of melodies, but like day and night, Rachel and you appeared at the expense of one another. The night I lost Rachel was the day I found you. In you, Xûan, I held onto the only link left to my childhood and fell in love all over again. Your presence extended my youth, allowed me to relive it and be reminded how brief and unattended that time was."

Then Xûan said to me, "I came home from the hospital and learned you were sent home. I joined Habrasham in gathering your belongings. I wanted some things for keepsake. I learned then, why you wanted to meet me, Mel, and why you stared at me so strangely. We saw the photos of Rachel and I was frightened. She looked so much like me. I learned your secret, the one you kept from me, and the source of the smiles you often hid. Habrasham told me how Rachel died. I am sorry, Mel."

Lon approached us and Xuan placed her hand on his shoulder, then looked at me.

"Lon and I have talked," she began. "Our wish is that he goes with his father, and learn his father's ways. Your family, your wife, this will be okay, yes? Take our son, Mel, take him with you and I will always know he is well. Someday, give him a choice to come back."

I wrote out my address and gave it to Xûan. In a silence foreign to me, I rose to my feet and embraced the woman and the likeness forever a part of me. There were no tears between Xûan and Lon, or last minute packing. When Xûan focused again, on me, in the half-light of her home, her huge passionate eyes reminded me of the woman I loved years earlier. I felt no guilt for the wishes that swirled inside me. Although no one could ever replace Sandra and Tillie, Xûan was as much a part of my life as the childhood she preserved. Once again, the feel, the taste and sentiment of an eternal voyage, offered via the brown of her, the black of her; her tan, and bronze. Xûan then turned to Lon and spoke in their tribal language.

"Remember that I love you," she said. "I will miss you. Someday I hope you will come back to me and I will be waiting." She called upon the village elders who gave their blessings to Lon's departure, then we headed to the south gate and the idled Huey.

In a drizzle of rain that came unnoticed, a fine, soft, rain that fell through the sunshine and the rainbow, I thanked Xûan for her gifts of wisdom that helped me define a sense of identity and community. Our walk in the fine spring rain brought us again to the gates of goodbye, the gates that forever separated yesterday, today, and tomorrow. Just beyond the small, grassy clearing, Xûan paused, stood straight with her hands clasped behind her. She narrowed her eyes against the force of the rotors and squinted more as the Huey banked into the afternoon sun. It's not certain for whom Xûan cried, for me, for Lon or for herself, but she cried. Xûan did not wail, did not shout, nor fall to her knees. She stood still and erect, her hands clasped behind her, allowed the tears to flow freely down her cheeks, and watched as the helicopter grew smaller in the distance.

Lon sat nervously in the cargo bay, clutched the railed edge of the bench seat, when finally he, too, cried. With tightly clinched eyes, he pinched the tears into small masculine drops and wept in an agony all too new to him. Below and behind us, was Lon's world of mutual order and predictability. A world still hinged to the mystical, to the rhythms, the flux, and the phases of the moon. Lon braced himself in the banking turns of the helicopter, and still with tightly clenched eyes, chose not to view the warm, green earth that fell silently beneath him.

THE MOON OF TWO SONS

APRIL 1975

Tan Son Nhut Airport remained a mass of moving bodies that charged in panic at any vehicle that attempted to land or lift off. In order to land without incident, Habrasham breached the airspace of incoming helicopter traffic and settled near the main terminal. General Stretch and the team of pilots watched in dismay a rapid decline of civil authority. Our proximity to the end of an era was unfathomable.

Lon and I, in particular, became the subject of conversations as everyone struggled to internalize circumstances that surrounded Lon's presence and my serious dilemma. Lon, dressed in a striped pullover T-shirt, short pants with a ribbon of cloth that tied at the waist. He mirrored the mode of public desperation.

The general then said, "April stateside might be a little rough on him dressed as he is. Once in the Philippines, you can get him squared-away."

I gave considerable thought as how best to inform my family. Lucky for me, there remained two days to decide. I looked over the papers and documents pertaining to Lon. A birth certificate, record of inoculations and a post office address in Kontum. We talked, shared again the photos of Sandra and Tillie as I taught him how to pronounce their names. I wondered, too, how he really felt about his loss of friends, how quickly would he adjust to vast changes and modernity? When Lon asked about our destination, my thoughts rested on Washington, D.C. Prominent among such thoughts were, how was I to explain him to Sandra?

217

"Are we going to Wain Cid (Rain Seed)?" Lon asked.

I nearly choked. I couldn't believe he knew so much about me, my childhood, and names of people from my past. The idea was appealing, that he met and was introduced to the entire family in Rain Seed County. My parents knew of Xûan and my efforts to reconcile her presence. They would help clarify any frivolous thoughts or misconceptions Sandra might encounter. The weather, too, in Florida would provide an ideal transition to the colder temperatures of Washington, D.C.

"What else did your mother tell you about me?" I asked Lon.

"She said you are tall, say you can do many things. I know you have a one sister and a one brother."

One of the pilots scrounged a pair of sandals and a baseball cap for Lon as faint explosions of mortars on the horizon signaled the advance of communist troops. At mid-morning, the team gathered our gear and headed for a vacant stretch of tarmac and a transport bound for the Philippines. Seven long years culminated with the events of the past eight weeks. I did not look back, did not peer out the window at the velvet-covered mountains, nor the beautiful terraced farms along the hillsides. I did not worry about Xûan or her village or the thousands that crowded Saigon. I watched Lon from the corner of my eye as he struggled with the effects of cabin pressure. I laughed and told him to swallow and his ears would clear. In route between worlds, Lon and I bonded, communicated, and studied our personal mannerisms. To my delight, he was an astute child, a quick learner.

So I'd take Lon to my home in Rain Seed County, to the Red Hills and Ancient Oaks of the south. I'd take him to the country lane near the bend of the railroad tracks where folks still told time by the noon and 9 P.M. trains. I'd take him home where once I was a child, to tadpoles in summer, and frost covered fields in winter. I'd take him where the old folks would hold his hand and tell him stories about me, where relatives would happily make a big fuss over him, squeezed him in long embraces.

Once again in San Diego, we gave up our weapons and ammo, watched news reports of the fall of Saigon and cringed at the sight of airworthy helicopters pushed from crowded ship decks into the sea.

"Let's keep in touch, Navy?" Habrasham said. "I'd like to see what becomes of Lon."

"I don't know, Hab. Just knowing you is a liability. Any word from you in the near future and my wife will kill me for sure."

General Stretch was supportive throughout the ordeal. He praised Lon and me for our courage. More importantly, I would not deny my whereabouts the past two months. The national news was full of the fall of Saigon and supported the story I'd tell.

At 4:00 P.M., Pacific Time, on Friday, I called home and Tillie answered the phone.

"It's daddy," she said. "Daddy, are you coming home now?"

"Yes, tomorrow, and I can't wait to see you. Put mommy on the phone."

"Mommy's already here," Sandra answered from an adjacent phone. With a velvety softness, she was relieved and elated to hear my voice.

"Where are you? You're not saying 'over,' so I take it you're back in the States?"

"God, I can't wait to see you. I'm in San Diego and I wonder if you and Tillie would meet me in Rain Seed, at mom and dad's. Get the first flight you can and I'll do the same from here. Will you do that for me?"

"Why? I've kept mom and dad informed. We want you to come home," she said in a pouting and sad voice.

"I have so much to say, and I don't know where to start or how to say it. Sandra, something's come up, something big and important—a change and a challenge for each of us. We'll need some time, and mom and dad's is the best place."

"Mel, what are you talking about? I hope they haven't talked you into re-enlisting and made you some big promises. Not now, Mel, please."

I wished for something so simple. "I have some good news for us, something to be shared with all of the family. I don't want to say anymore or discuss it over the phone. It's too important. Now, will you and Tillie meet me at mom and dad's?"

Her intuitive wheels began turning, and I heard the swell and wrath of concern.

"Are you all right, Mel? Is everything all right? Have you been injured?"

"No, dear."

Tillie, excited by the inflection in her mother's voice, asked,

"Mommy, what's wrong with daddy?"

"Daddy is fine, Tillie," I answered. "We have a great deal to talk about and I want the two of you to meet me at mom and dad's in Florida." To Sandra,

I continued, "Darling, I want to come home, too. I want to see you and hold you; I miss you both, but there is something I can't ignore."

"You're pushing it, Mel. Really pushing it," she said.

Having said little, I felt relieved, but knew the real task was ahead. "Great, now how's everything around the house, work, and your last doctor's appointment?" I asked.

"You gotta be kidding!" Sandra said. "How do you expect us to talk about anything else, when you've filled us with such mixed emotions and curiosity?"

"Trust me. All is well."

Sandra would not leave it alone. She wanted assurances. "Mel, you are telling me you're alright? Nothing's wrong with you?"

"Yes, darling, I'm alright," I muttered.

Reluctantly, she surrendered and said, "Okay, we'll see you at mom and dad's."

Lon was mesmerized by the enormity of new surroundings, it enveloped and overwhelmed him. Newly clad in route to L.A. International, Lon inhaled a bevy of revelations and discovery. To minimize the shock, I anticipated his questions, stayed close, explained, and demonstrated the things he encountered.

Often, in the years that came, he and I talked for hours about his arrival. To no end, we stood at the gates of yesterday, remembered the fine, soft, rain that fell through the sunshine and the rainbow.

At boarding time, near 6:00 P.M., Lon and I stood at the edge of the world. He and I watched the sunset, watched the sun hover above the surf. A huge, orange, ball it was, demur, but magnificent as it sunk ever so slowly, sipped from the surface of the ocean, simmered and shimmered, then lowered itself until only the orange, glow remained.

When evening came, and things of old had passed away and morning seemed long, long ago, I reflected on the times. I likened my life to one single day and remembered those who lived only a few hours. I accepted the good and the evil that life presented, but dared not forget those that fell short of the evening. I remembered the good boys who lived only in the morning. Ramey's frail whisper was wet with dew when he died, still green and undeveloped. His was the opening chorus to the song of summer.

"Let's," was the sound Tommy made. The quiet leader, all full of ideas, and Tommy died this morning. The laughter of Packy, Leo, and Beenie in the clubhouse as each shouted above sounds of the noontime freight train. Packy,

Leo, and Beenie died this morning, too. The sound of the good shepherd was a song that echoed near noon. Matured, it bellowed full of sanctity and full of redemption. It was near noon when Rachel died. All those voices drifted in memory, quieted in life's stormy expression. Sleep, in a wallow of words that occasionally connected, mended slowly. Perhaps, the lives of Sleep and I represented a visual reminder, the final chorus in the song of summer. The sound of my voice, once stilled, now called to the hollow breeze that is their memory.

CPSIA information can be obtained
at www.ICGtesting.com
Printed in the USA
LVHW052123131021
700374LV00004B/14/J

9 781636 615301